THE RIGHT DIRECTION

RAY HOBBS

Wingspan Press

Published in the United States and the United Kingdom

by WingSpan Press, Livermore, CA

The WingSpan name, logo and colophon are the trademarks of WingSpan Publishing.

ISBN 978-1-59594-655-3 (pbk.)
ISBN 978-1-59594-967-7 (ebk.)

First edition 2020

Printed in the United States of America

www.wingspanpress.com

1 2 3 4 5 6 7 8 9 10

This book is dedicated to the staff of Discovery Blossom suite at Applecroft Care Home in Dover, whose dedication and professionalism made my wife Sheila's last two years infinitely happier and more comfortable than they would otherwise have been.

Ray Hobbs

AUTHOR'S NOTE

There can be few challenges more irritating for a reader than a text littered with jargon that calls for a specialised dictionary or, more usefully, a tame expert. To avoid that state of affairs, I have set out below a guide that I hope will help enlighten those who find the language of music trying, if not forbidding. Of course, there will be readers who will have no need of this service, and I ask them to bear with me, or even to skip this section altogether. I shouldn't be offended in the slightest if they did.

To begin with, I should point out that most musical instructions are expressed in Italian. There is nothing affected or precious about this except, of course, when words such as *concerto* or *scherzo* are trotted out with perfect pronunciation at social gatherings. Otherwise, their language is an accident of birth or, more accurately, rebirth, as they originated in Florence during the Renaissance.

First, let's consider the *oratorio*, of which George Frederick Handel's *Messiah* is the best-known example. Imagine an opera performed statically and without costumes, scenery or acting, and you have an oratorio. Most, although not all of them, have a religious theme, and that is because the entertainment was conceived at a time when theatrical and operatic performances were forbidden during Lent. Singers, actors and the like were regarded as trollops and debauchees throughout the church year, but were particularly vulnerable at this time, so the singing of biblical texts afforded them a degree of camouflage, at least until after Easter, when the establishment resumed its policy of pious condemnation.

Before leaving the subject of oratorio, I should explain that the tradition of standing for the chorus 'Hallelujah', at the end of Part Two of Handel's *Messiah*, is said to have begun in 1743, when King George II was so enchanted by the music that he rose spontaneously to his feet. There is no reliable evidence that this actually happened, but who cares? Cosy traditions are increasingly coming under attack from the iconoclasts around us, so if you're similarly enthralled by the music, don't hold back. Stand up and be counted. You won't be alone.

An *aria* is simply an air or song, but its Italian label gave it welcome gravitas when opera was under siege.

A *cantata* (literally a piece which is sung, as distinct from a *sonata*, which is played) is shorter than an oratorio, it may comprise several movements, and like its grown-up cousin, it is usually, but not always, sacred.

In music, a *bar*, or *measure*, to give it the earlier name still favoured by American musicians, is a metrical division. Think of the waltz with its *one, two, three* pulse. Each set of three beats, or pulses, constitutes a bar. A march has two beats in each bar: *left, right.* The numbering of bars provides a convenient means of checking that everyone concerned is at the same place in the score. Conductors swear by the facility, knowing that without it, they would probably swear a great deal more.

A *recitative* is a passage of sung text, accompanied either orchestrally or by a spinet or harpsichord, that leads into a music number. It is seldom tuneful, but it does an honest job and should be respected for that.

A *mezzo-soprano* is a female singer whose vocal range is a little lower than that of the soprano, but not as deep as that of the contralto. Whilst not all mezzos are fortunate enough to share the glamorous appeal of the beautiful and talented Katherine Jenkins, they are in great demand for their versatility as well as for recognised mezzo roles.

Tempo is simply the Italian term for 'pace'. Think of the Bianchi pedal cycle, the 1400cc Moto Guzzi Audace, and everything in between.

Adagio is a broad and leisurely tempo with the calming effect that chilled Pino Grigio has at the height of the Italian summer.

Falsetto is an unnaturally high voice affected by the counter tenor, or male alto, as he is known in Anglican church music. The technique is admittedly clever, but of rarefied and limited appeal outside the confines of sacred and early music.

Thankfully, the *castrato* is now extinct. The castration of prepubertal choirboys was common practice in 16th century Rome and for far too long after that, the object being to preserve the unfortunate victim's treble voice in adulthood. During the Renaissance and Baroque periods, some adult *castrati* also found acclaim on the opera stage. More latterly, a recording still exists of the Bach/Gounod *Ave Maria,* sung by the last of the *castrati,* Alessandro Moreschi, 1858-1922, evidence that he was recognised during his lifetime for the unnatural facility he possessed, rather than for the natural facility he no longer possessed.

A pastoral symphony (not to be confused with Beethoven's 6th) was, at the time of Handel, a fairly short piece evoking a pastoral scene. The word 'symphony' described a multitude of compositions before the Classical period of ca. 1750 to 1810, during which it was given a recognisable form and therefore a new identity, and Josef Haydn was credited with its paternity.

Sight reading is the skill of playing previously unseen music. Accompanists and organists pride themselves in their adeptness in this discipline, whilst solo pianists keep quiet and hope no one will ask them to attempt it. British orchestras are superb at sight reading because they are so underfunded that rehearsal time is almost non-existent.

Finally, if you're still with me, thank you for buying this book. I hope the foregoing has not put you off reading it, and if you do read it, I sincerely hope you enjoy it.

Ray Hobbs

1

Adam was on his hands and knees, sweeping the carpet with a stiff hand-brush and a dustpan. There was little carpet in the caravan, but the necessary obstacles, the table and beds, made it an annoying, fussy job. His publisher had asked him to work on a second edition of *Book One* of *Keyboard is Cool*, and he wanted to make a start on that, but the caravan, which had spent the winter in the farmer's barn, had to be relieved of its dust and cobwebs before his conscience would allow him to attend to other matters.

He brushed the last bit of carpet, and was about to stand up, when he heard a busy, scrambling noise in the open doorway. He turned to see what was making the noise, and found himself nose to wet nose with a Jack Russell terrier. It was clearly friendly, because it was licking his face with obvious enthusiasm.

'Hello,' he said, standing up to take a break from the licking. 'What brings you here?' It occurred to him that it might possibly have been more sensible to ask *who*, rather than *what*, because there was presumably someone on the other end of the extending lead.

The answer to his question became apparent when a child's face topped with fair, windblown hair peered innocently round the doorway.

'Hello,' he said again. 'Did you think you'd lost your dog?'

The girl shook her head decisively. 'No, I knew where she was. She went inside and I couldn't stop her.'

'Oh, well, don't worry. There's no harm done.' He picked up the

1

Jack Russell and carried it to the door.

'I have to keep her on the lead,' the girl told him, as if he might find the information helpful.

Adam guessed her age at about eight or nine. 'Quite right,' he agreed. 'There are sheep everywhere, and we don't want them worried, do we?'

That gave the girl cause to think. She asked, 'What do sheep worry about?'

Still holding the dog, he sat down in the doorway to consider the question. 'The usual things, I imagine. The cost of living, interest rates, where Mr Blair's next foreign adventure might take place. Most of all, though, they worry when a dog chases them, because it's fun for dogs, but very frightening for sheep.' He looked around for signs of human life, and asked, 'Is there a grown-up with you?'

The girl nodded and said, 'My mum,' adding by way of explanation, 'She can't run as fast as me.'

'I expect she'll be here soon.' He stroked the dog again and asked, 'What's her name?'

The girl gave him a strange look. 'Mrs Thorpe,' she said. After a few seconds, she offered further information. 'I'm called Nicola Thorpe.'

'I'm pleased to meet you, Nicola, but I meant the dog's name. I'm sorry, I should have made it clearer.'

'Dottie.'

'That's a good name for a Jack Russell.'

'It's because she has black dots on her.'

'Yes, she's lovely.' Dottie responded to the compliment by licking him again.

'She belongs to my grandma, really, but she can't control her. My mum has to do it for her.'

Adam wondered a little about Nicola's ability to control her. 'Jack Russells aren't the easiest dogs to keep,' he said.

'She's a handful,' agreed Nicola, 'and her hair falls out all over the place.'

She seemed content to pass the morning in friendly conversation, until a new voice called from the gateway.

'Nicola, I've told you before, you mustn't run away like that, and you mustn't go bothering people either.' As the woman, who Adam presumed to be Nicola's mother, drew closer, she said, 'I'm ever so sorry.' There was a boy with her, older than Nicola, but it was the mother who caught Adam's attention. Her hair was a little darker than her daughter's, and a woollen hat shielded most of it from the wind, but she had the same light complexion and bright blue eyes. She walked with a pronounced limp.

'Please don't apologise. Nicola is charming company, although I should be inclined to warn her about approaching strangers.' Dottie was clearly unconvinced, licking him industriously as he spoke.

'I've told her that as well. I mean, I'm sure you're above suspicion, but she'd no way of knowing that.'

'We can only nag,' he said. 'I remember having the same conversation many times with my children when they were young. They were friendly souls too. Thankfully, they still are, although I don't need to warn them nowadays. Instead, I spend much of my time warning young women about my son.' He was aware that the boy had been staring at him and was now whispering in his mother's ear.

'Gareth, it's rude to whisper in company,' his mother told him. Somewhat embarrassed, she said, 'My son thinks he's seen your photograph on a music book at school.'

'It's possible he has. What was the book called, Gareth?'

The boy looked to his mother, who gave him an encouraging nod. 'Donkey Ride to Bethlehem,' he said diffidently.

'Has your school done that show?'

Gareth nodded.

'And were you in it?'

The boy nodded shyly, leaving Nicola to speak for him. 'He was the innkeeper that let Mary and Joseph sleep in the stable,' she told him.

'That's a very important part. Did you enjoy it?'

Gareth nodded again, still staring, as if he expected a bright light to appear in the firmament, and Adam to morph into the Archangel Gabriel.

'It was a lovely play,' said Mrs Thorpe. 'I really enjoyed it.'

'Thank you. I'll tell you what. I've got some hand bills, just advertising stuff they put inside music books. Excuse me for a second.' He went into the caravan and took two handbills from his briefcase. He signed them and handed them to Nicola and Gareth. 'There you are,' he said. 'Now you can tell your friends you've met me, and the photograph is better than the real thing.'

Nicola looked uncertainly at hers, and said, 'Thank you.'

Mrs Thorpe nudged Gareth, who also thanked Adam.

Reading his name on one of the handbills, Mrs Thorpe said, 'That was very kind of you, Mr Watkinson. Thank you.'

'They're only bits of blurb about forthcoming publications, and they're not all mine.' He considered that modest disclaimer and added, 'Most of them are.'

'I mean it was kind of you to take the trouble, and we've already taken up too much of your time.' She winced, as if something were causing her discomfort.

Adam asked, 'Is something the matter?'

'I'm all right, really. I broke my ankle some time ago, and I've probably walked too far on it. It's not all that long since they took off the plaster cast.'

'How far do you have to go?'

'Only two miles or so.' Her attempt to minimise the journey was unconvincing. 'We live in Thanestalls,' she explained.

'That's too far with a weak ankle. You'd never make it. Let me run you all home.'

'I couldn't put you to that trouble, Mr Watkinson. Besides, you'd get dog hair all over your car. She sheds it all the time.'

'Now I've cleaned the caravan, the car's next on my list. A bit of dog hair won't make much difference, and you can't possibly walk home in that state.' He forestalled another refusal by saying, 'Come on, all of you. Get in the car.' He closed and locked the caravan door and then led the way to a silver Rover 45 parked behind it.

'Gareth, Nicola and Dottie, you can all get in the back, and then I'll pull the passenger seat back so that your mum doesn't catch her ankle when she gets in.' He opened one of the rear doors to let them in and then adjusted the front seat.

Settling into the driving seat, he turned his head to say, 'You'll have to make your walks a bit shorter, Nicola, and give your mum's ankle a chance to heal.'

'I feel guilty,' said Mrs Thorpe, 'putting you to this trouble.'

'You've done nothing to feel guilty about, and it's no trouble as far as I'm concerned,' he said, turning up the farm track.

They joined the main road, and Mrs Thorpe asked, 'Do you make your living writing plays for schools?'

'Partly. I write all kinds of things, really. I published an electronic keyboard tutor some years ago, and it became quite popular. The royalties made it possible for me to give up teaching.'

'It *must* be popular.'

'Oh well, it also helped that I'd no mortgage to worry about.'

'Lucky you.' After a moment's thought, she asked, 'Didn't you enjoy teaching? I mean, you seem very much at ease with children.'

'Yes, I loved it, at least until the last few years. It was what the politicians did to it that turned me sour.'

If that meant anything to her, she gave no sign, saying instead, 'You mentioned you had children. It was a brave thing, to give up your job when you did.'

He turned on the wipers to cope with the squalling rain. 'It was three years ago. My son was eighteen and my daughter was fifteen. My late wife and I had made provision for them some time ago. They're secure enough, believe me.'

'Your late wife?'

'Yes, she died four years ago.'

'I'm so sorry. I didn't realise.' She was looking guiltily at the pink silk badge on his anorak.

'Of course you didn't. Why should you?'

It was beginning to rain harder, so he flipped the switch on the steering column so that the wipers swept continuously.

'I'm sorry I asked you all those questions, now. I feel as if I've intruded on your private life.'

He smiled good-naturedly. 'You're no more inquisitive than most wom... people, Mrs Thorpe,' he said.

'I hope not.' A moment later, she said, 'It's left at the next junction, and about two hundred yards up the lane.'

Okay.' He took the next left and followed her instructions, stopping outside a stone-built cottage with an ample conservatory and a small, tidy garden.

'Thank you again, Mr Watkinson. I really don't know how I'd have coped with the walk home.'

'Will you be all right?'

'Yes, thank you. I'm more concerned about you.'

'About me?' He looked at her in surprise.

'Staying in a caravan in this awful weather.'

'Oh, I'll be all right. I'll be going home soon, anyway.'

'Where's home?' Immediately shamefaced, she said, 'I've done it again.'

'Huddersfield, and don't worry. I'm told that nature designed woman to be inquisitive so as to compensate for man's indifference to all but the task in hand. It's all to do with evolution, they say.'

'I shouldn't be at all surprised.' She got out and collected the children, who had all but fallen asleep in the car. Dottie was as alert as ever.

'Goodbye, Mrs Thorpe.'

'Thank you again, Mr Watkinson. Goodbye.'

Adam took his leave of them and drove up the lane to find a place where he could turn round and get back to the main road. As he did so, his eye fell on an estate agent's sign, and he pulled up to look at the house that was for sale. Even through the rain, it looked rather promising, and it set him thinking.

* * *

With the children fed and off to bed, Jenny Thorpe dropped a log on the fire and sat down beside it to rest her ankle.

On the occasional table beside her were the hand-outs that Adam Watkinson had signed for the children. She picked one up to read it. It seemed he'd been busy again, writing musicals and cantatas. It sounded odd; as a rehearsal pianist she'd encountered cantatas, many of them by Bach, but none of them seemed at all suitable for children.

He'd joked about looking better in the photograph than in real life, but anything else would have been impossible in the March wind. His hair had greyed to some extent since the photograph, although he only looked to be about forty or so, and his brown eyes had lost the twinkle that the photographer had captured, but that wasn't surprising, considering what the poor man had been through.

In spite of his assurances, she winced when she thought of the way she'd asked him about his private life. She recalled the breast cancer badge on his anorak, which presumably told its own story, and she wondered what made him want to wear such a thing only four years after losing his wife.

She'd told him nothing about her life. Why would she? It had been a chance meeting, if a fortunate one, considering the state of her ankle. At all events, though, he was almost a stranger, and she was unlikely to see him again. It was a shame, because she'd rather liked him.

2

Leanne stared glumly through the passenger window at the repeated advance and retreat of the rain-soaked landscape.

'Chin up, love.' Adam had persuaded her with some difficulty to forsake her studies for one day, basically because she needed the break.

His daughter was unconvinced. 'Why am I here, Dad?'

'What, metaphysics at this time of the morning?'

'No, it's a practical question. Why were you so keen for me to come with you today, when I could have been working?'

He slowed down behind a struggling lorry and waited until it was safe for him to overtake. 'Everybody needs a break from work, Leanne.'

'I didn't need a break.'

'I thought you did, and you haven't had my long experience. You'll find some jelly babies in the glove compartment, by the way. I've just remembered them.'

Smiling in spite of her misgivings, Leanne opened the compartment and took out the bag of sweets. 'I'm eighteen,' she said, 'and you're still trying to bribe me with jelly babies.' With her fair hair and teasing eyes, she looked very much like her mother. Kate had also been susceptible to the lure of confection.

The road widened, and he overtook the lorry. 'It worked, though. You're in a better frame of mind already.'

'Mm.' It could have meant anything. 'Will we have to look at lots of houses?'

'I hope not.'

'We always used to.'

'We've only moved twice in your lifetime.'

'I know, but we still looked at lots of houses.'

'That was with your mum. She was the house-buying expert. That's why I left it to her.' As he spoke, he saw a look of amused scepticism cross his daughter's features.

'You were too lazy to go with her. That's why I had to do it.'

'And that experience is going to be invaluable. You're the expert now.'

'You're just full of it, Dad.'

They drove on without speaking, until Adam said, 'After we've seen the house, we'll find somewhere nice for lunch.'

'That's the least you can offer me.'

With a sigh of nostalgia, he asked, 'What happened to the sweet little girl I knew?'

'She grew up, Dad. That was years ago.'

'Do you remember it?'

'No, I'm just going by what people have told me.'

He looked at her, and saw that she was smiling.

After a while, she asked, 'Are we meeting an estate agent?'

'Not at this stage. We're meeting the owners of the house.'

'When?'

He looked at the dashboard clock and said, 'Hopefully, in about ten or fifteen minutes.'

Leanne regarded the surrounding countryside with new interest.

Presently, they came to Thanestalls, and Adam drew into the side of the road.

'Why are we stopping, Dad?'

'I don't want to arrive too soon. We'll give it ten minutes before we knock on the door.'

She delved into the packet for another jelly baby.

He asked, 'Have you nearly finished them?'

'No, do you want one?'

'No thanks. You know I prefer wine gums.'

She shook her head in disapproval. 'That's living dangerously,' she said.

'I can handle it.'

When enough of the ten minutes had passed, he started the engine and drove on, turning into Brocklehurst Lane. The weather was just as awful as it had been when he first noticed the property. He drove past Mrs Thorpe's house, wondering inconsequentially what use she had for such a large conservatory.

According to the estate agent, the house that was for sale had been on the market almost eighteen months, and the owners had reduced the asking price twice. Foot-and-mouth disease had blighted a great deal more than farms and livestock. Living as he did in West Yorkshire, he'd been aware of it, but now he was beginning to appreciate the reality.

He pulled up beside the 'For Sale' notice and got out of the car to stand on the side of the road, taking in the immediate features. There was a reception room to the left, with a bay window, and a smaller window, possibly looking out of the dining room, to the right. Three windows looked out of the first floor.

He rang the doorbell and waited. They were five minutes or so early, but it wouldn't matter.

A man of around Adam's age opened the door. He was neatly dressed in a navy-blue cardigan and dark-grey trousers, and his expression was welcoming.

'Good morning,' he said.

'Mr Hibbert? Good morning. I'm Adam Watkinson and this is my daughter Leanne. I hope you were expecting us.'

'Of course. Do come in, both of you. Let me take your coats.' He relieved them of their outer clothing, which he hung in a hall cupboard. 'My wife's out shopping,' he said, 'but I'll show you around and do my best to answer any questions.'

Leanne asked, 'Do you mind if I use your loo?'

'Not at all. You're standing in front of the downstairs cloakroom,' said Mr Hibbert, pointing to the door behind her. 'You'll find us in the sitting room.'

Adam followed him into a generously-proportioned room, the one with the bay window.

Mr Hibbert asked, 'Do you work locally?'

'No, I work from home.'

'Do you really? There's a study upstairs that might interest you. I'll show it to you later.'

'That's likely to interest my daughter, actually, but I need something on the ground floor, where I can put a piano.'

'A piano?'

'I write music resources for schools.'

'I see.'

Before either of them could say more, Leanne reappeared, holding something in her hand.

Adam asked, 'What's that, Leanne?'

'A compass. You didn't bring one, did you?' She tutted. 'A compass is essential house-hunting equipment.'

It was news to Adam. All he could say was, 'What does yours tell you?'

'North is that way,' she said, pointing to the left side of the bay window, 'which means that the back garden is basically south-facing.' She thought again and corrected herself. 'South-south-east, actually.'

'That's right,' said Mr Hibbert, a little surprised.

'I've done this before,' Leanne told him casually.

Mr Hibbert took them on a tour of the house, during which Leanne paid special attention to the second bedroom and the study he'd mentioned earlier.

As they followed him downstairs, she motioned to her parent to stop for a moment. 'Don't make an offer yet,' she whispered. 'Tell him you'll phone the estate agent.'

Adam realised he had much to learn about the buying and selling of houses. Fortunately, he seemed to be in good hands.

* * *

They ate at the Golden Lion. It was rather splendid, but Adam felt that his daughter had earned a good lunch.

'Don't offer him the asking price,' she advised over coffee.

'They've lowered the price twice since they put it on the market,' he reminded her, 'and it really fits the bill.'

'Are you sure you want to buy it?' Leanne was wearing her serious look, the one that made him forget she was only eighteen.

'Don't you like it?'

'Yes, if I can have the second bedroom and the study.'

'There's no problem there.' He'd already decided that part of the dining room would serve as his work area. Jimbo came home only occasionally, so the small bedroom was quite sufficient for him.

'In that case, see if you can get another five grand off the price.'

'A whole five thousand US dollars?'

She gave him an impatient look. 'You know what I mean.'

'I usually know what you mean, Leanne, even when you forget to speak English.'

'The extra cash will pay for a new loo and wash hand basin for the downstairs cloakroom,' she told him. 'They need replacing.'

'I didn't look in there.'

'I know. It's just as well I did.'

* * *

Adam was working on the new edition when the doorbell rang. He wasn't expecting anyone, and it was late for any of Leanne's friends, so he was curious about the visitor.

As he went into the hall, he saw the inner flap of the letterbox move. The outer door was unlocked, and someone had got into the porch and was obviously crouching to peer through the letterbox.

Instead of going to the door in the normal way, he crept around the wall and stationed himself beside the doorframe. It seemed distinctly odd that an intruder would ring the doorbell, unless it was to find out if there were anyone at home. Adam's curiosity was aroused.

The mystery was laid bare when an adolescent voice said, 'Are you there, Leanne? It's Matthew Dewhirst.'

Adam reached for the doorknob, and detecting movement within, the caller said, 'You are there, aren't you? I came round 'cause Gary said your dad would be off to his caravan tonight. Come on, Leanne, open this door. Now you're not going out with

Gary anymore, I wondered if you fancied hanging out with me.' He waited and, getting no response to his plea, said, 'Come on, Leanne, you know I've always fancied you.'

Seized with uncontrollable mischief, Adam crouched in front of the letterbox and lifted the flap further.

'You *are* there,' said the voice. 'Don't play games. You know I fancy you something rotten.'

'You wouldn't if you saw me first thing in the morning,' said Adam.

In a startled voice, the caller asked, 'Who's that?'

'Leanne's dad. Now, bugger off and try your luck somewhere else.'

As Matthew scrambled for the outer door, Adam heard Leanne's voice behind him.

'Dad, I can't believe you just said that.'

'I'd say it again and confirm it for you, but he's gone now.'

'It's just as well. He only ever has one thing on his mind. He's well known for it.'

Her casual dismissal shocked him as well as serving as an unnecessary reminder that there was one area of lone parenthood in which he felt completely inept. He needed bracing.

'Come and have a drink, Leanne,' he said, 'seeing as it's a special day.'

'All right, but what's special about today?'

'If you remember, we bought a house.'

'No we didn't.' She held up a cautionary finger, one of the gestures that made her seem older than her years. 'You made an offer. At this stage, you don't know whether they'll accept it or not.'

'I think they will. What would you like to drink, by the way?'

'What are you drinking?'

'I opened a bottle of Merlot earlier.'

'Okay, I'll join you with that.'

He poured two glasses and handed one to her.

'Thanks.'

'You're welcome.' He sat beside her, thoughtful and uneasy.

'What's on your mind, Dad?'

'Is it so obvious?'

13

'That you have something on your mind? Yes, it's quite noticeable.'

'I must be transparent.' He said it almost to himself.

'You are.'

'I was thinking about tonight's mysterious visitor.'

'"Dickhead" Dewhirst? Don't waste time thinking about him.'

'It wasn't about him specifically, but boys in general. You see, when I was a lad....' He hesitated.

'Go on, Dad. I didn't know it was going to be a history lesson.'

'The thing is....'

'Are you going to tell me about the goings-on in Bonksville, Arizona? I learned about that some time ago.'

'Yes, I'm sure you know all about that.' He hesitated again, closing his eyes helplessly. 'If only your mum were here.'

Leanne shook her head dismissively. 'She'd have struggled too, Dad. It's not a thing that comes easily to parents. Tell me about when you were a lad,' she suggested helpfully.

'It's just that young lads generally... well, they have just the one thing in mind, you see.'

'And don't I know it.' She took pity on him and said, 'So you wanted to warn me about the predatory male and the dangers associated with that nuisance, and you probably wanted to satisfy yourself that your only daughter is not yet sexually active. Is that basically what you had in mind?'

Wincing, he said, 'You really don't mince words, Leanne. Yes, that's basically what I wanted to say.'

'Just those three things?'

'Yes.'

'Okay.' Counting unnecessarily on her fingers, she said, 'One, I'm aware that where there are trousers, danger lurks within.'

'Good.'

'Two, I know about unwanted pregnancy and sexually transmitted diseases.'

'Good.' He was beginning to feel easier.

'As for Number Three....'

'Yes?'

'It's none of your business.'

'I thought you might say that.'

'But credit me with an ounce of common sense, Dad.'

Defeated, he took her hand and held it. 'You have common sense to spare,' he said. 'If you could hire it out, you'd make a fortune.'

It might have been a cosy picture, father and daughter in agreement, with all questions answered, or rather, most of them, but Adam was embarrassed. He'd just discussed something with his daughter that was deeply personal and once regarded almost as taboo, and he needed another drink. He reached for the bottle of wine.

'You're embarrassed, aren't you, Dad?'

There was no point in denying it, as she seemed to be reading his thoughts. 'Yes, I am.'

'All right, let's talk about the house. You never told me why you wanted to move.'

'That's because to begin with I didn't know why. I just saw the house, thought of the caravan parked in a boggy field, and suddenly, I wanted a house in Netherdale.'

'It's not all that surprising. You like Netherdale.'

'And I'm famous there, at least at Thanestalls Primary School.'

'Yours should be a household name in every school, Dad.'

'Thanks, love.' He patted her hand, thankful for the recognition.

'It came suddenly, wanting to move, didn't it?'

'I don't know. I think it's been creeping up on me, so it's possibly overdue.'

'What do you mean?'

He wanted to give her an honest answer, so he spent a moment or so, thinking about it. Eventually, he said, 'When your mum died, I stopped thinking about the future and concentrated on the present, because that was where I was needed. I had to do what I could for you and Jimbo, as well as all the practical things.' His mind returned to the seemingly endless list of tasks. 'There were so many,' he said, 'I sometimes thought, when I was besieged by demands on my time, that I was neglecting you two. Did you ever think that?'

'Not even for one minute.' She lifted his arm so that she could sit closer to him, and he saw that her eyes were wet. Four years was a short time.

'I've gone along with things, you see, just letting the world pass by, because that's what bereavement does to you. It says so in all the leaflets, so it must be true. I've been standing still instead of moving in any direction, and now, suddenly, I've made a decision.' He stroked her hair as he used to when she was little, and it pleased him that she made no protest. 'Maybe this is what people call "getting on with life",' he said.

'It can't be easy, Dad,' she said, pulling a crumpled ball of tissues from the pocket of her jeans, 'but it seems to me you're getting the hang of it.'

3

AUGUST

'Go up to the crossroads,' Adam advised the driver. 'You can turn round there.'

'Cheers, mate. All the best in your new home.' The driver wound up his window, so Adam simply waved. He and Leanne stood and watched the removal van disappear.

There was the sound of footsteps behind them, and Adam turned to see a young woman, whom he recognised a little belatedly as the mother of the little girl whose dog had invaded the caravan and the boy who had taken part in *Donkey Ride to Bethlehem.*

'I'm sorry,' he said. 'It's been a while since we met, and I didn't recognise you at first.'

'It's only to be expected after all this time, but I was surprised when I saw you with the removal van. I'm glad you're going to be a neighbour, and I wondered if you'd like a cup of tea or something after your ordeal.'

'How very kind. We'd like that, wouldn't we, Leanne?'

'Mm. Yes, please.' She offered her hand. 'I'm Leanne Watkinson.'

'Glad to meet you, Leanne. I'm Jenny Thorpe.'

'Adam,' said Adam, relieved that he no longer had to admit that he'd forgotten Mrs Thorpe's name.

'Jenny,' said Mrs Thorpe, rounding things off.

'I thought we'd better introduce ourselves,' said Leanne. 'My dad's hopeless with names at the best of times, and I'm sure he was struggling to remember yours.'

'I'm only two doors down,' said Jenny, leading the way.

'There are usually three of us,' said Adam, recovering from

Leanne's embarrassing disclosure, 'but my son's on holiday with his friends. We don't expect to hear from him until he returns.'

'Or until we get a phone call from the embassy in Paris,' said Leanne.

'What?' Jenny looked round in surprise.

'Leanne's just being rude about her brother. He's quite a character, larger than life but otherwise difficult to describe. You'll form your own impression when you meet him.'

'I'll look forward to that.' She unlocked the door and invited them inside, taking them through to a small but cosy sitting room with a three-piece suite and an upright piano. Dottie, the Jack Russell, greeted them enthusiastically.

'It took me ages to stop her leaping up at people,' said Jenny. 'She's almost civilised now. I'm just going to put the kettle on. I shan't be a minute.' She re-emerged from the kitchen to ask, 'Is tea all right, or do you prefer coffee?'

'Tea would be lovely, thank you.' Adam was stroking Dottie, who seemed to welcome the arrangement. Leanne was examining some watercolour landscapes. She asked, 'How did you two meet?'

'I was cleaning the caravan, and Dottie turned up inside it with Jenny's little girl on a lead.'

'She's nice.'

'Dottie?'

'Yes, but I meant Jenny.'

'She is. She was a bit embarrassed when we met, because she found her little girl talking to a strange man. Actually, I had quite a conversation with her. You'll meet her before long. There's a boy as well, a bit older than the girl.'

'Does he talk to strange men too?'

'I hope not. Now I think of it, I couldn't get him to say very much, except that he was in *Donkey Ride to Bethlehem* when they did it at school.'

Jenny came into the room with a tray of tea things, which she set down on a low table. 'We'll just let it brew for a minute,' she said. 'The children are in the garden. They'll be in soon.'

Adam asked, 'Do they play together?'

'Play? Not really. They're tidying the woodshed before the next delivery.' Before he could say anything, she asked Leanne, 'What do you do when you're not moving house?'

'Not much, really. I suppose I should do something soon about getting a job.'

'Leanne got her A level grades last week,' said Adam. 'She's taking a gap year.'

'What a good idea. What did you get, Leanne?'

'Two A stars, an A and a B.'

'Hey, well done. What kind of career do you have in mind?'

'I don't know. That's why I'm taking a year out.'

'I see. I'm being nosey, but what are your A levels?' She inspected the tea and then poured it out. 'I'll let you do your own milk and sugar,' she said.

'Art, Photography, English Literature and German,' said Leanne. 'I took the three subjects I enjoyed most,' she explained, 'and German because I felt sorry for the teacher. It's not a popular subject. What do you do, Jenny?'

'I'm an artist,' she said, adding with a mischievous smile, 'and photographer, but I came to that more recently.'

'Did you paint these watercolours?'

'Yes, do you like them?'

'They're brilliant.'

'Thank you.'

While Leanne was re-examining the watercolours, Jenny asked, 'How old is your son, Adam?'

'He's twenty-one. He's just finished his first year at the Guildhall School of Music.'

'His *first* year?'

'Yes, his first study is singing, and they don't take male singing students until they're twenty. They say male voices take two years longer than female voices to mature.'

'I see.'

'It'll take longer than that for Jimbo to mature,' said Leanne.

Amused by the remark, Jenny asked, 'Is that what you call him?'

'According to his birth certificate, his name is James,' explained Adam, 'but we decided quite early in his life that he wasn't quite ready for such a grown-up name, so we called him "Jimmy". That was all right until he reached his teens, when we changed it to "Jim", but even that sounded somehow adult, and then, when Leanne started calling him "Jimbo", it sort of stuck, and he's been "Jimbo" ever since.'

'I'm looking forward to meeting him.'

'Be careful what you wish for,' said Leanne.

'Believe it or not,' said Adam, 'they're actually quite close.'

'Like these two,' said Jenny, as her children came into the room. 'Gareth and Nicola, do you remember Mr Watkinson, who wrote *Donkey Ride to Bethlehem*? This is his daughter Leanne, and they've come to live two doors up.'

'Hi.' Leanne offered her hand to Gareth and then to Nicola, who asked, 'Have you still got the caravan?'

'No,' said Leanne, 'it found a new owner, someone who'll use it for nice things, like holidays.'

Gareth was whispering in his mother's ear.

'Gareth, don't whisper in company. Nicola, Gareth says you have a splinter in your hand. Weren't you wearing your gloves?'

'Yes, but it went straight through and stabbed me.'

'Show me. You'll have to take your glove off, darling. I haven't got X-ray vision.' Jenny helped her remove it and examined her hand. 'I'll get it out for you,' she said, 'but you need to wash your hands first.'

'Why?'

'Because you don't want your hand to be infected, and because washing them will soften the skin and make the splinter come out more easily.'

Leanne said, 'To save you getting up, I'll take her to wash her hands.'

'That's kind of you, Leanne. She's quite good at doing it without being asked, but she doesn't always do a thorough job.'

'Right, Nicola,' said Leanne, 'lead me to the bathroom.'

When they were gone, Jennie said, 'Leanne's a lovely girl.'

'Thank you. She has a playful sense of humour, but a good heart as well.'

'I got that impression. You know, I'm glad you've come to live here, Adam. We obviously have things in common.'

'It seems so. Who plays the piano?'

'Nicola, when I can get her to practise, and I do, although I hesitate to say that to a musician.'

'Don't be fooled. I'm rubbish, really.'

'I don't believe that. Anyway, I only play at rehearsals for the Choral Society.' Correcting herself, she said, 'At least, I did. The Choral Society has rather lost its way, I'm afraid.'

Leanne ushered Nicola into the room. 'Her hands are clean,' she announced, 'and we've soaked the splintered one in warm water.'

'Oh, thank you, Leanne.'

Adam got to his feet and placed his cup and saucer on the tea tray. 'Thank you, Jenny. The tea was very welcome, but we should be on our way.'

'If there's anything you need,' said Jenny, getting up to let them out, 'you know where I am.'

* * *

Adam's mobile phone chirruped while he was unpacking. It turned out to be a text message from Jimbo:

Hi Pop, had a gr8 hol. Not sure when UR moving, so good luck and stuff. Lol. Got a job as barman in the smoke for hols. CU sometime. Jimbo.

Leanne asked, 'What does he say?'

'I don't know. It's all in code.' He handed his phone to her.

' "Gr8" means "great", "lol" means "laugh out loud", and by "smoke", I imagine he means London. "CU" is "see you".'

Adam shook his head at the wonder of it all. 'It's like that programme we saw about the Enigma code,' he said. 'If you'd been born sixty years earlier, Leanne, you could have done this country a great service as a codebreaker.'

'The twenty-first century is just too much for you, isn't it, Dad?'

'It seems so at times. I spent my holidays from the College working for my Uncle Fred. You never knew him, did you?'

'No.'

'He was a locksmith, and we spoke to each other in plain English.'

He lifted a cardboard box labelled *L's U/W*. 'I wonder what this is.'

'My underwear.' She took it from him hurriedly. 'Something else that's secret.'

Adam's thoughts were already elsewhere. 'I wonder when we'll see Jimbo,' he said.

4

SEPTEMBER

Leanne had found a job as a waitress at Netherdale Tea Rooms, so Adam was alone when he heard the sound of a motorbike at the end of its journey, and saw something large, black and threatening glide past the dining room window.

He opened the front door to find Jimbo on the doorstep, crash helmet in hand.

'Hi Pop.' He held out his arms for a hug. 'How's things? Getting plenty?' It was one of Jimbo's stock greetings, and like so many irritating features of family life, it refused to go away. There was, however, the minor blessing that no response was necessary, because Jimbo never waited for one.

'What a journey,' he said, sighing theatrically.

'What would you like? A cup of tea?'

'No, Pop, something stronger.'

'A cup of strong tea, or very strong tea?'

'Try again, Pop. You're nearly there.'

'Beer?'

'Now you're speaking my language.' He unzipped his leather jacket and then removed his boots. When Adam returned with a glass of bottled Black Sheep, he was almost undressed. 'Thanks, Pop,' he said, squinting at the brew. 'Haven't you got any lager?'

'That's not a word we use up here,' warned Adam. 'You're in real ale country now.' He decided to take pity on his son. After all, it was a long way from London to Netherdale. 'I'll look in the fridge.'

He found a can of lager, which he handed to Jimbo, taking the Black Sheep for himself.

'Thanks, Pop. Nice place you've got here.'

'I'm glad you approve. How are things with you?'

'Don't ask, Pop.' He shook his head sorrowfully.

'Now you've whetted my appetite, I have to ask.'

Jimbo closed his eyes, an indication that the information he was about to impart was causing him great suffering. Eventually, he said, 'I went through all the trials of adolescence and puberty, if you'll pardon my directness, to get the voice I wanted, and now my professor wants to take it from me.' On brief reflection, he added, 'Actually, it's been going on for a year.'

Knowing his offspring as well as he did, Adam waited for him to explain.

'He wants me to lose three semitones at the bottom end and gain three at the top. In short, he wants me to forsake life as a *basso profundo* and become a bass-baritone.'

'How do you do that?' Adam's musical education had been reassuringly instrumental, so he knew very little about vocal training.

Jimbo shrugged. 'Concentrate on the top end,' he said, 'and the bass notes will simply lose the will to survive, victims of an academic whim.'

'It makes sense, Jimbo.'

'*Et tu, Brute*? My bass voice is my fortune. Bottom D flat up to E, but who gives a damn for the high notes?'

'How do you work that out?'

'A deep voice indicates a high level of testosterone, Pop. Girls can't get enough of it. I speak, and they melt into my arms. How am I to survive as a bass-baritone, a virtual *castrato* among basses?'

Adam nodded wisely. 'You could start by curbing your fondness for exaggeration.I can't imagine that the adjustment your professor has in mind will make all that much difference to your vocal quality, but it's bound to widen your options when you audition for parts. There's far more work for bass-baritones than there is for basses.'

'That's what my prof says.'

'Exactly. With a bottom E, you could still sing Sarastro in *The Magic Flute*, and you'd have access to a great many more parts as a bass-baritone with a top G.'

Jimbo looked unconvinced.

'Incidentally, you didn't acquire your bass voice at all. It was a gift of nature.'

'I was using poetic licence, Pop.'

'And you know more than most about licence. But, you know, I think you could be on to a good thing. Imagine yourself, for example, as Don Giovanni.'

It was as if a long-disused part of Jimbo's mind had suddenly become connected, and a new realisation had dawned. The magical name of the great seducer had done what Jimbo's singing professor had failed to do in three terms. He was an instant convert.

When he could speak, he said, 'Thanks, Pop. You've taken a load off my mind.'

'Think nothing of it, Jimbo. It's a father's job, after all, but there's something else you should remember.'

'What's that, Pop?'

'It really is time to start thinking further than the end of your... the blunt instrument in your trousers.'

* * *

Jimbo's unexpected arrival meant that Adam had to buy extra food. They could eat at the pub that evening, of course, but thereafter, adjustments had to be made, so he left Jimbo to unpack while he made a trip to the supermarket.

He found everything he needed and headed for the shortest checkout queue. The woman in front of him picked up a divider and placed it behind her shopping.

'Thank you,' he said, only half-recognising Jenny from behind. A moment later, he saw the children.

'Hello, Adam.'

'Hi, Jenny, Gareth and Nicola. I thought it was you. I'm shopping in a hurry because my son's just arrived home unexpectedly. He does everything unexpectedly,' he explained.

'Do you want to go ahead of me?'

'I'm not in that much of a hurry, but thank you all the same.'

Jenny had a full trolley, and Adam noticed, quite by accident, several bars of chocolate on top of the pile. He couldn't reconcile chocolate with Jenny's trim figure, and he was making a point of looking elsewhere, when she said, 'The chocolate is for my gran. She's in a long-term care home. It's one of her remaining pleasures.'

'That's a shame. I'm sorry.' It was a lame remark, but the best he could offer.

'She has dementia,' Jenny told him. 'Her behaviour's quite eccentric sometimes, and her language can be downright lurid. She never used to swear, but she's taken to it readily since dementia took hold. I can't take the children in to see her. I have a friend who looks after them. She's having them tomorrow morning.' As an afterthought, she said, 'I have to take her TV set in for her as well. I've been storing it in my conservatory.'

'How big is the TV set?'

Jenny held out her arms. 'About so big. I don't know what use she'll get out of it. She used to forget how to switch it on.'

Adam nodded understandingly. 'My granddad suffered from it.'

'What kind?'

'They called it Lewy body dementia.'

She nodded. 'That's what my gran has.'

The woman in front of Jenny finally packed her shopping into bags and paid for it. It was Jenny's turn.

'Look,' he said, 'you're going to need help with that TV set. I'll gladly give you a hand tomorrow.'

'I couldn't possibly let you do that.'

'It's no trouble.'

The checkout assistant started running Jenny's items past the barcode reader. 'Let him help you, love,' she said. 'He's right about a telly being too much to carry. I've done my share of carting things for elderly relatives and I know.'

'All right. Thank you, both of you.'

* * *

'Wouldn't you rather be with your son this morning?'

'No.' Adam stretched as far as he could in the passenger seat of Jenny's Renault, enjoying the unusual luxury of not having to drive. 'I gave him a year's worth of fatherly advice when he arrived home.'

'Friendly advice, I hope?'

'Of course.' He told her about Jimbo's dilemma and his shock realisation that he could still set hearts a-flutter as a bass-baritone.

'I've got all that to come,' she said, 'teenage, adolescence and beyond.'

'It doesn't last forever,' he assured her. 'They grow up eventually, and you have to sympathise with them while it's all going on. Just to appreciate what they're going through, you've only to remember how awful it was for you.'

'Yours are lucky to have an understanding dad.'

'They don't think so. Jimbo's a wild child, and Leanne thinks she understands a great deal more than I do.'

'Even so, you seem to have things under control,' she said. 'When my husband went on his way, my greatest worry was that I had to shoulder all the responsibility for the children.'

It was the first time Jenny had mentioned her husband, but Adam made no comment. Instead, he said, 'You seem to be doing a pretty good job too.'

'Thank you. In case you're wondering, we parted company four years ago. He was serially unfaithful, and I decided I could take no more. It was difficult at first, but I've come to enjoy the space he left behind, particularly since the divorce.'

'Exactly, and the fact that he was drawn repeatedly to pastures new is no reflection on you. It never is.' He was currently admiring pastures that were quite new to him. The trees on the wooded hillside were just beginning to turn with the onset of autumn, and the hedgerows were a wine-red blur of autumn fruits.

'I wondered about that for some time.'

'Honestly, you shouldn't.'

'No, I came to terms with it a while ago.' The situation still puzzled her, though, because she asked, 'Why do men do it?'

Having no real knowledge of such things, Adam had to think about his answer. 'I can only think it's the thrill of the chase,' he said, 'the prospect and the pursuit, because once they've made their conquest, the game's over.'

She nodded. 'I think you have something there.' She turned into a long drive leading to a large building and a carpark. 'Here we are,' she said. 'I'll get as close to the entrance as I can.'

'Don't worry, I can manage.'

When she'd parked the car, he lifted the hatch and picked up the TV set.

'Are you all right, Adam?'

'Absolutely.'

Jenny led the way, punching the PIN into each lock until they arrived at a suite labelled 'Honeydew'.

'Are you sure you want to come in, Adam?'

'I need to carry this in for you. At the very least, it'll give her something new to think about.'

'It will,' she agreed, 'but you could turn out to be her late father or the Archbishop of York. It's an even shot.'

'I'd prefer the latter. I've never worn gaiters and a shovel hat, and Leanne keeps telling me I should be more adventurous with my wardrobe.'

Jenny operated the lock and let them both into a large room with smaller rooms along opposite walls. Waving to a member of staff, she continued until they came to a room at the far end, where Jenny's gran sat, clothed and looking as if she were expecting something to happen.

'I wondered when you'd come,' she said, accepting a kiss from Jenny. 'You've left it a bit late.'

'It's ten-thirty, Gran.'

'Is it really? My watch must be wrong.' She gave Adam an appraising look and asked, 'Who's this, then?'

'This is Adam, my new neighbour.'

Adam put the TV set on top of a convenient chest of drawers and said, 'How do you do?'

'I see. What's he like in bed?'

Jenny tried not to look at Adam. 'I don't know, Gran. He's my neighbour.'

The information seemed lost on Jenny's gran, who was

convinced that Adam was her granddaughter's latest suitor. 'You'll have to try him out, you know. Try before you buy. That's what I always say. Try before you buy, and then you don't find yourself short-changed when it's too late to back out.'

'What are you reading, Gran?' In her embarrassment, Jenny picked up a paperback from the top of her gran's locker.

'I can't read it. My eyes are completely buggered.'

Adam took the book from Jenny and asked, 'Would you like me to read to you?'

'You can if you like. If you're no good in bed, you might as well make yourself useful somehow.'

It was a novel by Danielle Steele, not Adam's usual choice of reading, but he opened it and did his best.

As he read, the old lady hauled herself on to her bed and laid her head on the pillows, closing her eyes. Adam continued to read until he could detect no movement other than deep and regular breathing. Jenny motioned towards the door, so he put the book down.

They'd reached the doorway when the old lady opened her eyes and said, 'Remember what I told you, Jenny. Try before you buy.'

Adam sensed a presence close by. He turned to face a man who was wearing nothing but a pyjama jacket. The man came to attention, saluted him smartly, and said, 'I'm sorry, sir. It won't happen again.'

'I know it won't,' said Adam, who had dealt with similar incidents. 'You're a good man.'

'Thank you, sir.'

'You're welcome.' The man was standing so stiffly, Adam wouldn't have been surprised to find him in the same attitude a week later. He must have been a good soldier. 'At ease,' he said, 'and carry on.' As he recalled, it was what they said in films.

'Very good, sir.'

When they were in the car, Jenny said, 'Thank you for coming today and reading to her.' She turned to face him. 'And for being so understanding.'

'Any time.'

'You really mean it, don't you?'

'Yes, as long as you promise not to tell her my secret.'

'What's that?'

'That I really am rubbish in bed.'

'My lips are sealed.' She started the engine. 'Anyway,' she said, 'that's quite enough embarrassment for one day. I've been meaning to ask you if you've ever conducted a choir. I mean, I'm sure you have, but I thought I'd better ask.'

'Do you have a particular choir in mind?'

'Yes, I have. It's the Netherdale Choral Society. I play the piano at rehearsals.'

'Yes, I remember.'

'Of course. The trouble is, the society has no conductor, its numbers are depleted, and it hasn't met for several weeks.'

'What happened to the conductor?'

Jenny negotiated the turn-out into the main road before answering his question. 'He walked out on us,' she said, allowing him a few moments to digest the information. 'He came highly recommended. Apparently, he was a choral scholar at Cambridge.' She stopped at a pedestrian crossing and waited for the green light. 'I always felt awkward when I played for him,' she said. 'He never criticised my playing, as such, but he used to get very impatient if I didn't know immediately where he wanted to start in the middle of the score.' The lights changed, and she moved off again.

'Was he as impatient with the members?'

'No, he was worse with them.'

'No wonder numbers have fallen off.' He wondered if the society meant more to her than she'd admitted.

'Foot-and-mouth didn't help, of course. That was the greatest tragedy, but for some, the society was a welcome distraction from it. That was until Nicholas, the conductor, became an *un*welcome distraction.'

They were almost home when she asked him, 'Is it something you'd consider doing? I mean, it's not up to me, of course. The committee would have to decide, but if I could put your name forward, I don't think there'd be a problem.'

'Let me think about it, Jenny. I'll let you know.'

5

Leanne enjoyed childminding. She'd known very few naughty children, and the other kind allowed her to watch television or read, usually without interruption, and so, when Jenny asked her to look after Gareth and Nicola while she visited her parents, she was happy to agree.

As she'd anticipated, it was a quiet evening, with only one minor incident.

She was reading, with Dottie half-across her lap, when she heard what sounded like a gasp from upstairs, and then someone crying. It sounded like Nicola. Jenny had told her that Nicola was prone to bad dreams.

She went to the foot of the stairs and found the child on her way down, still crying. 'Come on, Nicola,' she said, 'come and tell me about it.' She steered her to the sofa, where she sat down with her. The poor child was incoherent at first, but her sobs ebbed after a while, and Leanne asked, 'Did you have a bad dream?'

Nicola nodded.

'That's awful, but we know how to deal with bad dreams.' She held out her arms to her, and said, 'Cuddle up and make it go away.' It was what her mum used to say. It made no sense at all, but it always seemed to work. 'Send it on its way, Nicola,' she said, rocking her. 'It can't beat the cuddle.'

She was still holding her when Jenny arrived home.

'Oh,' she said, taking Nicola, now almost asleep, into her arms, 'was it a bad dream?'

'Yes, but we sent it packing, didn't we, Nicola?'

'Thank you, Leanne.' She held Nicola until she was almost asleep. 'I'll take her up to bed. Will you stay and have a drink?'

'Mm. After all that, I think I will.'

When Jenny came down, she opened a bottle of wine and filled two glasses.

'She started the bad dreams when my husband left us. It's the only way it seems to have affected her. Gareth, on the other hand, just withdrew into himself. He was never as shy when his dad was around.' She looked down at the carpet, no doubt remembering past incidents.

'They'll both adjust in time, won't they?'

'I hope so.' Looking up again, she asked, 'How did you send the bad dream packing?'

'My mum's old formula. "Cuddle up and make it go away." Just saying it made it work.'

'That's something you'll always remember, isn't it?'

'Yes, it is. We forget some things too easily.'

'That's true.' Jenny gave her an enquiring look. 'Are you thinking of something in particular?'

Leanne looked down into her wine, thinking about the day they'd viewed the house and her dad had chased Matthew Dewhirst away, when they'd sat together and talked.

'On the day my dad made the offer for the house,' she said, 'I asked him why he wanted to move, and he told me it was about moving on, and that it was the first positive decision he'd made since my mum died. I realised, as he said it, that it was. Even packing in his teaching job had been a negative reaction. It turned out to be a good move, but it was a knee-jerk at the time.' She sipped her wine thoughtfully, because she wanted to make sense. 'Anyway, it all became a bit emotional – for me, that is, because my dad always holds his feelings in check – and he saw I was upset, so he did something he hadn't done for years. He stroked my hair. You know how girls go through that thing when they don't want to be treated as if they're little?'

Jenny nodded.

'I used to say, "Gerroff", and I wish now that I hadn't, but that's how we are when we're growing up. Teenage girls can be horrible. But, you know, it was nice, him stroking my hair like that, and I think he found it as comforting as I did.'

'I'm sure he would.'

'That was something I'd forgotten.' She finished her wine and put her glass down. 'When my mum was ill and when she died, it was too horrible for words, but we could always go to him, and he always made time for us. The trouble was, he had no one to go to.'

'No family?'

'My uncle lives in New Zealand, my granddad died in an accident before I was born, and my grandma died a few years before my mum.'

'What about the other side, your mum's family?'

'She was an only child, and her parents and my dad didn't get on.' She stopped, like someone getting her bearings. 'Am I making sense?'

'Perfect sense, but it wouldn't matter if you weren't. You're talking about something that's important to you, and that's what matters.' She refilled Leanne's glass and her own. 'Talk when you need to, Leanne. I'll always listen.'

'You're easy to talk to as well, Jenny.'

'Good. Hopefully, we've all got some special quality tucked away somewhere. Did your dad tell you about this morning?'

'Visiting your gran? Yes.'

'He was very good with her.'

'He would be. It takes a lot to faze him.'

Jenny seemed unsure. 'I may have asked too much of him,' she said.

'No, he didn't mind.'

'I mean, when I asked him if he'd consider taking on the Choral Society.'

'Oh, that.' Leanne dismissed her concern. 'He's thinking about it. Jimbo's tried hard to sell the idea to him, but Jimbo's like that. If someone said, "Let's cross the Sahara Desert tomorrow", he'd say, "That's a brilliant idea," and he'd pack his bucket and spade without considering the implications. But don't worry, Jenny. He'll do it, basically because he finds it difficult to say "no".'

'I wouldn't want him to do it on that basis.'

'He'll convince himself it's a good idea, put heart and soul into it and wish he'd thought of it earlier. Trust me.'

* * *

The Choral Society Committee welcomed Jenny's suggestion, but insisted that all candidates for the honorary role of Conductor must be auditioned. Jenny was painfully embarrassed on Adam's behalf, whereas he was inclined to take a philosophical line. After all, they'd made one ill-judged appointment. Why would they want to risk making another? Maybe they needed the practice. Accordingly, he agreed to audition in the school hall before those members of the society who could be persuaded to attend. Jimbo invited himself as an observer, and Adam told him to stay out of sight.

The Chairman of the Society addressed Adam.

'Mr Watkinson,' he said, sounding like a local dignitary, 'what are your qualifications?'

'Graduate of the Royal Schools of Music, Associate of the Royal College of Music and Postgraduate Certificate in Education.'

The Chairman conferred with his fellow committee members before re-addressing Adam. 'We had a much-qualified conductor until recently, Mr Watkinson, and he turned out to be a disappointment.'

'He must have been infinitely better qualified than I am; in fact, my meagre qualifications hardly deserve a mention.'

'Really?'

'In any case, I think that ability is worth a whole wall of diplomas.'

'Do you really?'

'I only took them so that I could practise as a teacher, and to make my grandmother happy. She always wanted me to get my name in the local paper, hopefully for something that wasn't embarrassing.'

The Chairman eyed him uncertainly and then entered into further discussion. Eventually, he said, 'Very well. Let's see what you can do. We've chosen a chorus from Handel's *Messiah* for you to conduct. We imagine you're familiar with "And the Glory of the Lord"?'

'I'm well-acquainted with it, Mr Chairman.'

'Good. Please proceed.'

Adam surveyed the modest collection of choristers before him and picked up his stick. 'Altos,' he said, 'will you identify yourselves, please?'

Four hands were raised.

'Thank you.' He surveyed the rest of the chorus and said to the altos, 'It's a bit like Custer's Last Stand for you, isn't it? Never mind.

I'm sure you'll give a good account of yourselves.' Turning to Jenny, he gave her the downbeat for the ten bars of introduction, and on the second beat of the next bar, brought in the altos.

' "And the glory, the glory of the Lord—" '

He stopped them. 'I'm sorry, altos. Sopranos, tenors and basses, you missed your entry. I know you haven't sung this for a while, but please watch me. We'll start again with just an "A", please, Jenny.' He resumed, and the errant choristers made their entry successfully. All went well until the forty-third bar, when he stopped them again. 'Tenors,' he said, 'you missed your entry. Just the "E" chord, please, Jenny, and we'll start at the tenor entry.'

' "And all flesh shall see it together".'

Adam beamed at them, and then at the altos, as they repeated the phrase. They continued up to the last three bars, which was where Adam stopped them once more. 'This chorus is where Christmas begins for a great many people,' he told them, and a stirring climax at the end is what does it. Let's hear some Christmas cheer. Just the notes of the "A" chord, please, Jenny. He brought the now enthusiastic chorus in for the last three bars. 'Excellent. I think we'll run the whole number from the beginning.' Leaning over to speak to Jenny, he said quietly, 'At the end of the number, go straight into "Thus Saith the Lord". I fancy a bit of fun.' She looked at him in surprise, but he simply stood upright again and gave her the downbeat for the introduction.

They sang quite well, each section making its entries cleanly. There was still much to build on, but Adam enjoyed the number right to the end.

The committee were smiling; it was clear that they had good news to impart, but their smiles gave way to surprise as Jenny played the first bar of the following *recitative*, and their consternation deepened when a rich and resonant but anonymous bass voice sang, ' "Thus saith the Lord, the Lord of Hosts; yet once a little while, and I will shake the heavens and the earth, the sea and the dry land." ' The mystery bass sang to the end of the *recitative*, when it was clear that the chairman and his committee were in a state of shock.

'The bass solo,' Adam told them afterwards, 'was provided by my son. He can never resist an audition, even when it's someone else's, and that is the only excuse I'm prepared to offer on his behalf.'

There was a hurried discussion, and the Chairman stood to announce their decision.

'The Committee has decided to offer you the honorary post of Conductor, Mr Watkinson. We also wonder if your son might be available for solo work from time to time.'

'Regarding the Conductor's post, Mr Chairman, I'm pleased to accept it, but I have to let my son speak for himself. I think you'll find him hiding in the cloakroom. It's an old habit.'

After thanking the members and Jenny for their efforts, he and Jimbo retired to The Craven Heifer, where Jenny joined them. Some of the members trickled in and greeted Adam politely, as if they were as yet unsure of him.

'We never use The Golden Lion,' Jenny told them. 'The landlord is a colossal bore. He's an ex-army officer, who thinks he's still in a position of authority, and he wheel-clamps any non-patrons' cars he finds in his carpark, even when it's almost empty, and parking is always at a premium on market day and weekends.'

'I'm not keen on wheel clampers,' said Adam.

'It's true,' said Jimbo, grimacing, possibly at a memory best left untold.

'Official wheel clampers are bad enough, but the cowboys shouldn't be allowed to do it.'

'It's a one-man crusade, Jenny,' confirmed Jimbo.

Adam eyed his son seriously. 'Jimbo,' he said.

'Yes, Pop?'

'Stop talking nonsense, will you?'

'And I thought I'd walked in on a double act,' said Jenny. Others apparently agreed with her. Some of the members had been covertly following the conversation, and now they looked embarrassed, as if they'd been caught out.

'In a sense, that's what we are,' said Jimbo. 'It's fair to say that I helped Pop get the conducting job tonight. Goodness knows, I'm a semi-orphan and a first-year student; a pitiful scrap, you might say, but I know where my loyalty lies, and if I can help my elderly parent in any way possible, I will.'

'No one who heard you sing tonight,' said Jenny, 'would have guessed that you were a first-year student, let alone a semi-orphan.'

There was a murmur of agreement among the members.

'I'll be a second-year student later in the month,' he said, patting Adam's shoulder, 'and, as for the semi-orphan thing, as long as I've got the Old Man, I'll be all right.'

'Only until I disown you.' Adam pushed his empty glass and a ten-pound note in front of his son, and said, 'Make yourself useful and get the drinks in.'

'Not for me, thank you.' Jenny finished her drink and got up. 'Leanne's minding the children for me, so I must get back to relieve her. Well done, both of you.'

As she left them, one of the members asked, 'Do you mind if I join you?'

Adam welcomed him with a hand gesture. 'Feel free.'

'I will an' all,' said another, drawing out a stool. 'That's if you don't mind.'

'You're welcome.'

'We're known as "The Gospel Writers",' the first man told him. 'We're brothers. I'm Mark and he's Matthew.'

'I thought you looked rather alike.' They were both about fifty, with innocent, cheerful faces. They even wore their hair in the same style, with a side parting and a crown that sprouted a defiant cone of standing hair.

'Have you any other brothers?'

'No,' said Mark. 'We get asked that quite a lot, don't we, Matthew?'

'We do, but no, our parents never managed a Luke and a John.'

'We're glad you got the job,' said Matthew, changing the subject, allusions to the New Testament having possibly worn thin over time. 'That other fella couldn't speak to us without being insulting, and he treated poor Jenny shamefully. It's only because she's a lady that she didn't tell him where to put his conductor's stick, and it were a treat to hear you thank her nicely after your audition.'

'Jenny and I are friends, and she's doing a good job.'

Mark leaned forward confidingly to say, 'The Society needs you, Mr Watkinson.'

'Adam.'

'Na'then. What I'm trying to say is this.' He put his glass down for emphasis. 'The Choral Society is a sort of guide to the state of the Dale.' He stopped for a moment, and his brother said, 'I don't think "guide" is quite the right word, Mark.'

'Well, what word am I looking for, Matthew?'

' "Barometer",' suggested Jimbo, putting a pint of bitter and one of lager on the table.

'All right, it's a kind of barometer that tells you how things are, how folk are feeling, and that sort of thing. Foot-and-mouth did horrible things to the Dales, and a lot of folk are still suffering, and I don't just mean financially, although many are. No, they're in need of a lift, a sort of tonic.'

'Aye,' said Matthew supportively.

Mark waited politely for his brother to say more, and then, when he was satisfied that nothing was forthcoming, he continued. 'Members came to the Choral Society because it was a social thing as well as a way of making music, and folk made a point of coming to hear us. We were a....' He struggled again to find the right word.

'A feature,' suggested Jimbo.

'That's right. We were a feature of the Dale.'

'And now you're not?'

'That's right, Adam, and most of it's down to that Nicholas Davies, that... blasted conductor we had. He turned something enjoyable into a toil.'

'Aye,' said Matthew, 'he turned honey into mustard.'

'Hang about,' said Mark. 'I'm partial to a spot of mustard in a ham sandwich.'

'Well, happen t' young chap can think of a word.' Matthew looked expectantly towards Jimbo, who waxed thoughtful.

After a few seconds, Jimbo spoke. 'He turned pleasure into purgatory.'

'Aye.' The description seemed to appeal to the brothers. They returned their attention to Adam, who felt obliged to say something.

'I can't work miracles,' he told them, 'but I do know something about motivation. I think, if we all pull together, we can revive the Choral Society and restore it to something of its former self.'

6

'I don't see why we can't perform *Messiah* this December,' said Adam. 'If the members have done it several times, they'll just need to lose a few bad habits.' It was Sunday morning, and the two families were at Adam's house. Jimbo and Gareth were outside, and Leanne was showing Nicola her old Enid Blyton books.

Jenny asked, 'How do you know they've learned bad habits?'

'I understand they've always used the Prout Edition,' said Adam. 'That's a whole string of bad habits in itself.'

'Will they need to buy a new set?'

'No, I can correct things as we go.'

'I see. We could put it to the committee.' Jenny considered other implications. 'We'd need to hire a church as well.'

'Why?'

'For the organ. We'd need an organist, too, because it's not something I'm confident to do, especially something as big as *Messiah*.'

'I disagree. We have a perfectly good accompanist. We could hire the old Council Offices and use their piano. I'm told there's a Steinway there in reasonable condition.'

'Thank you for that vote of confidence, but I don't know what the committee will....' She broke off to say, 'What on *earth* is going on out there?' She was looking through the kitchen window.

Adam joined her and shrugged. Jimbo was hopping on his left foot and patting his head with his right hand. Gareth followed in his wake, hopping and stopping as he repeatedly lost his balance.

'It's the first time in ages that Gareth has played at anything,' said Jenny. 'Look,' she said in disbelief, 'he's laughing.'

As she turned to speak to him, Adam saw that her eyes were wet. 'Jimbo either annoys or pleases,' he told her sympathetically. 'He doesn't offer a third option.'

Gareth was still following Jimbo, who was now walking like Charlie Chaplin.

'I can't believe it. I've been so worried about him, I've even wondered about seeking medical advice.'

'So have I,' said Adam, watching Jimbo. He handed her a box of tissues.

'Thank you,' she said, dabbing her eyes. 'I'm sorry.'

'Don't be. It's the effect Jimbo has on some people. I've considered marketing it, but I don't think many people would take crackpot therapy seriously.'

'Oh, but I do.'

Leanne came into the kitchen and asked, 'Who's not taking what seriously?' Then, seeing Jenny red-eyed, she asked, 'What's the matter?'

Adam pointed towards the window, 'Jimbo's playing with Gareth,' he explained.

'Ah.' Leanne observed the phenomenon briefly and then held out her arms to Jenny.

Nicola walked into the kitchen. She stared at her mother and asked, 'What's the matter, Mum?'

'Nothing, darling. I'm all right.'

'Did you have a bad dream last night?'

'Yes, and not just last night, but I think it's over now.'

'It will be,' said Nicola, confident that her mother was in good hands.

The outer door opened as Jimbo and Gareth entered the kitchen.

'Gareth needs to water his donkey,' announced Jimbo. 'I'll show him to the downstairs bog.'

Jenny waited until Jimbo was back, and then said, 'Thank you, Jimbo. You've worked a miracle with Gareth.'

Jimbo shrugged modestly. 'It was nothing,' he said. 'He just needed to chill out. Everybody does sometimes.'

'Whereas you do it all the time,' said Adam, who'd been feeling a trifle spare until that moment.

'All that flies out of the window after tomorrow, Pop. It's back to the grindstone for me. No time for fun and frolics, no taking time out, no partying, no rumpty-tumpty, just hard work.'

'I'll believe that when I see it.'

'Oh, you of little faith, Pop, and after I helped you get that conducting job as well.'

Leanne took Nicola's hand and said, 'Come with me, Nicola. I'm going to give you one of those *Famous Five* books, and then, if you like it, I'll give you some more.'

As they climbed the stairs again to Leanne's room, Nicola asked, 'What's rumpty-tumpty?'

Leanne considered the question. 'It's a game that boys think is just for their benefit,' she said. 'The only trouble is that they need a girl to play it as well.'

'Is it like *Trivial Pursuit?*'

Leanne frowned. 'What made you think of *Trivial Pursuit?*'

Nicola paused on the landing to explain. 'Most boys are hopeless at reading, so they need a girl to read the questions, and then the boys try to answer them, but they usually get everything wrong.'

'Right, Nicola, I think you've hit the nail on the head there. It is a kind of trivial pursuit. At least, it's certainly seemed so in my short experience.'

* * *

A few days later, Adam was working on a new musical for schools. It was about the story of Moses and the great exodus. Strangely, or perhaps reassuringly at a time of political correctness and the questioning of accepted values, children still wanted biblical stories set to music. He thought he might call this one 'Promised Land', although titles were seldom definite until they went to print. In view of the long-running Middle Eastern dispute, the publishers had forbidden the use of the names 'Palestine', 'Israel' or 'The Holy Land', a constraint that struck Adam as faint-hearted. In any case, he reasoned, what were the odds on a copy of his musical finding its way into the hands of either of the opposing forces?

He was working on a song about the plague of frogs when the phone rang. Hoping it wasn't the Foreign Office phoning to ban the musical, he answered it.

'Hello.'

'Adam, it's Jenny. I'm sorry to disturb you.'

'That's all right. I was only marshalling an army of frogs. How can I help you?'

'I'm really sorry.'

'Don't be. I prefer you shameless and unrepentant.'

There was a pause, and then Jenny spoke again. 'My mum went to see Gran yesterday, and she was going on and on about how I'd brought this man, and he'd read to her. Apparently, no one reads as well as you, and she wants to know when you're going to read to her again. My mum told her how busy you are, but she was adamant that she wanted to see you again. Once she gets a bee in her bonnet, it takes some shifting.'

'That's all right. I'll read to her again.'

'Oh, will you, Adam?' She sounded relieved but still embarrassed. 'With any luck, she'll get it out of her system and I shan't trouble you again.'

'Don't worry. It's little enough to do for her. I remember what it was like with my granddad, except he used to demand a live cricket commentary, even when there was no cricket being played. I had to switch the TV on, turn the sound down, and describe an imaginary match to him. His eyesight was almost gone, so it didn't matter what was happening on the screen.'

'It's very kind of you, Adam.' She hesitated again. 'Could you bear to do it tomorrow morning?'

'Of course. What time?'

'If we leave by ten, we can spend an hour with her. Is that all right?'

'Right as rain.' With Jimbo back in London, he was making good progress with the musical, and an hour or so away from it would make little difference.

* * *

'Gareth's missing Jimbo,' said Jenny as she started the car.

'His absence seldom goes unnoticed.'

'I've told him he'll be back at Christmas, but in the mind of a ten-year-old, that might as well be a year in the future.'

'Has he got a mobile phone?'

She laughed shortly. 'Haven't they all? Refusing a child a phone is tantamount to cruelty nowadays.'

'I'll get Jimbo to text him.' He thought for a moment. 'I think that's what they call it.'

'That would be lovely.'

'Just as long as Gareth knows the code. I must say, it defeats me.'

'I prefer plain English too.'

'Changing the subject, I've been meaning to ask you, have you always been a Jenny or are you a sawn-off Jennifer?'

'Always,' she confirmed. 'I was abbreviated in the womb. When my gran was in charge of her faculties, she cited a radio programme in which someone used to say, "What's your name, little girl?" and the little girl said, "Jennifer" in such a simpering way that it put my gran off the name forever, and my mum, who is always good for a compromise, settled for "Jenny".'

'I'm glad she did. I like it.'

'Thank you.'

His attention was taken again by the changing autumn scene. The trees were still clinging forlornly to their foliage in its various hues, and he was reminded of the first autumn Jimbo, Leanne and he had spent in the Dale.

After a moment, Jenny surprised Adam by saying, 'It's my turn now.'

'Your turn for what?'

'To ask you a personal question. When we first met, you told me the politicians had put you off teaching. What did you mean?'

'Oh, that.' He wondered quite how to condense what had been for him a long tale of rancour. 'It was their cynical attitude,' he said eventually, 'buying votes by promising to get tough with teachers. Everyone's been to school, and most people have had a bad experience at some time, so they knew it was a vote catcher, and I'm not being partisan; the current government is just as bad as its predecessor.'

'Were you inspected?'

'Yes, twice. It was the second inspection that killed my pig. The Ofsted inspector didn't find anything wrong with my teaching. How could he when he was a mere child with precious little chalk-face experience of his own? No, he snagged me on documentation.'

'What?' She took her eyes briefly off the busy road to register her surprise.

'Oh yes, documentation is far more important than teaching kids. The most important document is the Department Policy Document, and there are certain buzz words and phrases that must appear in it. One of them is "high expectations". However, with the best will, I couldn't see my least-able and semi-literate students getting scholarships to Oxford, so, tempering piety with realism, I adopted the phrase "high *aspirations*".'

'That sounds quite acceptable to me.'

'Ah, but you have to get the wording just right.'

'Was that all?'

'Not by a long chalk. I refused to allow one inspector into my classroom because he was chewing gum.'

'Surely not.'

'He wasn't one of the education inspectors. He was the one responsible for fire extinguishers, dustbins and toilet tissue, but I had to tell him that he would only be welcome once he'd removed his gum. I didn't allow the kids to chew gum in class, and I wasn't going to let him set them a bad example.'

'What happened?'

'He reported me to the Registered Inspector – that's the head of the team – who wrote an adverse report. You see, an inspector must be allowed to roam without let or hindrance, regardless of whether he's chewing gum, picking his nose or mooning at passing traffic.'

She turned into the road leading to the home. 'How petty,' she said.

'Well, with Kate less than a year in her grave, it wasn't a good time for me, as you can imagine, and I'd had enough of the whole charade, so I told the Head and the Registered Inspector to divide my job by two and insert each half into a place of intimate seclusion.' He paused to enjoy the memory of that meeting. 'It was the right decision,' he concluded.

'I'd no idea it was like that,' she said, switching the engine off.

'For most people, it isn't. They're usually all right as long as they go along with the system. It was just unfortunate that, in my case, they picked on a novice member of the singles club.'

She reached out and patted his arm. 'What a rotten time you've had,' she said.

'It's improving for me. Jimbo's bouncing back, although he has his moments, but I'm mainly concerned about Leanne. She and Kate were almost joined at the hip, they were so close.'

'And she's concerned about you.'

'What?'

'Yes, she told me. It worries her that, at the worst time, they had you, but you had no one to turn to.'

'I had them, Jenny. I think it's what the psychologists call "projection". They came to me for comfort, and that helped me.'

'I'm glad.'

'Okay,' said Adam, releasing his seatbelt, 'let's go and read to your gran.'

'Yes.' She removed the ignition key and opened her door.

Adam waited for her beside the car, and then offered her his arm.

'How nice.' She smiled her appreciation.

Adam asked, 'What's your gran's surname?'

'Sanderson. Why do you ask?'

'So that I can be polite and address her properly.'

'Of course.'

'Where are we going?' She was towing him away from the locked door.

'We have to sign in,' she said. 'I forgot last time. We were taking the television set in, and it went out of my mind.' She took the captive ballpoint and wrote *J. Thorpe + 1*, adding her car registration number and the time.

They went through the two locked doors, exchanged a brief

word with the nurse and one of the care workers, peered into the sitting room to ascertain that Mrs Sanderson wasn't there, and continued to her room.

They found her gazing through her window. 'Oh, you're here at last,' she said. 'I'd almost given you up. I was watching the bears play on the lawn, just to pass the time on.'

'It's not ten-thirty yet, Gran,' Jenny told her.

Mrs Sanderson looked sternly at her wristwatch and said, 'This bloody watch is no good. I don't know why I bother wearing it.'

'I've brought Adam to read to you.'

'I thought he was too busy.'

'No, Mrs Sanderson,' said Adam, 'I'm not too busy.'

'He's taken over as conductor of the choral society,' Jenny told her.

The old lady eyed him sharply. 'That's where I've seen you before.' She nodded, as if in confirmation. 'Next time you conduct the Last Night of the Proms,' she said, 'tell those hooligans in the audience to stop waving things. It's most annoying.' She pulled herself back on to the bed and swung her legs up so that she was lying on her back.

'I'll do my best to put a stop to it,' said Adam. Looking at the books on her table, he asked, 'What would you like me to read?'

'Not that Danielle Steele. Suddenly everyone's American. I don't know why.'

'Maybe it's because Danielle Steele is American.'

Mrs Sanderson merely snorted.

'How about Rumpole?' He picked up *Rumpole for the Defence*.

'That'll do. At least he's not American.'

'Are you comfortable, Mrs Sanderson?'

'As comfortable as I can be on this bloody boat.'

'Good.' He began reading. Almost immediately, her eyes closed, and she lay still. In the light of previous experience, he continued to read.

Presently, a resident leaned over the wicket door, and Adam recognised him as the man who had spoken to him on his last visit. Surely enough, he saluted Adam smartly and said, 'Sorry, sir. It won't happen again.'

Adam broke off to say, 'I know it won't, You're a good man.'

'Thank you, sir.'

'At ease. Carry on.'

'Very good, sir.'

Mrs Sanderson opened her eyes and said, 'Tell him to bugger off. He's ga-ga, you know. Most of the passengers on this boat are.'

'He's gone now.'

'Good. Why have you stopped?'

'I'm sorry.' Adam read on.

After a while, she opened her eyes and said, 'You can stop there. I've guessed the ending already. It was the cat that wrote the letter. They're always walking across typewriter keys.'

They took their leave of her, but not before she'd offered Jenny a nugget of advice. 'If he's no good at sex,' she said, 'get him to read to you. It'll be better than nothing.'

As they walked back to Jenny's car, she asked, 'How old are you, Adam?'

'Forty-two.' He could see the arithmetic going on behind her eyes. 'Jimbo was conceived when we were still under starter's orders,' he explained. 'It caused a stir at the time.'

'There's no shame in it,' she assured him.

'It made life difficult enough, and it was so expensive at the time that we decided, as things improved, that we couldn't face the idea of our children struggling as we had, so we took out insurance to help them through higher education. We didn't know then that tuition fees were going to be introduced, but it was a relief when it happened that we didn't have to worry about it.'

'You told me something about that when we first met.'

'Did I?'

'Yes.' She fished in her bag for the car key. 'It was when you told me you'd given up teaching.'

'Of course.' He opened the passenger door and got in.

'I know you want to get back to your work,' she said, 'but, as you've been so kind and accommodating this morning, will you let me buy you lunch?'

'I was about to offer you the same.'

'But I got my offer in first.'

'In that case, thank you, I think I can allow that.'

7

OCTOBER

' " And the government shall be upon his shoulder, and his name shall be callèd Wonderful, Counsellor, The Mighty God, The Everlasting Father, The Prince of Peace, The Everlasting Father, The Prince of Peace." '

Adam let Jenny play out the final eight bars, and then put his stick down. 'Thank you, Jenny and everyone,' he said. 'We've made excellent progress tonight. I'm looking forward to seeing you all next Thursday.' A rough headcount had come to forty-seven. It was an encouraging response, as Jenny said later in the Craven Heifer.

'It's wonderful to see them returning. Most of them had given up on the Choral Society, but word's got around that things have improved, and it's bringing them back again.'

Mark and Matthew nodded in agreement. 'It's like being reborn,' said Mark, adding hurriedly, 'the Society, that is, not us.'

'Aye.' Matthew added his customary support.

'Will young Jimbo be singing with us?'

'He will, Mark,' assured Adam, 'and he'll be in good practice if last Christmas is anything to go by. He'd sung in two *Messiah*s by the time he came home.'

'He has a grand voice,' said Mark.

'Aye,' said Matthew.

Jenny asked, 'What are we going to do about "The Trumpet Shall Sound"? It won't be much of a sound without a trumpet.'

'We'll bring in a trumpet player.'

She looked at him in surprise. 'Just for that number?'

'No, he or she can join in with the "Hallelujah" and "Amen" choruses as well.'

Mark asked, 'What about the other principals? The people we used to use are all a bit long in the tooth now, and we haven't done *Messiah* for three years or more.'

'I'm waiting for the committee to give me the go-ahead,' said Adam, 'and I'll book some people I know. I have in mind a soprano, a tenor and a mezzo who'll do it without breaking the bank.'

'That's another thing,' said Jenny. 'The Society's funds are depleted after recent events.'

'Aye,' said Matthew, surprising everyone by going on to say, 'that Nicholas Davies has a lot to answer for.'

'The principals shouldn't cost the earth,' said Adam. 'The biggest expense will be the hire of the old Council Offices.'

'I don't know why.' Jenny got up to put her coat on. 'It's hardly used for anything these days.'

'Well, we'll see.' Adam helped her on with her coat.

'Thanks, Adam. I must get back for Leanne.'

'I gather she's going to one of your watercolour classes on her day off.'

'Yes, she's very keen.' She fastened her coat and said, 'Gareth got a text message from Jimbo as well. He was thrilled to bits. I think there's a lot of hero-worship going on there.'

Adam smiled at the thought. 'Jimbo's an unlikely role model,' he said.

'Well, I'm very grateful to him.' She looked at her watch. 'Must go,' she said. 'Are you okay for ten o'clock tomorrow?' In response to a further demand, Adam had agreed to read again to Mrs Sanderson.

'Yes, I'll see you at ten o'clock.'

* * *

'This is ever so good of you,' said Jenny, punching the PIN into the lock on the second door.

'Not at all. I feel desperately sorry for anyone in her position.'

One of the care workers saw them and came over to speak to them. 'She's in her room,' she said, 'waiting for her mother. She's been very impatient.'

'Thank you,' said Jenny. 'We'll calm her down if we can.' To Adam, she said, 'This happens sometimes. You just have to lie like a trooper and tell her something to satisfy her.'

'Did her mother have a favourite place to visit?'

'Yes, Scotland. She came from Kirkcudbright.' She pushed open the door.

'Where have you been until now?' The question came like the prelude to a rant, but Jenny said calmly, 'It's not ten-thirty yet, Gran.'

'So you keep saying, and where's my mother?'

Jenny was caught for a moment without an answer, but Adam said, 'Didn't she say Kirkcudbright?'

'Yes,' said Jenny, grabbing the lifeline, 'she's gone to Kirkcudbright.'

'What the fuck is she doing there?'

Adam thought quickly. 'She's working for the SNP, trying to get a candidate elected.'

'And just what is the SNP when it's at home?'

'The Scottish National Party,' said Jenny.

'Oh well,' said Mrs Sanderson, 'if that sort of thing amuses her.... I saw her on the bus this morning, and she didn't even look the side I was on.' She made a dismissive gesture and sat on her bed. 'As soon as this train stops, I'm getting off.'

'Would you like me to read to you?' Adam picked up *Rumpole for the Defence* in readiness.

'No, I can't be bothered with that now.'

'Adam made a special journey to come and see you, Gran,' said Jenny.

Mrs Sanderson stared at him. 'You look very much like that other chap,' she said, 'the man who reads to me. He's a pleasant enough chap, but he's hopeless in bed. I don't know what Jenny sees in him.' She hauled herself into her usual dorsal position and said, 'Go on, you may as well read to me, seeing as you're here.'

Adam opened the book and found the story *Rumpole and the Gentle Art of Blackmail*. He read for a good twenty minutes, and when he and Jenny made their exit, Mrs Sanderson was sleeping soundly.

* * *

It was Adam's turn to buy lunch, which he did at the Craven Heifer.

'The food is probably better at the Golden Lion,' he said, 'and I have to confess that I took Leanne there the day I made the offer on the house.'

'You didn't know any better in those days.' Jenny was happy to make his excuse for him. 'Anyway, it's pretty good here.'

'Actually,' he said, squeezing lemon juice on his haddock, 'I had to sweeten Leanne somehow. She wasn't at all pleased to be taken away from her studies.' He thought about that day, and something else occurred to him. 'Kate was the same when we were students.'

'Was she a musician?'

'No, a biochemist. She was at Imperial College, which is next door to the Royal College of Music. That's how we met.'

'What was she like?'

'Physically, an older version of Leanne. They were similar in temperament too. I look at Leanne sometimes and I see Kate. The only difference is that Leanne's not remotely scientific.'

'No.' Jenny smiled at the thought. 'Leanne is an artist through and through.' As if to reinforce her point, she said, 'She showed me some of her work. It's very good.'

'You and Leanne get on well together, don't you?'

'Yes, and Nicola thinks she's wonderful. It's like Jimbo and Gareth.'

Adam closed his eyes tightly at the thought.

'Give him credit for something, Adam.'

'Oh, I do. He has a good heart. It's his amorous inclination that worries me.'

'He has quite a talent,' she reminded him.

Adam nodded. 'He'll sing *Messiah* from memory.'

'Will he really?'

'Yes, he has a prodigious musical memory, but he doesn't always use his talent. Singing means everything to him, but in all the time he was at home he never once touched the piano.'

'Is that part of his course?'

'Yes, all singing students have to take piano as their second study, and usually an orchestral instrument as a third study.' He laughed shortly. 'Jimbo does just what he needs to do in order to survive. No more than that.'

'So that's what was worrying you, that Sunday, when he said he was going back to the grindstone.'

'I was just being my usual sceptical self. Jimbo will find his way eventually, but he'll deliver a few shocks on the way.'

* * *

Later in the day, Adam remembered that he was out of tea, so he set out to the supermarket to get some. As he made his way along the main street in Thanestalls, he pulled up at the pedestrian crossing and, in doing so, noticed Jenny's car up the side street that led to the Golden Lion carpark. She was talking with another woman, and her arm movements suggested that she was agitated.

As soon as he could, he turned back and drove into the street, where he found Jenny still beside her car and in what appeared to be a state of distress. Lowering his window, he asked, 'What's the matter, Jenny?'

'Look at that,' she said. 'I'm maybe a couple of inches into his entrance and he clamped me while I was in the newsagent's.'

'The landlord of the—'

'Yes, Tom Harrison,' said the other woman, who seemed equally outraged. 'He thinks it's clever. It shouldn't be allowed.'

'I have to pick up the children from school, and he's nowhere to be found,' said Jenny.

'Just give me a minute.' Adam got out and lifted the hatch to open his toolbox. He picked up a bunch of tiny skeleton keys and crossed the road to where Jenny's car stood captive. He tried one key and then another until he found one that was the right size.

Jenny's friend asked, 'Should you be doing that?'

'Probably not, but he shouldn't go around clamping cars, as I believe you just said.' He gave the key a final twist and lifted the clamp off the wheel. 'There you are, Jenny. You can collect the children and I'll return this to its owner after I've had a friendly chat with him.'

'Oh, Adam.' She hugged him. 'Thank you. You're wonderful.'

'I'm just handy with locks and keys,' he told her modestly. 'Put it down to early training.'

Jenny slid gratefully into the car and drove off, leaving her friend to eye Adam nervously.

'I spent my student holidays working for my uncle, who was a locksmith,' he explained to the anxious woman. 'I'm not a criminal,' he assured her, picking up the clamp and inclining his head towards the pub, 'but he is.'

He walked up to the kitchen door and pushed it open. A youth in kitchen whites and checked trousers looked at him in surprise.

'Is the landlord about?'

'I think he's back.' The boy seemed uncertain.

'Tell him retribution has caught up with him. I'll wait here.'

The boy left the kitchen, reappearing a few moments later with a large man dressed, rather as Adam had always thought of it, like one of the cast of *The Archers*, in a tweed jacket, a checked shirt and a green bow tie. He wore a handlebar moustache and his manner was immediately truculent.

'What the hell do you want?' His moustache quivered.

'I'm returning this toy to its rightful owner, the Cowboy Clamper of Thanestalls. That's you, I believe.' He held up the clamp for Harrison to see.

'You'd no right to touch that.'

'And you've no right to impede innocent motorists.'

'I give the money to charity.' He seemed less certain, but the bluster was still there.

'It's not for you to decide where other people's money should go. Believe it or not, there's a limit to a publican's powers, and you've over-stepped it.'

Harrison picked up a cleaver. 'Give me that wheel-clamp,' he demanded.

'Gladly, when I've told you what I'm going to do.'

'Give it to me now!' He was brandishing the cleaver.

'What are the odds, I wonder, against your being able to fillet me with that thing before I drop this on your toes? It's only a toy, but it's bloody heavy.'

'All right. What have you got to say?'

'Only this. Whenever I see a car that's been clamped either by you or by one of your staff, I'll remove the clamp and leave it somewhere that you'll find very embarrassing. Then, I'll photograph it and give the picture to *The Netherdale Reporter*. That way, in no time at all, you will be the laughing-stock of the Dale. I wonder what that'll do to your takings.'

Harrison was shaking with anger. 'Who are you, anyway?'

'I'm just someone who has no time for injustice or bullying, and I like to prick self-important bubbles, especially when the bubble is, itself, a self-important prick.' He placed the clamp on the nearest table and said, 'You've been warned, Harrison, and I shan't warn you again.'

* * *

'He won't clamp you again, Jenny.'

She handed him a fresh cup of tea. 'Thank you, Adam, but I'll keep clear of his property in future. Anyway, how can you be sure of that?'

'He and I reached an agreement, and I think, also, he saw the error of his ways.'

'I'm very grateful.'

Adam was about to shrug off the incident again, when the doorbell rang and Leanne came in.

'I thought I'd find you here,' she said.

'Are you going to join us, Leanne?'

'Okay.'

Jenny went to the kitchen for another mug. When she returned, she said, 'Your dad took a clamp off my car today, Leanne.'

'Not an official one, presumably?'

'No, a Golden Lion one.'

Leanne bridled. 'I've heard about that man. He shouldn't be allowed to do it.'

'He's not now.'

'Oh? What happened?'

'He just agreed with me that it was time he found another hobby,' said Adam.

'Oh, Dad. You came down hard on him, didn't you? He's just an old softie,' she told Jenny, 'but not everyone realises that.'

'I was in an awful state,' said Jenny. 'I rather over-reacted. I hope you didn't mind, Adam.'

'Not in the least.'

'What *did* you do, Jenny?' Leanne's question was loaded with mischief.

'I hugged him.'

'Oh, that's all right,' said Leanne, treating the disclosure as an anti-climax. 'He accepts hugs and kisses as a matter of course, don't you, Dad?'

Adam forbore to answer, reluctant as he was to encourage his irreverent daughter.

* * *

A week later, Jenny was scanning *The Netherdale Reporter*. She'd recently placed an advertisement offering extra classes in watercolour painting, and she wanted to know that it had been included in the week's issue. As she ran her eye down the page, she saw a new advertisement that gave her special satisfaction. It read:

For Sale
2 Wheel-clamps.
Ideal security for cars, caravans and trailers.
£15 ea.
Buyer collects.

The advertisement gave the telephone number of The Golden Lion.

She resolved to tell Adam, and then continued to look for her advertisement.

8

The Choral Society Committee moved rather like the wheels of eternity, or so it seemed to Adam, but, by mid-November, the principals and the piano tuner were booked, a special rate had been agreed for the hire of the old Council Offices, and Adam had secured the services of a local trumpet player he'd known for some time. The members, whose number had now reached a round fifty, were as enthusiastic as ever, although there was still room in their performance for improvement, as Adam pointed out one Thursday evening. The fault wasn't entirely theirs, but it had to be dealt with all the same.

'As most of you know,' he said, 'Handel's first language was German, and his setting of English texts could be clumsy. He insisted, however, that he "perfectly English spoke", and he didn't take kindly to being corrected, which leaves us to negotiate his heavy-handed word setting, when it occurs, with care, and this passage is a case in point. 'When you sing, "All we, like sheep", the accent should be on the word "sheep". If you accent "like", it sounds as if you're expressing a preference for mutton. So,' he demonstrated, ' "All we, like *sheep*...". Let's try again.'

' "All we, like sheep,' they sang, 'have gone astray. We have turnèd ev'ryone to his own way—'

Adam had to stop them again. 'That's word-painting taken to an extreme level,' he told them. You really have turned, everyone, to your various ways. Sopranos, from "We have turnèd". Just a "G", please, Jenny.'

Jenny gave the note, and the sopranos, followed by the altos, tried again.

'Not bad,' said Adam. 'Once more.'

'They made a further, determined assault, and Adam declared himself reasonably satisfied. They sang through the number without the need for correction until they came to the final sixteen bars, when Adam stopped them.

'At this point,' he said, 'the music is marked *Adagio*, which is considerably slower than the preceding tempo, so you'll need to keep an eye on me.' He demonstrated, 'One, two, three, four. Just a "C" for the basses, please, Jenny.'

' "And the Lord hath laid on Him,' they sang, 'the iniquity of us all".'

'Good, except that you need to paint the word "iniquity" by emphasising the second syllable. "in*iq*uity". Let's try again from the same place. A "C", please, Jenny.'

They sang again, to Adam's approval.

'Okay, let's sing the whole number through, and then we'll call it a night.'

* * *

Work kept Adam busy for the rest of the week and the whole of the next. Apart from at the Choral Society rehearsal, he saw nothing of Jenny almost until the end of the month, and that was at the supermarket.

'Christmas has caught up with me,' she said, putting a large jar of mincemeat into her trolley.

'I prefer not to think about it, but I'll have to face up to it sooner or later.'

'I know. It must be a rotten time for all of you.'

An elderly man walked past with a jar of pickled onions and a harassed expression.

'T' wife's buggered off wi' t' barrer,' he told them in a strong West Riding accent. 'I don't know where she's got hersen to.'

'Good luck,' said Adam.

When the man was sufficiently distant, Jenny asked, 'What did he say?'

'His wife has gone somewhere with the trolley, and he can't find her.'

'Poor man.'

'Kate used to do that,' he told her.

'What, bugger off wi' t' barrer?'

'Yes, I've lost her in at least three supermarkets.'

'That was just carelessness on your part.'

'That's what she said.' Changing the subject, he asked, 'How's your gran?' It was a silly question, because her health was never going to improve, but he felt nevertheless obliged to ask.

'She has a urine infection. She gets them all the time, and they always make her loopy. Other than that, she wants to know when someone's going to pick her up and take her home for Christmas.'

'I remember that one. It's always difficult, because if you ever did, you'd have an awful job getting her to go back into the home.'

A voice close by said, 'How do you expect me to know where you are when you keep buggerin' off wi' t' barrer?'

They couldn't hear the reply.

'My mum and dad are going to visit her on Christmas morning, and then they're going to eat at their local pub.'

'That's a good idea.'

'Yes, and I've had another. Tell me what you think about this. I know Christmas is a difficult time for you, Leanne and Jimbo, so why don't we join forces, and you three come to us on Christmas Day? It'll be different from being on your own, and that must help. Also, as far as Nicola's concerned, Leanne walks on water, and Gareth can't wait to see Jimbo, so it'll be a joyful gathering for them as well.'

Adam hesitated, but only because her suggestion was a complete surprise. 'I think that's a wonderful idea,' he said. 'To be honest, I'd been dreading Christmas.'

'Well, now you can look forward to it.' She looked at her watch and said, 'Good grief. Is that the time?'

'Don't let me keep you.'

'I'll see you soon,' she said, turning her trolley round. 'It's time for me to bugger off wi' t' barrer.'

* * *

Not surprisingly, Leanne was in favour of the idea. Adam had to wait for Jimbo's response, which came inevitably in the form of a text. It read: *Gr8 idea, Pop. Looking 4ward 2 it already. That + Messiah. CU next month. Lol.*

'It's funny,' he told Leanne. 'Jimbo keeps sending me "Lots of love". It's touching, but strange, a bit like him, really.'

'Let me see.'

He handed her his phone.

' "Lol" means "Laugh out loud",' she reminded him patiently.

'What a strange language. I wonder what Shakespeare would have made of it.'

'If he'd been around today,' said Leanne, 'he would probably have shared your bewilderment. I think he'd have said something like, ' "What tongue is this the young ones have espous'd...?" ' She hesitated.

'You can't think of another ten syllables, can you?'

'Wait a minute. "That patriarchs' dismay it hath arous'd".'

'Okay, but do you really see me as a patriarch?'

She gave the matter brief consideration, and said, 'Not exactly, but it has three syllables.'

'What an analytical child I've created.'

She joined him on the sofa. 'It's a good idea of Jenny's,' she said, changing the subject.

'It'll be different.'

'That's right, a distraction.'

He had to ask. 'Are you coping, Leanne?'

'Mm. Are you?'

'I'm getting the hang of it, as you once said.'

'I worry about you sometimes,' she told him.

He took her hand between his. 'I know, and there's really no need.'

They sat in silence for a spell, and then Leanne said, 'There are times when I want to talk to her and tell her things, you know.'

'Why don't you? She's probably waiting to hear from you.'

She pulled a tissue from her pocket and said, 'I'm not sure we're having this conversation. I think I must be dreaming.'

'You don't have to talk to her aloud.'

'No, I suppose not.' She gave a tearful sniff.

'Have a good blow,' he advised her.

She obliged, and he reached for the box of tissues. 'Reinforcements,' he said.

They sat together without speaking, until Leanne, now dry-eyed and with her nasal consonants restored, said, 'There's a chap who comes into the café sometimes. He wants me to go with him to a Christmas party the Young Farmers are having.'

'Are you keeping him in suspense?'

'Yes, I'll have to give him an answer soon.'

Adam struggled to understand. 'What's the delay for?'

'I don't know. He's different from most of them.'

'How?'

'He's quite shy. He came to the café several times before he asked me, and when he did, it took a big effort on his part. Mind you, he's rather nice in spite of all that.'

Adam was encouraged by the description. 'There's nothing wrong with shyness, Leanne,' he said.

'Spoken like a true dad. The spirit that designed the chastity belt lives on in all of you.'

'Maybe you should bring him here so that I can vet him; in fact, maybe I should set aside a night of the week for interviewing potential boyfriends.'

'No way. It's bad enough when you impersonate me and talk to them through the letterbox.'

Adam recalled the event and it made him smile.

Leanne said, 'Jenny's mum and dad are going to look after the kids on the night of the performance. It's so that I can come and experience this ritual that's been taking place on Thursday nights.'

'Good. It's kind of them to do that.'

'I can barely wait.'

'You won't have to wait much longer, Leanne. It's nearly upon us.'

9

DECEMBER

'Adam Watkinson. Hello?'

The voice on the phone was almost a croak. 'Adam, its Helen Little.'

He knew already what she was going to tell him.

'I'm ever so sorry, Adam. I've got a throat like a furnace.'

'I'm sorry to hear that, Helen.'

'Where you'll find a mezzo or a contralto at this notice, I've no idea.'

'Don't worry, Helen. Just nurse your throat and get well again. I recommend port.'

'Thank you, Adam. I'll try anything. Sorry again. 'Bye.'

''Bye, Helen.' He put the phone down, trying to imagine a performance of *Messiah* without Isaiah's prophecy and the rest of the contralto repertoire, because the only course available to him was to omit those numbers.

He tried phoning Jenny, but there was no answer. He imagined she might be out with Dottie and, for some reason, her mobile was switched off. He would have to tell her soon, so that she could cross out the appropriate numbers in the score. He waited for the tone and then left his message.

It was a big disappointment, but there was nothing to be gained by dwelling on it, so he began preparing dinner. He was expecting Jimbo later. Happily, on this occasion, he'd given some warning of his intended arrival, so Adam had been able to buy the ingredients in the requisite quantities. Jimbo was a hearty trencherman.

He was working on *Promised Land* when Jenny arrived a little before three o'clock.

'I got your message,' she said. 'I'd had to turn off my mobile earlier because I was judging a painting competition, believe it or not, at the children's school. What are we going to do about a contralto?'

'We're not going to find anyone else at this stage. We'll just have to do it without her.'

'Just take out the contralto solos?'

'Yes, I don't see what else we can do.'

'It's an awful shame. There'll be quite a chunk missing.' After brief consideration, she added, 'It'll be like Christmas without mince pies.'

'Or a village without an idiot,' said Adam, as a motorbike roared to a stop outside the front door, 'but this village will soon be up to strength, as you'll see in a minute.'

Adam opened the front door, and Jimbo put down his helmet for the familial hug.

'How's things, Pop? Still getting plenty?'

'I'm not alone, Jimbo.'

'The situation's promising, then.'

'I mean, be a little more sensitive with your greeting.'

'Oh,' said Jimbo, looking over his father's shoulder, 'hello, Jenny. How are you?'

They exchanged greetings, and Jimbo initiated a hug while his father went to the fridge for a can of lager.

'It's a family secret,' he told Jenny, handing the offending beverage to his son, 'that he drinks lager.'

'I shan't tell a soul,' she promised.

'I usually put the kettle on at about this time. Would you care to join me?'

'Thank you,' she said, 'but I have things to do, including crossing the contralto recits and arias out of my copy of the score.'

Jimbo looked up from his remaining eighth of a pint, to ask, 'Have you declared war on contraltos, Pop?'

'No, I'm just making the best of a bad job.'

'What's happened?'

'Helen, who was going to sing with us, has a septic throat.

She's had to bow out, so all we can do is omit her bits from the performance. It's a shame, but there it is.'

'Don't do that, Pop. I can sing them. I did it last Christmas in Woolwich.'

Adam looked at him in astonishment. 'Did you? I didn't know.'

'Well, you know, Pop. Modesty is my *forte*, after all.'

'You hide it so well, Jimbo. Seriously, have you really sung all the contralto solos?'

'Yes, as a bass. I can't do the *falsetto* thing. Not without risking a permanent injury, anyway.'

'That's perhaps a mercy.' He could imagine the pantomime that would result from that. 'If you can sing them as a bass, that'll really get us off the hook.' He was feeling the relief already.

'Consider it sung, Pop.'

'Jimbo,' said Jenny, 'you're a trouper.' She hugged him again.

* * *

'You're a star, Jimbo,' said Leanne when Adam told her.

'You usually call me something else. If I remember rightly, it rhymes with "hillock".'

'That's because you usually behave like something that rhymes with "hillock",' she explained patiently, 'but I'm giving you credit for a truly noble gesture.'

'I suppose,' said Adam, 'they'll pay you Helen's fee as well as yours.'

'No, Pop.' Jimbo held out his hand like a policeman stopping traffic. 'I wouldn't hear of it.'

'What are you saying?'

'I don't expect to be paid for it. You told me the Choral Society was hand to mouth, and do you remember that night in the pub after our audition? One of the blokes told you how important it was to the Dale and everyone in it. No, I don't want any payment.'

Adam was stunned. 'Are you absolutely sure, Jimbo?'

'Positive, Pop. Anyway, I've just done a Messiah, and they paid me well for it, so I'm not skint. Not by a long way.'

'All that time, we kept wondering if we'd brought the wrong baby back from the hospital,' said Adam, 'but we needn't have worried.'

'And we knew the milkman wasn't responsible for him,' said Leanne. 'We used to hear him singing, and he couldn't carry a tune on a milk float.'

'I'm not so sure.' Jimbo looked as if he might be about to surprise them again. 'Sometimes, when I'm walking along Silk Street, I get this ungovernable urge to pick up the empty milk bottles and sing out of tune.' Becoming serious again, he said, 'We shouldn't be talking like this, should we? I mean, it's not what you'd call respectful in the circumstances.'

'I don't see why not,' said Adam. 'It's all part of learning to cope.' Looking at his family at that moment, it seemed to him that they were coping very well.

Leanne said suddenly, 'Is there anything I can do tomorrow night?'

'You could turn the pages for Jenny,' suggested Adam.

'Wow. Fame at last.' She looked at Jimbo and Adam, and said, 'Okay.'

* * *

Adam had seen the interior of the Council Chamber on one previous occasion, but he barely recognised it on the night of the performance, decorated as it was, with a huge Christmas tree behind the chorus, like an altar to the occasion. Most particularly, however, Adam's eyes were drawn to Jenny, who was wearing a long, royal blue evening dress. He was so used to seeing her in jeans or clad for the great outdoors that the effect was all the more dramatic.

As far as Adam could see, most of the seats had been taken, although a few latecomers were still filing in. He waited for them to find their places, and then stood, facing them.

'Ladies and gentlemen,' he announced, 'The performance is about to begin. Please take your seats, but feel free to stand during the 'Hallelujah' chorus.' He took his seat and nodded to Jenny. At her request, they had dispensed with the overture. She explained that she would have felt exposed and self-conscious, playing it as a piano solo. They had also agreed that Adam would conduct only the chorus items.

Accordingly, Jenny began the introduction to 'Comfort Ye, My People', and Nigel Thackeray, the tenor, rose to his feet. After weeks of rehearsal, Adam began to feel the familiar *Messiah* ambience.

As Nigel sang the next number 'Ev'ry Valley Shall be Exalted', Adam wondered a little about those seated behind him, the people of Netherdale, who must have thought their Choral Society had been lost forever. He imagined they must be as excited as he was.

The number came to its end, and Adam stood to wave the chorus to its feet. Confident that he had everyone's attention, he nodded to Jenny and gave her the downbeat for the introduction to 'And the Glory of the Lord.' He recalled telling the members that the number marked the beginning of Christmas for a great many people, and it was as if they, too, remembered it when he brought in the altos in the eleventh bar, and the rest of the chorus four bars later, so joyful was the sound they made. As its first line revealed, it was a glorious number, and Adam sat down happily at the end, to hear Jimbo's first solo 'Thus Saith the Lord'. It was the *recitative* he'd sung unofficially at the audition, and Adam imagined it would be as dramatic as it had been then.

Jenny played the one bar of introduction, and Jimbo began. He was tall, but his presence was magnified when he sang. He was singing from memory, as well, and that might have alarmed Adam, had he not been aware of his son's remarkable facility.

The glowering recitative gave way in turn to the menacing aria 'But Who May Abide the Day of His Coming?' It was one of the contralto numbers that Jimbo was to sing, and he hadn't forgotten. He simply picked up his score from his chair and prepared to sing. It seemed to Adam that, capricious and irresponsible though he was in so many ways, as soon as he set foot on a stage or a concert platform, he became a model of professionalism. It was a Jekyll and Hyde persona that continued to perplex Adam even after twenty-one years.

At the end of the number, he signalled his approval with a wink, receiving no more than a tiny nod in response.

The chorus 'And He Shall Purify' was followed by Isaiah's Prophecy 'Behold, a Virgin Shall Conceive', sung by Jimbo in place of Helen, and Adam waved the chorus to its feet in readiness for its entry during the next number. He was beginning to relax.

Jimbo remained on his feet for the bass numbers 'For Behold, Darkness Shall Cover the Earth' and 'The People that Walkèd in Darkness', and Adam began to fear, just for a moment, that it was an awful lot to ask of Jimbo to shoulder so much of the solo work, but his son seemed unperturbed. Even so, the chorus 'For Unto Us a Child is Born' came as a kind of respite, probably for them both.

Jenny played the Pastoral Symphony, without which the oratorio would have seemed incomplete, and the Christmas sequence proceeded in its own magical way, with its soprano solos and exhilarating choruses.

In fact, the whole performance felt breathtakingly special, including the 'Hallelujah' chorus, when the audience rose traditionally to its feet, and the chorus 'Worthy is the Lamb' with its towering 'Amen.'

At the end, Adam stood everyone up to take their applause, before shaking hands with the principals. At this point, Jimbo's professionalism deserted him and he hugged his father.

'Jimbo,' said Adam, 'I'm proud of you. Thank you.'

'No sweat, Pop. I'm proud of you too.' He seemed quite emotional.

Adam moved on to Jenny and Leanne, kissing them both on the cheek.

Afterwards, at The Craven Heifer, the atmosphere was jubilant. Mark insisted on buying drinks for the Watkinson family and Jenny. It was quite embarrassing, because he had to ask Matthew for the two pounds he was short, but that did nothing to quell his enthusiasm.

'You saved our Choral Society,' he said, setting a pint of Black Sheep in front of Adam.

'It wasn't just me,' Adam protested, 'it was all of us. We all pulled together.'

'Nay, we'd have been lost without you, Adam. You're the hero of the hour.'

Leanne said, 'He doesn't feel like a hero, do you, Dad?'

'No, and I'd rather not be called one, if you don't mind, Mark. It's a special word that's been devalued lately.'

'All right, Adam, I respect that. Let's just say we're glad you came. You an' all, Jimbo, an' Leanne. You've done a good job tonight, love. It's been nice meeting you.'

In a rare verbal contribution, Matthew said, 'Don't forget our accompanist, Mark. She's stood by us through….' He nudged Jimbo and asked, 'What are the words I'm looking for?'

'Through desolation and triumph alike,' suggested Jimbo.

'Aye. Well done, and thank you, Jenny.'

'You're welcome, but it's my Choral Society as well as yours, gentlemen, and I only did what was expected of me.'

'That's what we should all do,' said Adam. 'We should do what's expected of us and maybe a little bit more.'

Leanne put her glass down and adopted her grown-up look. 'Was that a general observation, Dad, a blueprint for the future of mankind, or do you have something specific in mind?'

'I was thinking of a way forward,' he said. 'Something we can do maybe next spring or later.'

'That's up to the Committee,' Mark reminded him.

'Of course it is. Whatever idea I have, I'll put to them for their approval.'

'Watch this space,' advised Leanne.

'Bags I a part in it,' said Jimbo.

'We'll keep you posted,' Adam promised.

10

Jimbo took Gareth's paper party hat and a felt marker pen that had been a stocking filler, and worked secretively behind the cover of his left hand.

Gareth asked, 'What are you doing, Jimbo?'

'You'll see in a minute.' He looked at his artwork and decided it was ready for exhibition. 'There you are,' he said, handing the hat back to Gareth, who expressed his delight at the skull and crossbones design.

'It must have been fun in those days,' he said.

'Not if you were captured by pirates,' said Jimbo, decorating his hat to match Gareth's.

'Well, I expect you had to be careful.'

Adam got up and said, 'I'll go and see if they need any help in the kitchen.'

'Good luck, Pop, said Jimbo. 'It's a closed shop in there.'

Adam peered into the kitchen to ask, 'Is there anything I can do? Any drying up or plates to hang on the line?'

'We're all done,' Leanne told him.

'Thank goodness for dishwashers,' said Jenny. 'I'll tell you what, though. You could make some coffee.'

'After such a glorious meal, it'll be a pleasure.'

'Coffee, cafetière, kettle,' said Jenny, pointing to each in turn.

Adam filled the kettle while Jenny and Leanne left the kitchen. Now alone, he was able to reflect on the day so far. It had been the perfect solution to a perennial problem, and he knew Jimbo and Leanne had felt the same. They all owed a great deal to Jenny for her kindness and hospitality. Gratefully, he measured coffee into the cafetière.

When he carried the coffee things into the sitting room, he found Jimbo and Gareth still arguing about pirates, Nicola looking for someone to groom, and Jenny and Leanne simply relaxing after the meal.

'Leanne,' said Nicola, 'can I do your hair?'

'You can comb it,' said Leanne cautiously, 'but don't cut it. It's short enough.' She opened her bag and fumbled inside it. 'Here, use my comb. My hair's used to it.'

'Right.' Nicola gave her client a professional looking-over and began combing.

'I don't really believe there were pirates,' said Gareth. 'It was only a film.'

'What a thing to say. Every pirate who ever made a victim walk the plank must be turning in his watery grave. There was Henry Morgan, Captain Kidd....' He scratched his head. 'I think there was one called Bluebeard as well.'

'No,' said Leanne, 'not Bluebeard. He was famous for something else.'

'He was the man who learned that paint sniffing could have colourful consequences. No, I think the pirate I had in mind was Blackbeard.'

'Was he a paint sniffer too?'

'No, Leanne, he had worse habits, being a full-time pirate.' As if in celebration, he sang, ' "Up with the jolly roger, boys, and off we go to sea...." '

Gareth asked enviously, 'How do you get a deep voice?'

'You're born with it.'

'I don't believe you.'

'It's true. I was singing "On The Road to Mandalay" when they cut the umbilical cord. My voice shot up an octave at the time, but it soon settled down again.'

'You're daft, Jimbo.'

'Well spotted, Gareth,' said Leanne.

'Keep still, Leanne,' said Nicola. 'I'm trying to do your parting.'

'Sorry.'

Adam pushed down the plunger of the cafetière and poured the coffee.

'Gareth and Nicola, go and get what you want to drink,' said Jenny.

'I'll go when I've finished this,' said Nicola.

Gareth returned from the kitchen with a glass of dandelion and burdock.

'I see you've found some rum,' observed Jimbo.

'No, it's—'

'It's all right, Gareth. Your secret's safe with me. "Fifteen men on a dead man's chest," he recited, "yo-ho-ho and a bottle of rum." '

Gareth looked puzzled. 'Why were they sitting on his chest? Is that what killed him?'

'There aren't many trees on a desert island, and all the furniture had been broken up for firewood. He was just unlucky enough to be the one they chose to sit on.'

'The chest was a trunk, Gareth,' said Leanne, taking pity on him, 'a wooden box, like a big suitcase, for packing his clothes and things in when he went to sea.'

Possibly in an effort to promote sensible conversation, Jenny asked, 'Have you had any more thoughts about the Choral Society's next event, Adam?'

'Yes, I'm thinking in terms of a cantata that I want to write as a kind of celebration of the Dales and maybe the county as a whole.'

'I thought cantatas were sacred.'

'Not necessarily. There are secular ones too. Believe it or not, someone once wrote one about Charles Lindbergh crossing the Atlantic. A cantata doesn't have to be sacred.'

Jenny digested the idea briefly, and asked, 'Will you write the words as well?'

'No, I think we could put out a request for people to send in any poems or pieces of prose on the subject, and then we could choose the most suitable items to be set to music.'

'Will it be a long work? Most cantatas I know wouldn't fill an evening.'

'Not an evening,' he agreed. 'I'm thinking in terms of an afternoon, along with something else, an exhibition or something, and it'll be the final part of an event occupying a weekend.'

'Don't keep us in suspense, Dad,' urged Leanne. 'What kind of event?'

'Yes, Pop, spill the beans.'

'It would have to be organised with the approval of the local authority, and local businesses would be involved, but I think we could mount a choir festival.'

'Like the Ilkley Choir Festival?' Jenny's interest was clearly aroused.

'Not exactly, but along those lines, and I'd better say from the start that, if I'm involved in the judging, the Choral Society won't be allowed to compete. That's why I'd like them to give a performance on the final day.'

It was a suitably positive announcement for a special Christmas Day, as Adam described it, with the wholehearted agreement of Jimbo and Leanne. When the time came for them to leave, they repeated their thanks to Jenny, who said, 'I think we made it special for one another, don't you?'

* * *

Adam put his idea to the Choral Society Committee, who considered it carefully before giving it their cautious approval, and arranged for him to address the Events Committee of the District Council. The meeting took place on a Tuesday evening two weeks later.

Councillor Beasley, chairman of the Events Committee, looked like a man who believed devoutly in his own authority. He looked quite imposing too; he wasn't particularly tall, but he was heavily built, with a frown that was clearly designed to intimidate. According to Jenny, he'd worked at Overton Pharmaceuticals since leaving school, but gave the impression of a man whose ambition to become something big in the shadowy underworld had been thwarted when fate made him a stock control clerk at a factory that made ointments for embarrassing conditions.

'Mr Watkinson,' he said, 'we've read your proposal, and it raises certain questions. The first is, why do you want to do this?'

'As I said in my proposal, I'm extremely conscious of the Dale's suffering during and after the foot-and-mouth epidemic, and I want to help in its recovery.'

'But why? You're not a native of these parts, are you?'

'No, I'm from Huddersfield. I only moved here last summer.'

'So, why are you so concerned about a place you've only known a matter of months?'

Adam summoned his patience. 'That's not the case. I first came to the Dale more than four years ago. It was shortly after my wife died, and I used to bring my children here so that they could find some peace and a distraction from their loss. I found that it helped me as well.'

'Oh, well,' the chairman shifted uncomfortably. 'I didn't know that.'

'Well, now that you do, you'll appreciate that the Dale has come to mean a great deal to me. With only a few exceptions, its people have welcomed us and made us feel part of the community, so it's only natural that I want to give them something in return. Can you accept that?'

'Of course I can. I simply wanted you to make things clear.'

The expressions of the other committee members gave Adam the impression that the Chairman was less than popular within his own circle.

'You say you want to compose a....' The chairman peered hard at Adam's proposal.

'Cantata,' said Adam, 'a piece of choral music celebrating various aspects of the county.'

'You've had some experience of composing music, then?'

'It's how I make my living.'

One of the other committee members seemed to come to life. He said excitedly, 'You wrote *Donkey Ride to Bethlehem*, didn't you?'

The chairman glared at him. 'Kindly address your remarks through the Chair, Councillor Slater.'

'Sorry, Chairman. Through the Chair, this bloke wrote the musical play my granddaughter was in two Christmases ago. It were a champion show an' all.'

'Thank you,' said Adam, recognising the first kind remark of the meeting.

'So, you know your trade, then,' concluded the chairman. 'The question is, what do you want from the District Council?'

'A Festival Committee needs to be set up, we need representation to the Yorkshire Tourist Board, and we need liaison with local businesses. We'll need car and coach parking, possibly camping facilities and catering. Most of all, though, we need a venue, somewhere big enough to house the choirs and the audiences that, hopefully, they'll bring with them. That's why the co-operation of the District Council is so vital.'

* * *

'I'm not kidding, Jenny, you'd think I'd gone there to undermine everything the council represents. The committee members were okay; in fact, one of them was very complimentary about my work, although I have to say that *Donkey Ride to Bethlehem* seems to follow me around like a love-sick shadow. The chairman, though, was uncompromising. I'd even describe him as aggressive.'

'Councillor Beasley? Being difficult is his way of life.'

'Well, he certainly lived up to his reputation last night.'

'But what was their final decision?'

'The proposal has to go before a full meeting of the District Council before anyone can proceed.'

'Oh well, that's democracy at work, I suppose, and we have to be thankful for that.'

'One thing that won't wait, however, is the cantata, because I don't need anyone's permission to write it. If I can just get some poems and articles together, I'll get on with it.'

11

Regardless of any decision by the District Council, the Choral Society had already approved Adam's idea of the cantata, and had gone ahead with newspaper notices asking the public for suitable poems and pieces of prose. However, the first to arrive were less than promising.

'There are two pieces of greeting card doggerel,' Adam told Jenny over coffee at her house, 'and a poem about the Three Peaks that someone must have sent in as a joke.'

'All right, let's hear it.'

Adam read:

‘ "When I've ascended Pen y Ghent,
With landscape worn and weathered,
At night, I crawl inside my tent,
Well and truly blethered.

‘ "Turning then to Ingleborough,
Picturesque and rugged,
The exercise is more than thorough;
And I'm completely buggered.

‘ "And finally, on Whernside's top,
I'm reasonably bucked,

'Oh, dear.'
'No, hang on.'

‘ "But then, inside my tent I flop,
In sleeping bag well-tucked." ’

'What a relief.' Setting the matter aside, she said, 'Let's hope you get something better soon.'

'I'm bound to.' His optimism was as harmless as it was baseless. On a whim, he asked, 'How are you at poetry?'

'I can't help, I'm afraid. All my creative impulses come out as brushstrokes.'

'They're a kind of poetry, though. You could have an exhibition as part of the finale to the festival.'

'I could,' she agreed. 'I'd have to put it to the committee.' Correcting herself, she added, 'I suppose that should be "committees".'

'There'll be a few before it's all over,' he agreed, putting his coffee mug down. 'By the way,' he asked, 'how's your gran?'

'As demanding as ever, but quite entertaining, as you can imagine. I'm going to see her in the morning. I thought I'd take Dottie in. She likes to see her.'

Dottie looked up when she heard her name, and Adam stroked her. 'Would you like me to come as well?'

'There's really no need, Adam, but it's good of you to offer.'

'No, I like the old girl. I enjoy seeing her.'

'In that case,' she said, smiling at the unexpected compliment, 'you're welcome to come.'

* * *

There was a new resident, or so it seemed to Adam, and he saw them come in. Immediately, he pointed to Dottie, and said, 'You're not bringing that dog in here.'

'She won't hurt you,' said Jenny.

'You can't bring it in here.' The man came towards them and, as Jenny picked Dottie up, he turned his attention to Adam. 'You're not going to bring that dog in here.'

'Why not? She's paid to come in.'

'I'm gonna knock your bloody 'ead off.'

'No, you're not. Come over here.' Motioning Jenny to continue to Mrs Sanderson's room, he moved to the opposite wall. 'What's your name?'

'Robert.'

'Mine's Adam. We should be mates, you and me.' He offered his hand, and Robert took it in a grip that was surprisingly strong for an old man. 'Mates, then?'

'All right, I'll let you off. Do you know where I can get a cup o' tea round here?'

One of the staff came from the sitting room to ask, 'What's the matter, Robert?'

'I wanna know where I can get a cup o' tea.'

'Come with me and I'll get you one.'

Robert shuffled after her, and then stopped and turned to say, as if to an old friend, 'See you again, Adam.'

'See you, Robert.' Adam walked down the passage to Mrs Sanderson's room, where he found her so delighted to see Dottie that she'd invited her on to her bed.

'Oh, it's you,' she said, recognising Adam. 'You're the man who reads to me, aren't you?'

'Yes, I've brought you a new book.'

'Good. I hope it's not American.'

'No, it's not.' He was about to tell her its name, when she wriggled purposefully off the bed.

'Must spend a penny,' she said, heading for her personal bathroom. 'When I need to go, I have to go straight away.' Despite that impediment, she stopped to explain. 'I have a weak ber, ber, ber.... What's it called?'

'Bladder,' Jenny told her. 'Come on, Gran.' She ushered her into the bathroom, where she was already wrestling with her clothes when Jenny closed the door on her. 'She's become completely disinhibited,' she told Adam. 'She'd do it with the door open if I let her.'

He nodded understandingly.

Jenny waited until the sounds from within suggested that the deed was accomplished, and said, 'Don't forget to wash your hands, Gran.'

'All right, I'm doing it now.' After a minute, she opened the door to say, 'Somebody's pinched the towel again.'

'They're paper towels, Gran.'

The door swung open. 'I don't like paper towels,' she said

dismissively. Finding Dottie still on her bed, she dried her hands on her instead. Dottie didn't seem to mind.

Jenny asked, 'Do you want Adam to read to you, Gran?'

'I want to speak to him first.'

'All right, he's here.'

Mrs Sanderson gave Adam a stern look. 'That Sibelius was far too slow this morning,' she said.

'It's a slow piece, Mrs Sanderson.'

'Not as slow as that. You need to get a move on, you know, or your audiences are going to fall asleep. I did this morning.'

'I'm sorry. I'll speed things up a bit.'

'Good.' She looked on her bedside table and asked, 'Where's the book you brought?'

'Here.' He opened it and found the first page of the story. 'It's *The Inimitable Jeeves* by P G Wodehouse,' he told her.

'Oh, lovely.'

He'd read as far as the top of the second page, when she interrupted him. 'Trevor bought the most hideous clothes, you know. I had to take him shopping.' She reflected on that and went on. 'Mauve shirts, mauve socks. He was hopeless.'

'I'm sorry to hear that,' said Adam.

'He was hopeless in bed, too.'

'It's not given to everyone,' said Adam, feeling that he should offer some defence on behalf of the hapless and mysterious Trevor.

'I told him straight. I said, "Put your pyjama trousers back on, for goodness' sake. I'd rather have a bar of chocolate." ' She looked up sharply at Jenny and demanded, 'Have you brought me some chocolate?'

Jenny opened the top drawer of the clothes chest and took out a bar of fruit and nut.

'Good. Leave it there and I'll have some later.'

Adam asked, 'Would you like me to carry on reading?'

'You might as well, seeing as you're here.'

He continued to read until he was reasonably sure she'd fallen asleep, and then Jenny picked up Dottie and they left.

They were on their way out, when a voice said, 'Do you know any good jokes, Adam?'

Adam stopped while Jenny unlocked the door. 'None that I could tell you with a lady present, Robert. Next time I come, maybe.'

'All right, only I've forgotten all mine what I used to know. I can't even remember me own....' He stopped and scratched his head.

'I know,' said Adam. 'It's a bugger, isn't it?'

Jenny said nothing until they reached the car. Adam sat Dottie on his lap.

'You'll be covered in hairs,' she said. She seemed preoccupied even as she said it.

'They'll come off, don't worry.'

She pushed the key into the ignition but made no effort to start the car. After a moment, she said, 'You can't imagine what she was like before all this began.'

Adam presumed she was talking about her gran. 'Tell me,' he said.

'She was unfailingly polite, and she'd have died rather than use what she called "a naughty word". Believe it or not, she would never dream of talking about sex, either. She was very prim.'

'Was Trevor her husband?'

'No, my grandpa's name was Geoffrey. I don't know who Trevor was, but the reference to mauve shirts and socks was triggered by the story you were reading.'

'It would be, but that's dementia. Fiction becomes interwoven with reality.' His mind went back to an earlier episode, and he said, 'My granddad underwent a character change too. He'd always been quite self-contained, and then, when dementia took hold, he'd tell anyone all that lay on his mind, often in embarrassing detail, and it often owed something to a story he'd heard.'

Jenny nodded. Her eyes were wet. 'I can visit her and not be affected by it,' she said, 'but, every now and again, it finds its mark, and I feel helpless.'

'We're all helpless,' he said, taking a tissue from the pack in his pocket and handing it to her. 'All we can do is remember the person we knew, and do what we can for the pitiful victim that's left behind.'

'Is that how you see them, as victims?'

'Yes, I do. Like cancer, dementia takes people prisoner and torments them and their wretched relations until it's run its course. The one difference with dementia is that another condition often intervenes, usually with merciful effect.' Jenny looked so abject that, almost without conscious thought, he put his arm round her, squeezing her shoulder the way he'd often given comfort to Kate and the children. It seemed the most natural thing to do, comforting Jenny and stroking Dottie so that she wouldn't feel excluded.

After a while, Jenny raised her head to say, 'I'm sorry. I didn't intend that to happen.' At least, that was how Adam interpreted it, her nasal consonants being temporarily in disarray.

'Don't be sorry,' he said. 'Have some more tissues.' He handed her the pack.

'I bust be ad awful sight,' she said, breaking off to blow her nose. 'I'b glad it happed afterwards ad dot whed we arrived.' She flipped open the visor mirror. 'Oh by good-dess,' she said, 'I *ab* a terrible sight.'

'Undeniably gruesome,' he agreed, 'but the damage is temporary and superficial, and if we stop at your place, you can carry out the necessary repairs before I take you to lunch, happy, smiling and with your eye make-up intact.'

* * *

Later, at the Craven Heifer, Jenny said, 'I feel guilty.'

'What have you done?'

'I mean for making a fuss this morning. You've suffered something far worse, and you don't inflict it on others.'

'It's the way I am, Jenny. We're all different.' He re-examined the menu and decided that he'd made the right choice after all. 'You've lost the gran you knew. She obviously meant a great deal to you, and it's quite natural for you to grieve.'

'But differently.'

'That's right. According to the leaflets, there's a basic grief model that describes the process for us all, but how we cope with it is an individual matter. I don't believe there's a strategy that works for everyone.'

'I've never thought much about it.'

The waitress came to their table with a tray of food. She said, 'You're the man who wrote *Donkey Ride to Bethlehem*, aren't you?'

'Yes.'

'Someone in the Choral Society pointed you out to me. My niece was one of the angels. We really enjoyed it.'

'I'm glad.'

'Have you written anything else?' It was what most people asked.

'Yes, lots of things, and I've just finished another one.'

'What's it called?'

'*Yoke up your Oxen.*' The publishers had given the title their official approval, and he preferred it to *Promised Land*.

'What's it about?'

'Moses and the Children of Israel.'

That seemed to please her. 'If it's about children,' she said, 'it'll be nice. I hope they do it at the school. It'll feel special, now I've met the man who wrote it.'

'We'll have to wait and see what happens.' He waited until she was gone, and said, 'It's like a tin can tied to my tail.'

'But it's a nice tin can. People always say good things about it.'

'Fortunately. Help yourself to the vegetables, by the way.'

'Thank you.' She took the serving spoons and took some cauliflower and broccoli.

'What were we talking about when the waitress came?'

'You said there was no coping strategy that was right for everyone.'

'Yes, when you go through something like that, there's no shortage of people who'll give you advice, and I'm not talking about the professionals, the bereavement counsellors. I mean people who imagine naïvely that they know best. My neighbour, for example, kept telling me to "let it out", as if, by opening a valve, I could unleash the grief monster, and everything would be all right and go back to normal.' He put carrots, broccoli and cauliflower on his plate.

'But you're finding your own way, presumably?'

'Yes, I told you how caring for the children helped me cope. I still have conversations with them that help them and me. What I've needed for some time, though, is a new direction.'

Jenny picked up the pepper mill and said, 'I've just remembered, I must put black pepper on my shopping list.' She smiled apologetically. 'I'm sorry. You mentioned a new direction. Is that the same as a way forward?'

'Yes, there are books about finding the way forward, but that's too much of a cliché for me. I prefer to think of it as a new direction, something I haven't done before.'

'Maybe revitalising the Choral Society was a start,' she suggested.

'Maybe it was.'

'Incidentally, I don't like clichés either; in fact, I go to some trouble to avoid them.'

'I wish Jimbo would. He even sends text messages in a strict code known only to the young and tech-savvy.'

She laughed good-naturedly. 'I know. I've seen some of the texts he's sent to Gareth, but I'm grateful to him for them, all the same.'

'Of course you are.' Her distaste for clichés interested him. 'How do you avoid falling into the cliché trap?'

'Practice, basically. I have a collection of idiomatic words and phrases of my own. I go for long walks with Dottie and make them up as I go.'

'Give me some examples. I'm interested.'

She thought briefly. 'Instead of "zilch" or "the square root of sod-all", I say "nought over zero". It's not brilliant, but I prefer it.'

'I like it.'

'Good, and I recently created a variation on "zero to hero". A friend, who'd left school with very little in the way of qualifications, was recently awarded a higher degree, and I sent her a card that I'd designed especially for her. On the front, I wrote, "Nothin' to Boffin!" In some cases, though, I resort to plain language, and "a wake-up call", for instance, becomes "a timely reminder". "A no-brainer" or "not rocket science" becomes "a nursery task". Boring, but grazing away from the herd, you have to admit.'

'Oh, I agree.'

'You know,' she said with sudden enthusiasm, 'I think you've found your "new direction".'

'Have I?' He hadn't been aware of it.

'The choir festival. If your idea can revitalise the Dale, it'll be a tremendous achievement.'

12

The District Council deliberated at length, finally giving its approval to the inauguration of the Netherdale Choir Festival. A Festival Committee was formed and Adam was naturally co-opted to serve on it.

On a more personal level, Adam's publishers were preparing to launch *Harness Your Camels*. In hindsight, it was generally felt that, as the ox was a castrated bull, *Yoke up Your Oxen* might offend animal rights sensitivities. Similarly, the inclusion of asses in the title might constitute an affront to lovers of donkeys. Camels, like every other species, had their champions, but saddling them and using them as transport was generally accepted. Adam had reached the stage when he couldn't have cared less what they called the play. He was only relieved that they'd finally made a decision.

He was enjoying the news when Jenny came to the door, clearly perturbed.

'Adam,' she said, 'can you help me? I left Gareth to close the door. It was on the latch, and he left the key inside. We're locked out.'

'Let me get my felon's toolkit from the car and I'll see what I can do.'

'Oh, if you could let me back in to get the key, that would be wonderful.'

They walked the short distance to Jenny's house, where they found Nicola looking worried and Gareth looking shamefaced.

'Chin up, Gareth,' said Adam. '*Errare humanum est*, as the Ancient Romans used to say whenever someone locked himself out of his villa.'

He selected a small key and used it to probe gently. His efforts had attracted the attention of a passer-by, who was now using a mobile phone. The observer was a slight man of middle years with a neatly-trimmed moustache. His tone was authoritative and demanding.

'Would you mind telling me just what you think you're doing?'

'Not in the least. I think I'm picking this lock. Have you come to see how it's done?'

'Certainly not. I've already called the police. I did it when I saw you behaving suspiciously.'

'They can come and watch if they like, and so can you. There's no charge.'

Jenny intervened. 'This is my house,' she said, 'and I've locked myself out, so I asked my neighbour to help me get back inside.'

'That's easy enough for you to say,' said the man, sounding like one who had heard a great many falsehoods in his long experience.

'I need a shorter key,' said Adam after a while. 'I'm pretty sure there's one in my car. I'll just go and get it.'

'The police are on their way,' warned the man with the moustache, nevertheless standing aside to let Adam past.

'Of course they are. They don't want to miss the excitement.'

He returned after a minute or so with a bunch of short skeleton keys. 'The levers in these locks are quite small, as you can imagine,' he told Jenny.

'This man says he's called the police,' she said anxiously.

'I expect it makes him feel useful.' Looking over his shoulder, he asked the man, 'Who are you, anyway?'

'I'm a member of the Neighbourhood Watch,' the man told him importantly.

'Well, watch this and you might learn something.' Adam searched and probed further until he heard another lever click open. 'That's two,' he said.

Jenny gathered the children together, keeping a wary eye on the police informer. 'I've already told you,' she said, 'this is my house.'

'We'll see how true that is when the police arrive.'

'How dare you!'

'All I'm saying is, we'll see, that's all.'

'You've got a cheek, whoever you are.'

'I'm just doing my duty as a law-abiding citizen.'

'Number three,' reported Adam.

'You ridiculous man,' said Jenny. 'Does this really make you feel important?'

'Number four.'

'The game's up,' said the man as a police car drew up outside. 'The police are here and they've got you bang to rights.'

'I wonder if they really say that,' said Adam. 'Maybe there's an official manual of clichés that they have to learn by heart at Police College and pass on to self-important busybodies like you.' He chuckled to himself as he located the remaining lever. 'Number five.' He turned the handle and pushed open the door.

'Thank you, Adam.' Jenny picked up the latchkey from the window ledge.

'Just a minute.' It was a woman's voice and it belonged to a police constable. 'We received a report that a man was breaking into a house.' She peered at the name on the wall. ' "Holme Cottage",' she confirmed.

'That was me,' said Adam, 'except I haven't broken anything, although I've been tempted.' He looked pointedly at the man with the moustache.

'This is my house,' said Jenny, 'and I locked myself out. My neighbour, here, very kindly picked the lock so that I could get in and retrieve the key.' Pointing to the man with the moustache, she said, 'That man has succeeded in annoying both of us and frightening my children, not to mention making the ridiculous and unnecessary emergency call that brought you on this fool's errand.'

The constable asked calmly, 'Have you some means of identification linking you to this address, madam?'

Jenny searched her bag and found a photo business card, which she handed to the officer.

'Thank you, madam. That's fine.' She turned to Adam and said, 'You were picking the lock, I'm told, sir?'

'At this lady's request,' he confirmed.

'Picking a lock isn't normal behaviour, though, is it?'

'I don't suppose it is, but I was once employed as a locksmith, which explains the skeleton keys. I have to say, though, that I ply my former trade only in emergency and at the request of the homeowner.'

'I see. And you asked this man for his assistance, madam?'

'That's what I said.'

Perhaps feeling left out of things, the man with the moustache said, 'I had no way of knowing that. I only reported what I saw.'

'Yes,' said Adam, 'a hardened criminal and his moll breaking and entering, and two children they'd brought along in case there was an open window or a coal chute they could wriggle through. And all this in broad daylight. The only missing elements were the black masks, the striped jerseys, and the sack marked "Swag".' He smiled at the absurdity of the situation.

'So,' said the constable, trying not to return his smile, 'what we have here is a misunderstanding on the part of the informant.'

Jenny was about to confirm that, when the said informant intervened. 'I'm a member of the Neighbourhood Watch,' he announced, 'and we take criminal behaviour seriously.'

'And you thought this might earn you promotion to Chief Snooperintendent,' suggested Adam.

'I need to take a few details from you, sir,' the constable told the man.

'She's going to charge you with wasting police time,' Adam told him gleefully. 'You'll get five years, at least.'

'Leave this to me, sir,' said the constable. Leading the man by the elbow, she said to him, 'Let's go and sit in the car.'

'It's people like him,' said Adam, 'that give law-abiding citizens a bad name.'

In her relief, Jenny could only say, 'Thank you, Adam. You got me out of another impossible situation.'

'You might even say, "This is another fine mess you've gotten me out of." '

'In these circumstances, I might,' she agreed. Turning to the children, she said, 'It's all right. No one's going to be arrested.' She glanced in the direction of the police car. 'She's probably advising him to think before making silly accusations, more's the pity.'

* * *

Since the early offerings of verse, nothing more had arrived, and Adam was impatient.

'It's too early to get despondent, Dad,' Leanne told him. 'How many pieces of poetry do you need, anyway?'

'About half a dozen.'

'Well, then.' She shrugged, as if the problem amounted to nothing. 'You're bound to have days when nothing arrives, and you can't always expect quality when it does.' As she spoke, she rubbed her wet hair with a towel.

'Your mature outlook on life is a perpetual tonic,' he told her, 'but I need to start rehearsals soon, and I can't do that without something to rehearse.'

'Why don't you set something that's in the public domain?'

'Such as what?'

She stopped rubbing and adopted a thoughtful expression. 'How about "The Ballad of Semerwater"? It's a poem by Sir William Watson. He died in nineteen-thirty-something, so it'll be out of copyright.'

'I don't know it.'

'I'll find a copy for you when I've dried my hair.' She looked at the damp towel in disgust.

Adam went to the linen cupboard and found her another, which he draped over her head.

'Dad, how obliging you are. You want me to finish so that I can get that poem, don't you?'

'Yes.' There was no point in denying it. 'What's the story behind the poem?'

'Semerwater is said to have been a settlement long ago,' she told him, 'and the legend is that a beggar – some call him an angel – called at each house, asking for food. Every household turned him away except one, where the poor couple who lived there took him in and gave him hospitality. His response was to put a curse on those who'd refused him, calling on the waters to engulf the settlement except for the poor couple's hovel.' She shrugged. 'Personally, I don't give it much credence, but that's folklore for you, isn't it?'

'It sounds like the kind of thing I'm looking for. Thanks, Leanne.'

'It's no trouble, Dad. I'm happy to be a prop in your declining years.' She stood up, giving her hair a final rub, and said, 'I'm going upstairs to use my hairdryer. I'll look for that poem while I'm there.'

'Thanks, love.' In her absence, he opened a bottle of claret and took out two glasses. Leanne had given him something to consider. There must be other poems in the public domain that he could use. Whether or not there was much of a response to the appeal, he would have something to work on. He sat down to consider the possibilities, and was still thinking about them when Leanne reappeared with her hair dried and caught back for the moment in one of those things that sounded like a chocolate bar. He experienced the familiar jolt at seeing her look so much like Kate.

'Here it is,' she said, breaking the spell by handing him an opened book.

'Thank you. Help yourself to wine if you'd like some.'

'Dad, you're leading me astray. Every time we sit down together, you ply me with booze, but don't stop, whatever you do.' She poured herself a glass.

'I can certainly use this,' said Adam, scanning the poem.

'What I'm wondering,' said Leanne, sitting beside him, 'is what kind of piece you're writing. Is it going to be folky or classical or what?'

'Not folky. That's not me.'

'Me neither.' She shook her head definitely.

'It's purely a matter of taste. I'm happy for people to enjoy whatever does it for them, whether it's The Dubliners or Guns 'n Roses, just as long as they don't inflict it on me.'

'That's the spirit, Dad. So, is it going to be in your usual style?'

'You'll have to wait and see. That's what I'm going to do.'

'I bet you can't wait.' Suddenly changing the subject, she said, 'I'll tell you what, though. I wish I'd been here when you picked the lock for Jenny. It must have been fun.'

'I enjoyed it. I don't think anyone else did.'

'I think Jenny was concerned most of all for the children.'

'Yes, it must have been a daunting experience for them.' He smiled as another thought came to him. 'It'll be something to write about at school.' He looked at her glass and saw that it was quite full. 'How's it going with the shy chap you told me about?'

'Craig? I went to the Christmas party with him. Hey, those Young Farmers are a predatory lot.'

'Why do you say that?'

'We hadn't been there half an hour before first one and then another tried to take me away from Craig.'

Adam frowned. 'There's no honour among young men nowadays,' he said.

'You're right there, Dad.'

'Mind you, I expect you can handle them.'

'They're like putty in my hands,' she confirmed.

He nodded, as if it were as he'd suspected. 'Will you go out with Craig again?'

'You'll have to wait and see, Dad. That's what I'm going to do.'

13

Adam was enjoying a rare luxury. It was almost eleven-thirty in the morning, and the phone hadn't rung. The peace was almost a distraction, and he was telling himself that, at the same time trying not to tempt Providence too far, when the phone rang. Philosophically, he picked it up. After all, a morning's tranquility was better than none.

'Adam Watkinson.'

'Oh, Mr Watkinson, it's St Thomas's Hospital, London.'

Adam felt the cold rush of adrenalin. Something must have happened to Jimbo.

The voice went on. 'There's nothing to worry about, but we thought you'd like to know that we admitted your son James this morning.'

'Jimbo? What's happened?'

'He was involved in a traffic incident earlier this morning. He's not badly hurt, but we're keeping him in for the next twenty-four hours for observation.'

It seemed to Adam that it must be fairly serious for them to do that. He asked, 'What are his injuries?'

'Slight concussion, cuts, abrasions, bruised ribs and a dislocated shoulder. He's going for a scan, shortly, to rule out any damage to the tendons in his shoulder now that we've manipulated it for him, and we're keeping a general eye on him.'

'But you say he's not badly hurt?'

'He's uncomfortable, as you'd expect, but there's nothing terribly serious.'

'Thank you for that. I'll come down, of course.' Traffic permitting, he reckoned he could be there in four to five hours.

'Oh, good.' She gave him the necessary details.

'Thank you. I'll be with you later today.'

He put the phone down and dialled Leanne's number at the café. Conveniently, it was she who answered the phone. Recognising her voice, he said, 'Leanne, listen, there's nothing serious, but Jimbo's had an accident. He's in hospital, and I'm going down there to see him.'

'Not without me, I hope. I can be home in ten minutes.'

'All right, it'll take me a few minutes to pack a bag.'

'Right, I'll see you there.'

It occurred to him that he should tell Jenny in case she wondered where he was, so he dialled her number. The phone rang until the answering service cut in, and he was able to leave her a message.

He was packing an overnight bag when Leanne arrived.

'Don't stress, Dad.' She kissed him. 'It doesn't sound too bad.'

'And I'm supposed to be here for you.' He gave her a quick hug.

'We're here for each other, aren't we?' Without waiting for an answer, she went to her room to pack, coming down five minutes later with her bag. 'I put some overnight bits together for Jimbo,' she said.

'It never crossed my mind. Thanks, love.'

'You'd be lost without me, Dad. Admit it.'

'I'd rather not even think about it.' He checked that everything in the kitchen was off, locked the back door and joined Leanne at the front. 'I'd like to think that the Neighbourhood Watch would be keeping an eye on the house, but I made myself unpopular with one of their number on Saturday.'

'You will have your bit of fun,' she said, fastening her seatbelt. Then, as they approached the main road, she said, 'I don't suppose they could tell you much about the accident.'

'No. Presumably he came off his bike, but we'll hear the rest when we get there.'

'I wonder when they'll let him come home.'

'I imagine that's something else we'll find out.'

* * *

90

The journey took a little over five hours, and Adam and Leanne arrived at the nurses' station at five-fifteen.

'I suppose we just look for the bed that has girls gathered round it,' said Leanne, looking around the individual alcoves.

'We'd better speak to someone first.'

Before long, a door opened and a nurse asked, 'Have you come to visit a patient? Visiting time was over some time ago.'

'I appreciate that,' said Adam, 'but we've driven more than two hundred miles to see my son.'

'Ah, you must be James's dad.'

'Yes.' It still sounded odd when people used Jimbo's proper name.

'In that case, you'll find him in the third bed on the left.'

'Thank you.'

'Visiting is from two p.m. until four.'

'Thanks again.'

Adam turned and found Leanne already at Jimbo's bedside, leaning over him to deliver a sisterly kiss while observing cautious regard for his bruised ribs, although her greeting was less than sensitive.

'What have you been up to now, you div?'

'Hello, Sis. Hello, Pop. It wasn't my fault.'

Adam took the chair beside the bed and asked, 'What happened?'

'A white van in the outside lane took a left turn into Wilson Street. I was on the inside lane.' He shrugged and then winced at the discomfort the gesture caused him.

'Did he stop?'

'No, another van driver stopped and called an ambulance. The police came eventually, but they said no one had taken the number of the white van, so he'd most likely get away with it.'

Leanne studied him carefully. 'This is the most serious we've seen you,' she said, 'since your famous double act in December. It's unnerving.'

'I'm feeling quite serious,' he confirmed. Then, looking a little more cheerful, he said, 'They say I may be allowed out tomorrow, after the doctor's seen me.'

'In that case, we'll take you home to recuperate,' said Adam. 'You'll need that.'

'Thanks, Pop.'

Practical as ever, Leanne asked him, 'Would you like me to pick up some things from your flat, Jimbo?'

'Oh yes, please. A week's worth of clothes and the usual overnight things would be good.' A little shamefaced, he added, 'There's a bit of dirty washing as well. I'd have done it this morning but for this.' He gestured painfully towards the locker at his bedside. 'The key's in there.'

The nurse who'd met them when they arrived came to ask them to leave. 'You'll be welcome after two o'clock tomorrow,' she said.

'He says he may be allowed to go home tomorrow,' said Adam.

'We'll know when the doctor's seen him in the morning. You could phone, and then if James is going to be discharged, you can come earlier to pick him up.'

* * *

They managed to find two hotel rooms and reserved a table for dinner before driving to Jimbo's flat.

Adam remembered it from taking Jimbo there with all his luggage when he first started at the Guildhall. His was the first floor flat, and he recalled that the ground floor was then occupied by two slovenly characters, who spoke an obscure language only distantly related to English. On entering the building, he found that nothing had changed.

'Waz crackin', dude?' On the face of it, the question sounded potentially helpful, rather than a challenge.

'We've come to get some clothes for Jimbo,' Adam told him.

'Wassup wiv Jimbo, den? We ain't seen him all day.'

'He's in hospital. He had an accident this morning.'

The ground floor tenant evidently understood English, because his eyes opened wide and he asked, 'Is he bad?'

'No, we'll probably take him home tomorrow.'

He seemed to digest that information before asking, 'Are you, like, his dad?'

'So alike, you can't tell us apart.'

It was Leanne's turn to be quizzed. 'Who you, den? Jimbo's boo?'

'No, I'm his sister.'

'Ball*er*! Where you live, den, homeskillett?'

'Miles away, in Yorkshire.'

'Sucky.' His expression left no need for translation.

'Let's get Jimbo's clothes,' said Adam, putting a protective arm round his daughter.

They let themselves into the flat, and Adam looked around him in distaste. 'He hasn't got any tidier,' he observed.

'I think I've found the "bit of dirty washing",' said Leanne, tearing off a plastic bin liner and stuffing it with at least a week's discarded clothes.

'Good grief.'

'What's the matter, Dad?' Leanne was hunting for a grip.

'Don't look at this, Leanne. It's too awful for words.' He was staring at a wallposter previously hidden by an opened wardrobe door.

Glancing quickly at the object of his disapproval, she said, 'I've seen naked females before, Dad.'

'Not like this one, I'm sure.'

She looked again. 'No,' she agreed, 'the girls at school never posed like that. Not publicly, anyway.' She found Jimbo's grip and lifted it on to the bed.

'What kind of clothes will he need, Leanne? Socks and underwear, obviously, but what else?'

'Leave it to me, Dad. If you go sorting through his clothes, you could find more than you bargained for,' she said, removing an opened packet of Durex Fetherlite from general view and dropping it discreetly into a drawer. She filled the grip with clothes and zipped it up. 'There'll be enough to see him through a week,' she said, 'although I reckon there's as much again in laundry.'

'Thanks again, Leanne.'

'No sweat, Dad.'

Adam picked up the grip and sack of dirty washing, and led the way downstairs, where the tenant was still lounging.

'Peace out, dawg,' said Leanne. 'We're gonna bounce.'

Mystified, Adam could only take his leave of the tenant in plain English before taking the bags out to the car.

As they set off, he asked her, 'What did all that mean?'

She gave him a look reserved for the elderly and obtuse, and said, ' "Peace out" is idiot-speak for "goodbye", "dawg" is a friendlier form of "dude", and "bounce" means "leave".'

* * *

Adam made his phone call to the hospital, as advised, after 11.00, and learned that Jimbo was to be discharged, and that he was allowed to call for him at any time. He and Leanne made it to the hospital by 11:30, and found Jimbo impatient to leave. They stood outside the screen while he changed, gasping and groaning, into the clothes Leanne had brought for him. Finally, he was obliged to ask for assistance.

'Will one of you tie my laces? I can't bend yet.'

Obligingly, Adam helped him, first with his socks, rather than let him leave without in the February chill, and then by tying the laces of his trainers. 'There,' he said. 'Soon you'll be able to do it all by yourself, just like the big boys we know.'

They left the hospital, Adam carrying the grip and Jimbo's boots, and Leanne bringing his leather jacket and trousers. Jimbo carried his battered crash helmet, swinging it by its strap, as if his discharge from hospital were an everyday occurrence.

Leanne volunteered to occupy the back seat on the journey home, allowing Jimbo the extra space in the front.

'Okay, dawgs,' said Adam, 'let's bounce.' In the mirror, he saw Leanne grimace, and he smiled at her reaction. 'As soon as we see somewhere promising on the A One,' he said, 'we'll stop for lunch.' Her frown gave way to a smile of approval.

As they left London behind them, Jimbo said, 'I must say, Pop, I really appreciate your pulling out the stops like this. You too, Leanne. I feel quite touched.'

'Think nothing of it,' said Adam.

There was no response from Leanne, so Jimbo turned painfully to peer into the back of the car. 'Leanne's asleep, Pop,' he reported.

'It's not surprising after all the excitement.'

'We'd better keep our voices down.'

Adam only ever remembered the most vivid dreams. Thankfully, they happened so infrequently that they didn't amount to a problem, but he'd just woken from one that left him in the grip of despair. It was a ludicrous dream, the kind of fantasy that only the unconscious mind in its nocturnal meandering could create and, for its own duration, make credible.

By celestial arrangement, he had been granted one more day with Kate, from breakfast time until six o'clock in the evening.

He remembered the joy of seeing her again, healthy and happy, her eyes shining with excitement the way they so often had before the disease claimed her.

They'd walked together in Greenhead Park. It was midsummer, and leaves and flowers abounded. Even the time of year had been changed for them. Anything was possible in a dream.

Every moment was precious, but the seconds were ticking away. No one could pause time, and each exquisite second spent with her was a second off the day. Always, at the back of his mind, and increasingly to the forefront, was the knowledge that six o' clock was creeping ever nearer.

In the end, there was no drama. Kate wasn't snatched or led away. Neither did she fade and become invisible. It ended when he opened his eyes, saw moonlight between the curtains, and reconnected with brutal reality.

He lay still, re-living the wretched countdown in abject misery, until his survival mechanism prompted him to get up. Further sleep was unlikely as well as undesirable. He knew the risk of a reprise was negligible, but he was disinclined to run the risk.

He walked to the bathroom, reluctant to look in the mirror until he'd splashed cold water over his face. Even then, he winced at his haggard reflection, a reminder of himself four years earlier.

The bathroom clock told him it was ten-past five. He would normally have been up at seven, so he brushed his teeth, shaved and showered.

Dressed for the day, he went downstairs and, having made tea, took it into the sitting room.

The dream must have been prompted by Jimbo's accident, the hospital, and probably the relief of knowing that his injuries were slight. The time element was a different matter. It had originated much earlier, with the devastating news that surgery and therapy had failed to eradicate the tumours, and that the condition was now terminal. The consultant had given Kate three to four months, although his estimate turned out to be a little optimistic, because her life ended after only ten weeks. That day, when he, Jimbo, Leanne and Kate's parents had gathered around her bed at the hospice to see her for the last time, would remain with them permanently, but even worse was the ten-week ordeal, when they wanted to spend every available minute with her, but always with the knowledge that time was running out.

He tried his tea and found it drinkable. As he was finishing it, the door opened and Leanne came into the room, visibly distressed. There was no need for him to ask what was troubling her. Only one thing could affect her so deeply. He held out his arms to her.

For some time, she simply wept, her shoulders shaking with each sob, and Adam held her, stroking and gently squeezing her shoulder. He knew from experience that she would speak when she could.

Eventually, she said, 'I had a... horrible... dream about... Mum.'

Adam nodded. 'I think Jimbo's accident might have brought that on,' he said.

'I was all... right last... night.'

'You would be. It was the relief, I think.'

'Is that... why you're down... here? I went... to your room. You... weren't there.'

'Don't worry about me.'

She fished in her pocket for a tissue, so Adam handed her the box from the table.

'I feel... so selfish. It's just as... bad for you.'

'Just cuddle up and make it go away.' He held her more tightly, as if that might speed the process.

'That's what... I told... Nicola.' Her breath was coming in shudders.

'Good girl.'

'It's what Mum... used to... say.'

'I know.' He squeezed her again. 'Cuddle up,' he told her again, 'and we'll make it go away.'

They sat for some time, Leanne with her head on Adam's shoulder, he squeezing and stroking, generating comfort the only way he knew, and feeling better for it as he did so.

After a while, Leanne sat up and said, 'I have to go to work today. I must look foul.'

Adam remembered Jenny saying something similar in the carpark at the care home. It seemed to be a common reflex with women. 'You'll be all right after a good scrub,' he told her. 'I've finished with the bathroom, and Jimbo's not likely to surface for a while yet.'

She adjusted the sash on her bathrobe and bent to kiss him. 'I love you, Dad.'

'I love you too, darling.'

It was as well, when the three of them only had each other.

14

Adam needed to think about a musical he had in mind, about the story of David and Goliath, and he decided to stimulate his brain with some fresh air. It would be a tonic, as well, after the disturbed night.

He often felt guilty that, despite living in beautiful surroundings, he spent so much time indoors, so it was with a feeling of belated virtue that he muffled up and ventured into the countryside above Thanestalls. Jimbo had expressed his intention, for some reason, to visit the café where Leanne worked, so Adam had to do it alone. In any case, Jimbo was still fragile.

The cold air was certainly bracing, and he wondered if he'd gone soft since his caravanning days, but he steeled himself and continued, almost without thinking, past the limestone outcropping that dominated the fell, towards the field that had been for so long his second home.

As he walked, he planned the musical. There would need to be baddies as well as goodies, a whole Philistine army, in fact, and Goliath himself called for careful thought. How could a nine or ten-year-old boy become a giant? He decided that Goliath would have to stand on a platform of some kind - his would be a static part – and he would need a special costume as well, one that would transform his small stature into the requisite number of cubits. He would be a giant with a piping voice, an impediment that only skilful production could minimise, but parents didn't go to school productions expecting grown-up voices.

He was distracted when he noticed a figure coming over the hill. He narrowed his eyes and made out a small, excited dog in attendance. He thought immediately of Jenny and Dottie and, as they came nearer, his hunch was confirmed.

There had never been any evidence that he was one of Dottie's favourite people, but her excitement intensified at their reunion.

'She never needs an excuse to behave like this,' Jenny told him, trying to induce calm. 'Which way are you heading?'

'Back home, I think. 'It's possible to overdo the hearty outdoor life.'

Jenny greeted the observation with an indulgent smile. 'You mustn't do that,' she agreed.

'I came out to plan, and, having planned, I'm going home to implement.'

'Implement what?'

'My idea for a musical about David and Goliath.'

'That should be popular.' She paused to check Dottie, who was trying to become airborne in an attempt to catch a robin. 'What age-group is it for?'

'Years five and six.'

She nodded, as if the information confirmed her guess, and asked, 'Was that the age-group you taught?'

'Good heavens, no. I wouldn't know where to start with tiny tots. I taught Key Stage Three and above.'

'What?'

'Sorry, ages eleven to eighteen. I write these things for primary schools because that's where the demand is. Secondary schools are moving towards mainstream rock and roll musicals.'

'So much lost innocence,' she mused. Then, glancing at the sky to the north, she said, 'There's snow on its way.'

'I haven't heard a forecast.'

'Neither have I, but just look at those clouds.'

Obediently, Adam followed her pointing finger and saw the leaden clouds that certainly seemed to contain the threat of something.

As the top of Brocklehurst Lane came in sight, she asked, 'How's Jimbo?'

'Was it the thought of lost innocence that made you think of him? He lost his some time ago. He's much better, though, thank you.'

'Good. He just crossed my mind.'

'He went to the Netherdale Tea Rooms this morning. I imagine there's a girl there who interests him. That's the only stimulus likely to get Jimbo moving before noon.'

She laughed. 'Go on. You think the world of him, really.'

'Of course I do. I just wish he'd concern himself with other things occasionally, such as work. That would set my mind at rest.'

'I don't imagine you ever had that problem with Leanne. I saw her this morning, by the way, when I took a painting in for them to exhibit. She looked tired.'

He nodded. 'She had a disturbed night. It happens sometimes. I'm afraid Jimbo's accident brought back memories.'

'It was bound to.' She transferred Dottie's lead to her left hand and took Adam's arm with her right. 'Don't feel you have to suffer in silence when there's a friendly ear just two doors away.'

'Thank you, but I'm all right, really.'

As they walked down the lane, Adam stopped suddenly.

'What's the matter?'

'They say the age of miracles is past, but I'm not convinced. Unless I'm greatly mistaken, that mysterious and seldom-heard phenomenon is Jimbo playing the piano.'

'You'd better go and investigate.'

'I shall.'

When Adam let himself in, Jimbo was playing one of Clementi's sonatinas with exaggerated presentation.

'I hate to interrupt you, especially now,' said Adam, 'but music of the classical period doesn't really call for a lot of interpretation, and yours is somewhat on the romantic side.'

Jimbo stopped playing and turned to address his parent. 'I'm venting my feelings, Pop, the anguish of the spurned.'

'What happened?'

Jimbo's face was a study in melancholy. 'I met a maiden in the tea rooms,' he said, 'full beautiful, a faery's child, but I got nowhere. And that is why I sojourn here, alone and palely loitering, and not even the sparrows have an awful lot to add to the conversation.'

Struggling to maintain a solemn expression, Adam said, 'I think

Keats would have preferred his version, Jimbo, but I take it you've suffered a rejection.'

'My heart is broken, Pop.'

'I suspect your pride has taken a knock, and you've naturally confused that with sorrow and despair. In your case, it's easily done.'

'Mock not, Pop. I've suffered enough already.'

'It was never a good idea,' said Adam, 'when you're about to return to London.'

'Some things transcend distance, Pop.'

Adam gestured towards the piano and said, 'Let Clementi continue to pour balm on your wounds.'

Sensitively, he made no further mention of Jimbo's misfortune until Leanne arrived home and the whole story emerged.

'He saw Lindsay, who works with me, and decided he was besotted with her,' she explained, 'although, in Jimbospeak, as we both know, that means she has "a fit body" and she turned him on. Words and their meanings have a confused relationship in his psyche.'

Jimbo appeared in the kitchen doorway, looking pained. He asked, 'Are you discussing this morning's catastrophe?'

'In somewhat less-colourful terms, yes,' said Leanne. 'I told you Lindsay wouldn't go out with you, but no, you wouldn't listen.'

'I took your warning as a challenge, Leanne.'

'More fool you.'

'I take it she has someone on the go?'

'Yes, she has. The reason you never stood a chance, though, is that she's just not interested in men.'

Jimbo appeared to consider that information. 'Maybe,' he said piously, 'she's suffered in the past at the hands of the insensitive and unscrupulous.'

'And maybe she's just never had experience of men,' said Leanne, breaking the news gently. 'You see, she's a lesbian.'

'Surely not.'

'Why not, Jimbo, when any girl who turns you down is, by definition, a lesbian?'

'No, but I mean, fully paid-up, not just part-time or giving it a try for the sake of idle curiosity?'

'She's a card-carrying member of the Women Only Club,' confirmed Leanne.

It was too much for Jimbo to take in. 'But she's so pretty, she can't be.'

'They don't all have big biceps and look like Harrison Ford, you know.'

'Suddenly,' said Adam, who had been following the conversation in the background, 'I'm alarmed that my eighteen-year-old daughter knows about lesbians.'

'It should worry you more, Dad, that your twenty-one-year-old son hasn't a clue about them.'

'I'll be twenty-two next month,' Jimbo reminded them.

'There must be a Ladybird book on the subject,' said Leanne hopefully.

'I think we should all go out to dinner this evening,' suggested Adam. 'Then we can forget about these things.'

'I'll vote for that, Pop.' Jimbo's natural resilience was seldom dormant for long.

* * *

Jenny's prediction turned out to be correct when, on becoming aware of an unusual silence, Adam opened his curtains and looked out on a white landscape. He would not, after all, be driving Jimbo to Leeds Station. He donned his dressing gown to inform his son of the change of plan.

At first, there was no reaction to his tapping on the door, so he knocked more loudly.

'Mm, mm, c'me in,' was the response. At least, that was what Adam thought he heard.

He pushed open the door. 'This is Planet Earth calling Jimbo,' he announced, as a tousled head emerged, tortoise-like, from beneath the duvet. 'You're not going to London today. There's two feet of snow outside.'

It took the information several seconds to penetrate Jimbo's final layer of unconsciousness. He blinked twice and raised himself on one elbow. Even then, he needed confirmation. 'Snow?'

'About two feet,' confirmed Adam, 'and, by the look of those clouds, there's more on its way.' He would give Jenny the credit, later, for telling him about snow clouds. For the moment, information was best fed to Jimbo in easy instalments.

'Great!'

'Don't you want to go back to London?'

'Yes, but... snow!' With unexpected enthusiasm, Jimbo threw the duvet aside and went to the window.

'Put something on, Jimbo.' Adam threw his son's dressing gown to him. 'It's a horrible sight.'

'Sorry.' He put the dressing gown on, still mesmerised by the changed landscape. 'Great!'

'Jimbo, you do for retarded development what Scheherazade did for the bedtime story. I'm going downstairs.'

He took the three pairs of wellingtons from the service room and parked them in front of a radiator. He could hear water running through the pipes now, so he knew Leanne was in the shower. He imagined she would have looked out and seen the snow. At all events, he would see that she went to work with a warm glow within. He switched the oven on and took sausages and bacon from the refrigerator, and eggs and mushrooms from the larder.

First to come down was Jimbo, impatient that Leanne had got to the bathroom before him.

'She has to go to work,' Adam reminded him. 'Anyway, I'm cooking breakfast, so that you can eat before you get ready to go out.'

'What are we having, Pop?'

'Bacon, eggs, mushrooms and sausages.'

'Sausages! Great!'

'It doesn't take a lot to make your life complete, does it, Jimbo?'

'Nothing goes unappreciated, Pop.'

Adam had to agree. One of Jimbo's great qualities was that he took little for granted and appreciated everything else. It was part of his genial nature.

Twenty minutes later, Leanne came down sniffing the aroma from the kitchen. ''Morning, Dad. 'Morning, Jimbo. What's cooking?'

'Bacon, eggs, bangers and mushers,' Jimbo told her excitedly.

'I want you to have something substantial before you go out in the snow,' said Adam.

'I'm not going to the North Pole, Dad, but thank you. You think of everything.' She kissed him gratefully before taking her place at the table.

Adam emerged from the kitchen with eggs, mushrooms and bacon. 'The sausages are on their way,' he told them.

'I was going to have cornflakes,' said Leanne.

To his son's delight, Adam served the sausages. 'Jimbo's impatient to play in the snow,' he told Leanne.

'Oh, bless.'

'I'll tell you what, Jimbo,' said Adam, 'I'll clear the snow from our footpath and drive and you can do the same for Jenny. I'm sure she'll appreciate it.'

'No sweat, Pop. What day is it?'

'Saturday,' Adam told him.

'Great. The kids'll be at home.'

'You'll have someone to play with,' said Leanne, smiling like an indulgent parent.

* * *

Jimbo cleared the snow from Jenny's path and drive, and then built an igloo with Gareth and Nicola in their back garden. He came home later and joined Adam in the dining room. The latter was working on *David and Goliath*, having decided that, as a working title, it was as good as any.

'Do you need the piano, Jimbo?' It was usually a silly question, but recent events had made it less so.

'Not just now, thanks, Pop.'

'If you've something to do in here, I can move to the sitting room easily enough.'

'No, Pop, don't do that.'

'What's on your mind, Jimbo?' It was unusual for him to be so quiet.

'Just, you know... things, Pop.'

'If you want to talk, I'm happy to listen.'

Jimbo was silent for a moment, possibly working out what he wanted to say. Then he said, 'It's just that, being out there with the kids and doing things I did when Leanne and I were kids, took me back. The worst bit was when Jenny called the kids in. She made me a coffee and then got them out of their wet clothes. She was just being... their mum, I suppose, and it made me think....' His head was bowed, but Adam knew how he was feeling.

'I'm not surprised it took you back, Jimbo. It's been quite a week for it.' He got up and put his hand on his son's shoulder and squeezed it the way he'd squeezed Leanne's.

'I don't make a habit of this, Pop,' said Jimbo, taking a tissue from the box on the side table.

'I know you don't, but there's no shame in it.' He continued to squeeze, knowing that Jimbo would talk when he was ready.

At length, he said, 'I'm sorry, Pop.'

'There's nothing to be sorry for.'

'I'm glad Leanne's out.'

'It wouldn't have made any difference, Jimbo. We're all in this. Anyway, you two need to stay connected.'

Jimbo was silent again.

Adam asked him, 'Do you ever talk to your mum? I mean, when you're alone?'

'Sometimes I want to talk to her.'

'You should. Leanne does, and I do sometimes.'

'When Leanne and Mum used to get talking, I couldn't get a word in edgeways.'

Adam laughed softly. 'I know, but you'll probably find it easier now, and you'll feel better for it.'

Jimbo looked up, red-eyed, but more collected. 'I think I will.'

'Stay connected with us as well, Jimbo. I know Leanne's always poking fun, but she loves you.'

'Okay, Pop.'

As the mood lightened, Jimbo went off to his room, leaving Adam to work, although it was far from easy. He was glad Jimbo had been able to air his feelings. He was adept at hiding them behind his carefree persona, and that was, at best, a temporary and risky palliative.

He was surprised when Leanne came home, and Jimbo met her at the outer door of the porch.

'Lean on me while you take your wellies off,' he offered.

'Thanks, Jimbo. That's downright civil of you.' She leaned on his shoulder to perform the action. Having done that, she eyed the tiled floor with dismay. 'It's all wet,' she said.

'No problem,' he said, picking her up.

'Remember your shoulder,' she warned.

'It's okay.' He carried her into the kitchen, where he set her down gently.

'Thanks again, Jimbo.' She looked puzzled when he held out his arms to her, but joined him, nevertheless, in a hug. 'What brought this on?'

'I'm just connecting with you,' he said.

'Oh, is that all?' She sounded matter-of-fact, but Adam could see the pleasure it gave them both. It pleased him as well.

15

MARCH

The District Council's decision to hold the festival in September rather than in May came as no surprise, and Adam was actually relieved, as it gave the committee four more months to organise it.

Given that the committee were happy to have him as head judge, he needed two others. That would be settled in committee, of course, but there was another matter that was entirely up to him, and that was the test piece for the competition. He discussed it with Jenny as they wheeled Mrs Sanderson through the rear gate of the home and across the park to the teashop.

'Just look at those bears,' said Mrs Sanderson. 'They've no fear at all of falling into the water.' She wore a thick, tweed coat, and Jenny had spread a rug over her.

'They can swim, Gran.' The only animal life near the lake were the swans and ducks that lived there and the dogs that people brought to the park for exercise.

'It needs to be something familiar but challenging,' said Adam, easing the wheelchair over a stony part of the footpath.

'What does?'

'The music, Mrs Sanderson.'

'Well, make sure it's not too slow. You're pushing me too quickly. I can't possibly see everything at this speed.'

'All right, I'll slow down.'

'But keep the music going. You have a tendency to conduct everything as if you're going to a funeral.'

'I'll try.' He relaxed the pace of the wheelchair.

'Where have all the children gone?'

'They're at school, Gran. It's Wednesday.'

'Good. I can't usually hear myself think for the noise they make.'

Jenny had been giving the test piece some thought. 'What about something popular?'

'No, I'm thinking of something that absolutely everyone knows, whether they're into pop, classical or whatever.'

'Are you two arguing again?'

'No, Gran, we're having a discussion.'

'Well, can't you discuss it more quietly? I want to hear the foxes talking.'

Adam looked at Jenny and asked, 'What noise do foxes make?'

'They make a sort of "yip" noise usually.'

'I've got it. "Greensleeves". Everyone knows it, and I can arrange it so that no one is at an unfair advantage. The melody will move between the parts, so that the sopranos, who usually get the melody, will have to work at it as well.'

'Make the buggers work.'

'I agree, Mrs Sanderson.'

'Are we nearly there yet?'

'Nearly, Gran.'

'Good. I need to spend a penny.'

Jenny pointed to the building next to the teashop. 'Can we go in there, Adam? The loos are separate from the teashop.'

'Quickly.'

'Yes, Mrs Sanderson.' Adam pushed her briskly, almost to the door.

Mrs Sanderson asked, 'What's he going to do?'

'He'll wait outside with the wheelchair, Gran.'

'Good.'

Adam stood outside, wondering a little about a world populated by bears, noisy children and talkative foxes. It was a private world, because no one else had ever been there.

Mrs Sanderson reappeared, guided by Jenny. 'I only just got there in time,' she announced to the amusement of two passers-by.

'Well, let's have a cup of coffee to celebrate,' said Jenny, leading the way to the teashop.

Once inside, Adam found it easy to navigate with the wheelchair, and he was able to push Mrs Sanderson the length of the display case that held cakes and pastries.

'What would you like, Gran? Chocolate cake?'

'Yes, if it's one I can eat with a fork.'

'What about you, Jenny?'

'No, thank you. Just coffee for me, please.'

Adam took a tray and wheeled the chair up to the counter. 'Three Americanos with milk, please, and a piece of chocolate gateau.'

'This is my son-in-law,' announced Mrs Sanderson. 'He's hopeless in bed, but he makes himself useful by pushing my wheelchair.'

Adam smiled benignly as the assistant struggled to contain herself.

They sat down at a table, and Jenny said, 'I think "Greensleeves" is a good idea.'

'As long as he doesn't make them sing it too slowly. He's a bugger for that, you know. This morning, I waited so long for him to finish "Finlandia" so that I could go and spend a penny, I wet myself.'

The assistant covered her mouth with a paper napkin and retreated into the kitchen.

* * *

'The best thing,' said Adam, as they drove into Thanestalls, 'is that I can laugh *with* her. She's good fun to be with.'

'I'm glad you see it that way.'

'There's only one minor problem.'

Jenny took her eyes off the road for a moment to ask, 'What's that?'

'If I ever wanted long-term female company again, I'd have to go into Wharfedale or Wensleydale to find it, because my reputation locally as a lover is in shreds.'

Jenny smiled. 'I don't think anyone is going to place any credence on what she says.'

'That's a relief.'

Jenny asked, 'Are we going to stop for lunch? If we are, it's my turn to pay.'

'If you really insist.'

'I really do.'

'You're so forceful, Jenny.'

'With two young children, I have to be,' she said, turning into the carpark of the Craven Heifer.

'I can't imagine they give you much trouble.'

'No, they're very good.' She locked the car and followed him into the bar. 'I have to say that meeting Jimbo has transformed Gareth. You saw what he was like when you first met him.'

'It's the strangest thing,' said Adam, 'but he seems to have done the trick.'

At the bar, Adam asked for a tonic water and a pint of Black sheep.

'If you're wanting to eat,' the barman said, 'we've no waitress today. Her little lad's poorly.'

'Nothing horrible, I hope.'

The barman shrugged. 'Just the usual, really.'

Adam could only wonder. 'Well,' he said, 'we'll appreciate her so much more when she comes back.'

They took their drinks to a table and studied the menu.

'Leanne's left her mark on Nicola as well,' said Jenny, continuing the earlier conversation. 'All the time, I have to hear about what Leanne's said and done.'

Adam considered the matter and said, 'It's a shame I can't hire them both out and make them self-financing.'

'As if you would.' She looked again at the menu and said, 'If you know what you'd like, I'll go to the bar and order it.'

'I'd like the quarter-pounder, please, done medium rare if they will.'

'I wouldn't. It's safe enough with steak, but not with a burger.'

'Okay, I'll be guided by you. Well-done is fine.'

While Jenny was at the bar, he thought about Mrs Sanderson's preoccupation with his perceived lack of sexual prowess. Maybe she could be persuaded to revise her judgement, so that she could say,

'This is my son-in-law. He's a famous conductor and he's brilliant under the duvet. I can recommend him heartily, but be prepared for a few surprises, because he's very inventive.'

Jenny returned from the bar with a pint of Black Sheep and a tonic water. She put them on the table and asked, 'What are you smiling about?'

He told her, and she gave him an embarrassed smile before conveniently changing the subject. She asked, 'Has Jimbo's motorbike been repaired yet?'

Adam gave her a long-suffering look and said, 'Yes, although Jimbo, being Jimbo, had insured it third party only.'

'Poor boy. That's more worry when he doesn't need it.'

'It didn't worry Jimbo. He just spoke to me, and let me worry about it.' He lifted his glass. 'Cheers.'

'Cheers.' As another thought occurred to her, she said, 'Our conversation in the park was downright surreal, wasn't it?'

'About the test piece?'

'Yes, although, with or without my gran's suggestions, it sounded like a good idea.'

'I've given it some more thought as well. I think I'll make it a *potpourri* of, possibly, three Tudor songs, beginning and ending with "Greensleeves". Then, they can perform a second, contrasting piece of their choice as long as it's no longer than, say, five minutes.'

'I like the idea.' It was clear that she was thinking. 'Will you just roll off photocopies of the Tudor thing and charge for them?'

'No, that's dicey. I'll persuade the District Council to publish it. They can do that quickly enough, and then the proceeds will go towards the cost of the Festival. I don't want anything for myself.'

'If that doesn't convince Councillor Beasley that you have the Dale's interests at heart,' she said, 'I don't know what will.'

'Oh well, it's that new direction we spoke about. If the Festival helps the people of Netherdale, I'll be delighted, because it's already working for me.'

'Is it really?'

Her interest was genuine and he welcomed it. 'I spent four years marking time,' he said. 'I worked because I had to, and I did what I could for Jimbo and Leanne. I took no interest at all in outside matters.' He gave a dismissive shrug. 'That changed when we moved to Thanestalls and you introduced me to the Choral Society.'

'I'm pleased that I had a small part in it,' she said.

He was about to tell her that she was playing a significant part in his revival, but he checked himself. There was no room in their friendship for misunderstanding, so he was relieved when a young woman in kitchen whites came to their table with the food they'd ordered.

* * *

Leanne was reading a prospectus, one of several that had arrived in the post during the past week or so, from various universities and colleges. Knowing his daughter as well as he did, he'd not commented on the development, but waited, instead, for her to raise the subject. His thoughtfulness was soon to be rewarded.

Leanne closed the prospectus and said, 'Right, I've made my decision.'

'Good girl. Drink?' It seemed to Adam that an important conversation was in the offing.

'Please.'

Adam opened a bottle of Shiraz and filled two glasses.

'It's still okay for me to go to university, isn't it?'

'Of course it is.'

'I just wondered, because of the money.'

'The money's there, Leanne, earmarked for the purpose.'

'How? I mean, Jimbo's costing a fortune, and now there's me.'

Adam realised that with so much to talk about, he'd never explained the matter properly to his children, and that explanation was now overdue, so he began.

'When your mum and I were first married,' he said, 'we struggled financially; it was very difficult for some time, but we decided, when things became easier, that we never wanted either of you to find yourselves in that situation, so we took out insurance for your future and Jimbo's.'

'Hey, that's really cool. It's bad, though, that things were so difficult for you at first.'

'To some extent,' he admitted, 'you could say that we brought it on ourselves.'

'I could say that,' she agreed, 'but I wouldn't dream of it.' Noting his embarrassment, she said, 'I worked it out ages ago, Dad. You were married in October nineteen-eighty-one, and Jimbo was born in March eighty-two.' She added in consolation, 'I don't think Jimbo's rumbled it yet. You know what he's like at maths.'

'Suddenly, I feel as if our roles are reversed, and I'm having to explain my actions to my daughter.'

'And after you grilled me the night you saw off "Dickhead" Dewhirst through the letterbox.' Smiling indulgently, she said, 'I didn't mention the dates-thing then. You were finding the conversation difficult enough as it was.'

'Tell me about your decision, Leanne,' he suggested, feeling like a drowning man grasping a lifebelt.

'All right. Spending time with Jenny and going to her classes has helped me decide that I want to study fine art and photography. I was keen already, but being with someone who does it for a living has made me think about all kinds of things that might never have occurred to me.'

Adam nodded approvingly. Leanne always made sense, even when she was teasing her hapless parent. 'Have you decided where you want to study?'

'Yes, the London Institute. It looks like an excellent place, and I shan't be all that far away from Jimbo, should he ever need me.'

That made sense too.

16

When the doorbell rang, Adam thought immediately of the young woman who delivered the post. She was cheerful and friendly, and he liked her. She'd even hugged him when he gave her a ten-pound note at Christmas.

When he opened the door, however, he was surprised to see the landlord of The Golden Lion on his doorstep.

'Mr Harrison,' he said, 'what can I do for you?' It was a fair question, because the visit was completely unexpected.

'It's a bit embarrassing, actually.' He looked embarrassed; even his handlebar moustache seemed to droop, as if he'd exchanged it for the drop design, rather than the usual flat, mountain bike variety.

'I'm a man of the world, Mr Harrison. I'm not easily shocked.'

'It's nothing like that.' The man shifted his weight nervously from one foot to the other. 'The things is,' he began, 'I clamped my car last night as a security measure....' He seemed at a loss as to how to continue.

'Go on,' urged Adam, 'get it off your chest.' He thought he knew what was coming.

'My wife has gone to Hampshire to visit her mother, and she's taken the house key with the clamp key on the same ring.' He looked as if, with little provocation, he might burst into tears.

'I see,' said Adam, enjoying the man's discomfiture. 'You might even say you're hoist with your own petard, although the phrase "held to account" springs almost as readily to mind.'

'I thought you'd find it funny.' He now looked dejected. 'I thought I'd throw myself on your mercy, but it looks as if I've wasted my time.'

'No, I'll unlock it for you. Just let me get my keys.' He couldn't resist the temptation of adding, 'I always keep them where I know I can find them.'

He locked the house door and took out his car key. 'Come on,' he said, 'I'll run you round to the pub.'

'I'm really very grateful for this,' said Mr Harrison.

'It's no trouble, and it's probably time to bury the hatchet, anyway.'

'Yes.' He seemed to welcome the truce. 'I believe you're involved in the planning of the choir festival, Mr Watkinson.'

'You could say that.'

'It could bring a lot of business into Thanestalls.'

'And the rest of the Dale, hopefully.'

Mr Harrison appeared not to have heard Adam's response, because he said, 'I have a number of regular patrons, but mine is mainly tourist and passing trade.'

Adam wasn't surprised, but he kept that thought to himself as a question occurred to him. 'How did you know my name and address?'

'I spoke to Mrs Thorpe, whose car you....'

'Unclamped.'

'Yes, and she wasn't in a hurry to tell me anything, but when I explained why I needed to speak to you, she told me who you were and where you lived.'

'Good for her.' He could imagine Jenny giving Harrison the cold shoulder. He smiled at the thought as he turned into the pub carpark and stopped beside the clamped Audi.

'I really am very grateful,' repeated Mr Harrison.

* * *

The following morning, the friendly postie delivered two letters. One, in an envelope marked *The London Institute*, was for Leanne, and the other was addressed by hand to Adam. He put Leanne's letter on the coffee table, where she would see it when she came home. When he opened the other, he found a covering letter, the official release form for the work to be reprinted and performed, and a poem printed on three sheets of paper. He read the covering letter, from which he learned that the poem was an evocation of the history of the Yorkshire Dales, from its birth as it emerged from the receding ocean, through the ice ages, to population, invasion, industry and tourism. It seemed a monumental programme for a poem; the poet had encapsulated the events of 150 million years into three sheets of A4, but she seemed to have done it rather well. He sat down to read it properly.

It was written in free verse; on such a scale, a rhyming scheme would have been a self-imposed millstone, but it had an insistent, compelling rhythm that held him in fascination to the end. He read it a second time, and an idea occurred to him. He would use it to provide an introduction, a series of links, and a glorious *finale*. He was excited already. He picked up the letter again and found the poet's phone number.

After several rings, she answered. 'Elizabeth Golding. Hello?'

'Good morning, Mrs Golding. This is Adam Watkinson. You sent me your poem "From the Depths", and I've just read it.'

'Oh, did you like it?' She sounded quite elderly.

'I think it's remarkable. I'd like to use it in the cantata.'

'Well, that's why I sent it.'

'It's so good, I'm surprised it's not in print.'

His observation caused her to laugh. 'Mr Watkinson,' she said, 'have you ever tried to get poetry published?'

'No,' he admitted, 'it was difficult enough with music.'

'Well, at least, you've had something published. There's no demand for poetry, and that means that most literary agents won't touch it with a long paper knife.'

'If its inclusion in the cantata causes someone to look more closely at it, it'll be no bad thing.'

'I can't argue with that, Mr Watkinson. It is "Watkinson", isn't it?'

'That's right.'

'Maybe it will see the light of day in my lifetime.'

'I hope so, Mrs Golding. The festival is only five or six months away.'

'Well, I'm eighty-six, so I'm hoping so too.'

When Mrs Golding had rung off, he looked at his workload. *David and Goliath* was complete and waiting for the approval of his publisher. Now he could start work on the cantata and the test piece. Ideally, the latter should be available to entrants as early as possible, so he resisted the lure of Mrs Golding's poem, and began work on it.

As well as 'Greensleeves', he'd decided to set extracts from Christopher Marlowe's 'The Passionate Shepherd to his Love' and Shakespeare's 'O Mistress Mine, Where Are You Roaming?' from *Twelfth Night*, and he set about structuring the piece prior to setting it.

With a day free from interruption, he completed the first draft shortly before Leanne arrived home.

She saw the letter from the London Institute immediately and opened it. 'Result!'

'So soon?'

'Yes, they don't bother with interviews and that sort of thing nowadays. They do it by points. You get a number of points for each grade.'

'I had to audition.'

'Poor old Dad. Things were tough in those days.'

'It's still the case with music colleges. Anyway, congratulations.'

'Thanks, Dad.' She carried out an investigative sniff and, failing to detect any recognisable aroma, asked, 'What are we eating?'

'I don't know.'

'Haven't you decided yet? Remember I'm a growing lass who's just done a full shift. I need sustenance, Dad.'

'And you'll get it. We're eating out tonight.'

'Don't tell me. You've won the lottery and we're going to be rich for evermore. Yay!'

'No, but we can celebrate your success.'

She gave him a suspicious look. 'I'm sensing an additional reason,' she said.

'I've done so much today, I wasn't able to cook.'

'Honesty's the best policy, Dad. Where are we going? The Craven Heifer?'

'No, the Golden Lion.'

Her eyes grew wide with exaggerated surprise. 'I thought you and he were sworn enemies.'

'He owes me a favour.'

* * *

The landlord was behind the bar when they arrived. He greeted Adam immediately.

'Good evening, Mr Watkinson.'

'Good evening. This is my daughter Leanne. She's just been awarded a university place.'

'Congratulations, and you've come to celebrate?'

'That,' said Leanne, 'and he remembered at six o' clock that he hadn't cooked anything for dinner.'

'I can't get away with anything when you're around, Leanne.'

'I told you, Dad, honesty is the best policy.'

'At all events,' said the landlord, 'your meal is on the house.'

'In that case, we're both grateful.'

Later, at the table, Leanne studied the menu, noticing the prices as she did so. 'It was a good job you had a skeleton key in your cupboard,' she said. 'Most families haven't.' She made her choice, closed the menu and said, 'I must say, Dad, it's good of you to do this.'

'Not really. It's only right to celebrate your success.'

'Not to mention the fact that—'

'I hadn't cooked anything. I know.'

'What were you doing that made you forget?'

'Writing the test piece for the festival. It's in draft form, so it'll need tidying.'

She nodded, accustomed to his bursts of creativity. 'I still think this is good of you. I mean, with a blank cheque like you have tonight, you could have brought Jenny.'

'Why Jenny, particularly?' He had a feeling he was already in deep water.

'Because you don't really know anyone else and because you take her to lunch at the Craven Heifer.'

'We take it in turns to treat each other, and it's only after we've been to visit her gran. Anyway, how do you know about that?'

'The kitchen window at the Tea Rooms overlooks the Craven Heifer carpark, and one of the girls is an awful busybody. She just has to tell me when she sees you two together.'

'And what's your reaction?'

'I just tell her what an awful philanderer you are.'

'Oh, Leanne.'

'It's all right. She thinks you collect stamps.'

The waitress came to take their order, and Leanne waited until she was gone before resuming the conversation.

'What I'm saying, Dad, is I know you see quite a lot of her, and, basically, it's okay by me.'

'As long as I'm in by half-past ten?'

'You know what I mean.'

'Yes, and it's good that you feel that way, but there's nothing going on between Jenny and me.'

Leanne's eyes opened wide as she feigned shock. 'I should think not. I hope you just go to the Craven Heifer to eat and talk about the olden days.'

'That's what it amounts to.'

'Well, just you keep it at that. I don't want you coming home with a problem.'

'I'll try not to.'

Leanne studied him thoughtfully and said, 'We need to have a sensible conversation, Dad.'

'I keep trying, honestly I do.'

'Mm.' It was clear she still had something on her mind. 'I spend a lot of time with Jenny, as you know, and for most of that time, she's just a friend, a good one, but a friend.'

'Yes?' He waited for her to go on.

'Some of the time, though, she's like a mum. I mean, she's twice my age, at least until my next birthday, so it's quite natural.'

Adam nodded.

'I tell her things, how I'm feeling, and that sort of thing. She's a "go to" person, if you know what I mean.'

119

'Yes, I do. I think it comes of having young children of her own. She caught Jimbo rather unawares.'

'How?'

'It was when he brought the children in from playing in the snow. She left him drinking coffee while she got the children out of their wet clothes and dried them off. He said it was just her being a mum that got to him.'

'Oh, bless.'

'Yes, he was very quiet when he came home. We had a chat and he was all right.'

'He met me at the door and helped me get my wellies off, and then he carried me across the wet floor and into the kitchen. He was really sweet.'

'I know. That was him connecting with you.'

She nodded. 'He said as much. I was quite touched.'

The waitress arrived with the starters. It was time for normal conversation to begin, so they discussed the Choral Society's Easter concert.

17

Two interesting suggestions for the cantata arrived by mail. Neither was original, but the ideas were useful. The folk song 'Fourpence a Day' was about lead mining, a significant feature of Dales history, and another song, by James Hook, 'The Lass of Richmond Hill', was also worth considering. Adam felt now that he had something on which he could work.

However, work called for fuel, which meant coffee, and that was running low, so a visit to the supermarket was necessary. Kate had always kept a list, adding to it whenever she saw that something was needed, and things never ran out, but nature had failed him profoundly in that respect. The other day was an example, when he'd been so engrossed in the test piece, he'd forgotten to prepare dinner. As a musician, he had to work cogently and systematically, but in every other aspect of his life, he was disorganised to the point of chaos, albeit of a gentle kind. And now he had to make a journey to the supermarket for coffee beans.

He drove down to the main road and turned left. Ideas were occurring to him all the time and he was keen to get started.

The carpark was relatively empty when he arrived, so he parked in the nearest place to the entrance that wasn't reserved for the disabled or for mothers and buggies, and locked his car.

In doing so, he noticed a familiar Renault Clio nearby and, on further examination, recognised it as Jenny's. As if further proof were needed, Jenny arrived at that moment, laden with two bags of shopping. As she flicked the remote switch, he opened the rear hatch for her.

She looked up in surprise, but then, when she recognised him, her startled expression became a half-smile. 'Hello,' she said.

'Hello. How are things?'

'Not so good. They took my gran into hospital this morning.'

'Oh, dear.' He took her bags and stowed them in the boot.

'Yes, her blood pressure's low and she's refusing food and drink. It's the fluid that's most important.'

It sounded ominous. 'Let's hope they can get her right.'

'Yes, she'll be eighty-six on Sunday.'

'Eighty-six?' Mrs Golding had told him she was eighty-six. Suddenly, it had become a landmark.

'We've been planning a party for her in the home.' Her expression was far from hopeful.

'If I can do anything, running about or anything at all, let me know. I mean it.'

'I know you do and I'm grateful.'

He gave her a quick hug of sympathy, thankful that the Tea Rooms didn't overlook the supermarket as well as the Craven Heifer.

'Thank you, Adam,' she said. 'You're very kind, but I must go.'

'Of course, but remember what I've said.'

'I will,' she said, opening her car door, 'and thank you.'

* * *

Jenny phoned late that afternoon. 'I've been to see Gran,' she said in a low voice. 'She didn't know I was there. It was the same with my mum when she went in earlier. She found her almost unconscious, but breathing rapidly, and she felt cold to the touch.'

Adam recognised the symptoms but kept his suspicion to himself. 'Let me know if you need company,' he said.

'I will. I'll let you know if anything happens.'

Had he been waiting, it would not have been for long, because the phone rang again an hour or so later.

'It's Jenny.' She sounded desolate. 'They called my mum to the hospital shortly after I phoned you. She arrived just too late.'

'I'm sorry, Jenny. Do you want me to come round?'

'Would you mind? When the children are in bed, about eight-thirty?'

'I'll be there.'

It was a sod. It sounded very much like septicaemia, the condition that had finished his granddad, and it was hardly surprising after so many urine infections. Her body must have developed a stoic resistance to antibiotics.

* * *

He told Leanne when she came home.

'Oh, poor Jenny,' she said. 'They were very close.'

'Yes, I'm going round there later, just so that she's not alone.'

'Do you want me to come as well?'

'Maybe not this time, Leanne. You could be a great help to her later. Just for now, though, one to one is probably better.'

Leanne nodded approvingly. 'Clear thinking, Dad.' A moment later, she sniffed the air like an Irish setter, and asked, 'What are we eating?'

'Beef stew, potatoes, peas and carrots.'

'Yay!'

Adam smiled. There were times when his daughter's customary eloquence deserted her. Her enthusiasm also reminded him of something else. He dialled Jenny's number. When she answered, he asked, 'Have you eaten yet?'

'No, I've fed the children, but I can't face cooking for myself.'

'I understand. I'll be with you at about eight-thirty.'

'Only if you're sure you don't mind.'

'Positive.'

At dinner, Leanne asked him about the cantata.

'I been sent two new ideas,' he said. 'One of them is 'The Lass of Richmond Hill'. It's a good song and I can do quite a lot with it. I think I'll give the solo to Jimbo.'

'It'll be just right for him,' said Leanne confidently.

'Do you know the song?'

'No, but it's about a girl, isn't it? Where you find girls you find Jimbo.'

'I suppose so.' He had to smile.

Later, he reheated some of the stew and vegetables, plated it up and carried it with a bottle of Bordeaux to Jenny's house.

She and Dottie met him at the door, and she saw what he was carrying. 'Adam,' she said, 'it's very kind of you, but there was really no need.'

Dottie seemed to think otherwise, because she followed him closely, enticed by the aroma of casseroled beef.

He put the plate down on the dining table and removed the dish that was covering it. 'No argument, Jenny. Tuck in. Leanne says it's good, and she doesn't bestow empty compliments on her elderly parent.' He looked around for a corkscrew, and seeing none, took out his penknife.

'I have a corkscrew,' she protested.

'Don't worry,' he said, pulling out the corkscrew attachment. 'This is a job for my Swiss composers' knife.'

'How many Swiss composers do you know?'

'Lots, and they all swear by the knife.'

Jenny sat at the table and inhaled the aroma as Leanne had earlier. 'You know,' she said, 'I think I'm ready for this after all.'

He filled two glasses with wine and took the seat opposite her. 'How's your mum?'

'She's taking it rather well. I think she sees it as…. What do they call it? A happy release, which I suppose it is. Gran could get very confused and frightened.'

He nodded. 'I can imagine so. And the children?'

'They hadn't seen her since she went into care, so it could have been worse for them, but they're quite upset.'

'Were they all right at bedtime?'

'Yes, they were fairly settled.' With a wave of her fork, she said, 'This stew is lovely, Adam. Thank you.'

'You're welcome. When you've had a shock like today's, cooking is the last thing you want to do.'

'And you know that more than most. I still feel guilty when you're like this.'

'There's really no need.'

He let her finish the meal and then took the dishes and cutlery to the kitchen.

'Just put them in the dishwasher, Adam,' she said. 'I'll return them when they're washed.'

'Okay.' On his way back from the kitchen, he picked up their glasses. 'Shall we sit down and have a leisurely drink?'

'Yes, I'll bring the bottle.'

She joined him quite naturally on the sofa. 'You've told me before not to feel guilty,' she said, 'but you've had so much to endure.'

'I have,' he agreed, taking her hand. 'You don't mind, do you? It's just that I'm not the most natural confider, and I need the contact if the conversation's running deep.'

'Of course I don't.' She patted his hand encouragingly with her free hand.

'When I first called to see the funeral director,' he said, 'I saw framed poems and quotations on his walls. Having other things on my mind, I took no notice of them at the time, but I remember going back to pay the bill, and I read one of them for the first time. I've always remembered it. It's by someone called Jamie Anderson, and it said, "Grief is just love with no place to go".'

'It sounds like a dead end, doesn't it?'

'Yes, it does, but much of it had somewhere to go, because I had Jimbo and Leanne to look out for.' He noticed that her eyes were wet. 'I didn't mean to upset you,' he said, taking a tissue from the box on the coffee table and handing it to her.

'You haven't.' She dabbed at her cheeks and said, 'You must think I'm feeble, always in tears. I assure you I'm not.'

'I know you're not. Anyway, you're allowed tears today, because of your gran, and when all's said and done, they're only liquid love. That's what I told Jimbo when his mum died. He was very self-conscious about it.'

'And what about you? Did you tell yourself that?'

'There was no need.'

'No?'

'No, it's not a macho thing, just the way I am. I have feelings but I don't show them.'

She squeezed his hand. 'A straight bat and a stiff upper lip.'

'I suppose so, but it's the way I've always been.' He studied her

125

briefly and said, 'Don't let me inhibit you. If you feel a sob coming on, feel free to give it full rein.'

'You know, I think I did most of my sobbing when Gran was alive and suffering from that awful condition.'

'I shouldn't be at all surprised. As I remember, it's like having someone taken from you. They're still alive, but not the person they were.'

'Of course, your granddad.'

'Yes.'

'It must have been worse with Kate. Breast cancer, wasn't it?'

He nodded.

'I noticed the badge on your anorak, the day we met, when you gave us all a lift home.'

He smiled at the recollection. 'Yes, it's rather like locking the stable door. It can do nothing for Kate, but if people take notice of it, it may help to save someone else's life.'

'You're a generous man, Adam.'

He wondered. 'I've done little enough for you tonight. It seems to me we've talked about my experience more than anything else.'

'It's taken my mind off things, so it's been good for me. I only hope it hasn't been too awful for you.'

'No, I'm coping better all the time.'

18

'This is very kind of you,' said Jenny, looking over her shoulder at the folded-down back seat of Adam's Rover.

'Not at all. After two years, her room must be full of clutter. My granddad's was. Mind you, he'd always been a hoarder.'

'Was that the one thing that didn't change with dementia?'

'One of the few.' He parked outside the home and turned to Jenny to ask, 'Will you be all right, going in there?'

'I think so.'

He locked the car and walked with her to the entrance.

'My last visit,' she said, keying in the PIN.

They signed the visitors' book before going on to the part that, until recently, had been Mrs Sanderson's home.

'You know,' said Jenny, repeating the process with the door lock, 'in all the time I've been coming here, I've never known what to call this unit.' She spoke the last word with a look of distaste. ' "Unit" sounds like something in a mental hospital, "Ward" is part of a hospital, and "Landing" is reminiscent of that Ronnie Barker show *Porridge*.'

'You won't have to worry about it after today,' he reminded her.

They closed the door behind them as a smiling, friendly woman came out of the office.

'This is Shirley, the nurse in charge of the shift,' said Jenny. 'Shirley, I'd like you to meet my neighbour Adam. We've come to collect Gran's belongings.'

'Of course. I'm sorry, Jenny, but it really was for the best.'

'I can see that now.'

Shirley turned to Adam and said, 'Joan always enjoyed your reading to her. She talked about you a lot.'

'Oh dear.'

She laughed. 'I shouldn't worry. No one took her chatter seriously.' She led them down the passage and opened the door. The room had been cleared, and Mrs Sanderson's belongings had been packed in cardboard boxes. It was as if she had never been there.

Adam gave Jenny a reassuring squeeze and asked, 'Is there a trolley or something that we can use?'

'Yes, we have a trolley. I'll send for it.'

As she returned to her office, a familiar voice said, 'Hello, Adam. Do you know any good jokes?'

'Hello, Robert. As a matter of fact, I do.' With an apologetic look in Jenny's direction, he began. 'A vicar was travelling on a train. It was back in the days of enclosed compartments, and he found he was sharing his with a group of actresses, so, being a friendly soul, he started handing round a bag of jelly babies. He asked them, "And what are you currently appearing in?" '

' "A pantomime," they told him, "Dick Whittington at Bradford Alhambra."

' "I say," he said, "how exciting. Help yourselves to jelly babies, by the way."

' "I'm Tom the cat," one girl told him.

' "And I take the part of Alice," said another.

' "Oh,' he said, still handing round the jelly babies, "and who takes Dick?"

' "We all do," they said, "but not for bloody jelly babies." '

There was a moment's silence, and then Robert began to laugh uproariously. 'A vicar,' he said, 'eating jelly babies.' His laughter continued unabated as he moved down the passage.

'I think he missed the point of the story,' said Jenny. 'It seems to go with the condition, because Gran always used to.'

When they'd loaded up the trolley and taken their leave of the staff, they took it down to the carpark, where Adam loaded the largest and heaviest items into the back of his car.

He asked, 'Where are we taking this stuff?'

'To my mum's, if you don't mind.'

They made the necessary detour to Jenny's parents' house. There was no one at home, but Jenny let them in with her key.

'It was a good thing I had this with me,' she said.

'I'd have got you in.'

'You probably would,' she agreed somewhat absently.

He realised her attention was elsewhere. She was staring at the cubist panorama that dominated the tiny sitting room.

'Everything she had is in those boxes,' she said.

'Yes, you need to leave them behind emotionally as well as physically.'

She blinked rapidly and followed him out to the car.

For a while, she looked silently through the windows. He glanced at her from time to time, but she remained apparently dry-eyed and seemed quite settled after her latest brush with nostalgia. Then, after a while, she surprised him by chuckling, and then the chuckle became an open laugh. In the circumstances, Adam was afraid she was going to give way to hysteria, but she abated.

'What was that all about?'

'The joke you told Robert, she said, laughing again. "We all do, but not for bloody jelly babies." '

'If you look in the glove compartment,' he said, 'you may find a surprise.'

'Oh?' She lifted the catch and opened it, taking out a plastic bag of sweets. Holding it up to read the label, she said, 'Jelly babies.' Once more, she gave way to immoderate laughter.

Emotions were strange and surprising things, or so Adam thought as he continued to the Craven Heifer. It was a strange kind of day, and there was every likelihood that it would become even stranger, because Jimbo was due to arrive later that afternoon.

* * *

Jimbo's arrival was as tumultuous as usual, from the roar of his engine to his unique doorstep salutation.

'Hi, Pop. How's things? Getting plenty?'

'You need to change your greeting, Jimbo. It's wearing thin.'

'Okay, Pop, I'll work on it.'

'Otherwise, welcome home. Sit down and I'll get you a can of the blonde tasteless stuff.'

'You're singing my song, Pop.'

Adam went to the kitchen and returned with a can of lager and a beer glass.

'Thanks, Pop.' Jimbo took them from him. 'You really know how to welcome a long-lost son back into the fold.'

'Think nothing of it, Jimbo, but tell me what you've been doing.'

'Deputising, Pop.'

'For whom?'

'Some Belarussian dude who fell ill before he could take part in Mozart's Requiem. My prof got me the gig.'

'Lucky you. Where was this?'

'St John's, Smith Square.'

Adam nodded. 'Yet another addition to your CV.'

'Too right, Pop. Anyway, what's the story with this Easter concert?'

'I couldn't get the tenor I wanted, so it's just going to be you and Helen Little. They just want you each to sing two solos.'

'Who's Helen Little, Pop?'

'The mezzo who was ill and couldn't take part in *Messiah* at Christmas. She's a third-year student at the Academy.'

Suddenly, Jimbo's brain leapt into full alertness. 'What's she like, Pop?'

'She's very good. I taught her at Aspley High before she went to the Academy. She has a remarkable range. She can go from the mezzo register, up into the soprano range with no difficulty at all. That's why I booked her.'

'I don't mean her singing,' said Jimbo impatiently. 'Describe her to me.'

Adam sighed, as he always did in matters concerning his son's carnal ambitions. 'She's about twenty-one, attractive, with dark hair and brown eyes, and she's tall and slim. Other than that, I can tell you no more. And, before you ask, I don't know if she has a boyfriend. I haven't seen her for a year, now.'

'You've sold her to me, Pop.'

'I was afraid of that.' He wondered what he'd done to the sweet girl who used to run errands for him and give him rock buns and raspberry volcanoes that she'd made in Home Economics. Arousing Jimbo's interest in her was like throwing a lamb to a wolf that's been on a diet for a week. He really should have been more careful.

'I've been working on *Ella giammai m'amo* from *Don Carlos*. Do you think they'd like that?'

'I don't know, Jimbo. It's maybe a shade obscure for our audience.'

'It's standard repertoire, Pop,' protested Jimbo.

'But not standard enough for our concert. Think *Classic FM* rather than *Radio Three*.'

'I never listen to *Classic FM*.'

'Neither do I, Jimbo.' He tried another analogy. 'Think of an opera prom performed in English.'

Jimbo thought, and then adopted a martyred, condescending look.

Before he could speak, Adam said, 'I have to compliment you on your acting.'

'Acting has nothing to do with it, Pop. You see before you the performer sacrificing his highest aspirations to entertain the masses.'

'Don't forget that those masses are paying good money to hear you, Jimbo.'

'I'm aware of that,' he said wearily, 'and I shan't labour the point, as I'm sure you've heard it all before.'

'I have,' agreed Adam. 'I've heard bullshit in every known form, so you can dispense with the histrionics and suggest two items that an uninformed audience would enjoy sung in English.'

'I happen to have with me,' said Jimbo with theatrical dignity, *The Magic Flute* and *The Abduction from the Seraglio*.'

'Excellent, and what will you sing from those two?'

' "O Isis and O Siris" and "When a Maiden Takes Your Fancy".' He delivered the answer like a condemned man accepting his fate.

'That's my boy. Now all we have to do is think of an encore.' He got up and went to the dining room, where his music scores occupied a series of shelves. He returned with the score of Bizet's *Carmen*, which he handed to his hapless son.

Jimbo stared in horror. 'Not the "Toreador's Song", Pop?'

'You sang it at the last school concert.'

'Pop, I was a mere child, too young to know better.'

'Don't be a music snob, Jimbo. There's no future in it.' He let the message linger, and then said, 'You'll possibly need another encore. Have you anything in mind?'

'I have a transposed copy of *Largo al Factotum*.'

'Perfect. What key is it in?'

'B flat.'

'That'll work nicely.'

'It will, as long as they don't expect a shave, a haircut and something for the weekend as well.'

'It's always a risk when you're called "Figaro".'

'Honestly, Pop, the more I debase myself, the more amusement it gives you.'

'Seriously, Jimbo, don't be a snob. It doesn't become you.'

Jimbo had never been one to sulk, and now he nodded his acceptance of his father's advice.

Adam stood up and said, 'I'll get you another can of coloured water as a reward for that, Jimbo.'

When Adam returned with the lager, Jimbo said, 'Of course, I'll have to sing *Largo al Factotum* in Italian.'

'Why?'

'Because it works better than it does in English, and because the audience doesn't need to know the words. It's enough for them to know that Figaro is a barber who's at everybody's beck and call, and he has to dash around like a blue-arsed fly.'

'Okay, I'll grant you that.'

Cheered to some extent by the concession, Jimbo asked, 'What's Helen singing?'

'I don't know yet, but my money is on "Softly Awakes My Heart" from *Samson and Delilah*. It'll be expected of her. It follows mezzos around the way *Nessun Dorma* stalks tenors. Oh, and I believe she wants to sing a duet with you. She mentioned "Give me thy Hand" from *Don Giovanni*. Of course, it'll have to be in English. I'll find out what translation she's using.'

'But Zerlina is a soprano role,' said Jimbo, controlling his excitement at the thought of playing the great spoiler of virgins.

'I told you, she has an extraordinary range.'

'I'm looking forward to meeting her.'

'I've no doubt you are.' Adam put aside his parental misgivings for the moment and said, 'I'll give her a ring tonight and arrange a rehearsal for you, her and Jenny. By the way,' he warned, 'Jenny lost her favourite granny this week, so be mindful of that when you see her.'

'I'll be at my most sensitive,' promised Jimbo.

* * *

Even when not at her most sensitive, Leanne was intuitive, and she could sense when all was not well with her brother. She raised the subject after dinner.

'Oh, what can ail thee, basest of basses?'

'Why should there be anything wrong with me?'

'It's a fair question in a liberal society, Jimbo, but your ears are back and your tail's not wagging, so something's either fallen off or stopped working. Whatever it is, you can tell your big sister about it.'

'You're not my big sister, you're my little sister.'

'I know. Nature's not always what it seems. Come on, tell me.'

Adam was working in the dining room, so Jimbo felt able to unburden himself. 'I came home all set to sing a couple of arias from *Don Carlos* and *I Lombardi* at the concert, and now the Old Man wants me to keep it low-brow.'

'Of course he does.'

Jimbo looked at her in surprise but said nothing.

'It's a concert for people who like what they know.'

For a moment, his face mirrored the struggle within, and then he asked tentatively, 'Don't you mean that they know what they like?'

'No, Jimbo. As I understand it, the operas you had in mind would appeal to two kinds of audience: the *cognoscenti* and the bullshit entity. By that, I mean those who can't get enough of Verdi, and then those who flaunt culture like holidays in the Maldives. The

Choral Society's audience is neither of those two. It consists of people who genuinely enjoy the music they know, but who might feel marginalised by something unfamiliar, and they deserve your consideration as much as anyone else. Do you see what I mean?'

'I do now.' He looked less convinced than he sounded.

'You still have something on your mind, Jimbo. What is it?'

'Just, well, how do you know all this?'

'As someone who only got as far as Grade Six Piano?'

'I didn't mean it like that.'

'No, you wouldn't.' She looked fleetingly guilty. 'You're better than that. No, I only know about these things because it's the same in art.'

'Is it?' It was a new surprise for him.

'Yes, it is, and shall I tell you something else that has nothing to do with what we've been talking about?'

'Go on.'

'We're going to be neighbours.'

Confusion returned once more to his features. 'Where, how, when?'

'I'm starting at the London Institute in somewhere called High Holborn in September.'

Suddenly, reason dawned. 'High Holborn? That's only a few miles from where I live.'

'I knew you'd work it out eventually, Jimbo.' She patted his shoulder in approval.

A shadow came across his face, and he said, 'You're not going to be bossy and judgemental, are you?'

'Who, me?'

'Yes, I mean, I have my life to lead, and I'm not going to live it like a monk, you know.'

'Jimbo, you couldn't live like a monk for one day, even for a dare.'

'Well, as long as that's understood.'

She couldn't help teasing him. 'I'll be there to support you and explain things to you, Jimbo.'

'More like, I'll be there to keep an eye on you.'

She narrowed her eyes at him in mock sternness. 'Fair's fair. You have your life to lead and I have mine.'

'I didn't mean that, although I hope you'll behave yourself. I meant I'll be there to see that no harm comes to you.'

'Oh, Jimbo,' she simpered, 'I'll have my personal protector.'

'Don't mock me, Leanne.'

19

The principals' rehearsal took place at Adam's house that Saturday. It was originally to have been on Sunday, but Helen wasn't available then. When she arrived, however, it became clear that she was the new attraction in Jimbo's life, although she was careful not to reveal any reciprocal interest, at least for the present.

Dottie, who was given to howling when anyone sang, was conveniently out of the way, enjoying a long walk with Leanne and the children.

'Before we begin,' said Adam, 'I'd better tell you both that some of the programme, at this stage, is sight-reading for Jenny. I just want you to appreciate that and be aware of it.'

'Of course.' Helen took her scores from her case and said, 'Feel free to hang on to these, Jenny. I shan't need them until after the concert.'

'Same here,' said Jimbo. 'I've taken a photocopy of *Largo al Factotum*, so you can keep the original.'

'Okay,' said Adam. 'Helen, would you like to begin with the *Samson* number?'

'Softly Awakes my Heart' was hackneyed, but no less beautiful for that, and Helen sang it to Adam's complete satisfaction; in fact, he was as delighted as ever with his *protégé*.

Jimbo followed it with 'O Isis and Osiris' from *The Magic Flute*, before joining Helen with the duet from *Don Giovanni*. The part might have been written for him, albeit two hundred or so years previously, so natural was his portrayal of the libertine, and Helen sang the part of the innocent but coquettish Zerlina with comic skill. It was an excellent choice.

Helen was to sing the solo aria 'Were I thy Bride' from *The Yeomen of the Guard* and, after a brief conference with Jimbo and Adam, suggested that she sang it with Jimbo as her stooge. They tried it, and her suggestion was adopted unanimously. Playing the love-struck dupe was child's play for Jimbo.

Having strutted as *Don Giovanni* and yearned as the love-sick Wilfrid Shadbolt, Jimbo turned to celebrity hubris with the 'Toreador's Song'. His best moment came, however, with 'When a Maiden Takes Your Fancy' from *The Abduction from the Harem*, which he sang with a full, rich tone, underlining the whole with a final, resonating bottom 'G'.

By the time, Jimbo and Helen came together to sing 'Bess, You is My Woman Now' from *Porgy and Bess*, it was clear to Adam that the two singers were as one, and he knew the audience would be enraptured with them.

Happily, they needed no prompting to express their gratitude and appreciation to Jenny, and the rehearsal ended comfortably before Leanne and the children returned with Dottie.

Afterwards, Leanne said, 'Jimbo and Helen seem to have hit it off, Dad. Mind you, it was always going to happen, wasn't it?'

'It was,' agreed Adam regretfully. 'I was responsible for that girl at one time, you know. I first knew her when she was eleven years old.'

'But she's grown up since then, Dad, and she's responsible for her own actions.' She gave him her older-than-her-years look and said, 'Growing up is what children do while their parents are living in the past.'

'Just wait until you have children of your own, Leanne. It won't seem so straightforward then.'

* * *

The concert took place a week later in the old Council Chamber and before a capacity audience. It pleased both Adam and Jenny that the Choral Society's popularity was not only restored, but possibly enhanced.

Jimbo and Helen, too, found immense popularity as soloists and as dramatic and sometimes comic duettists; in fact, their performance of Mozart's 'Give me Thy Hand', the great seduction scene from *Don Giovanni*, was so convincing that it renewed Adam's fears for his former pupil.

'Be realistic, Dad,' Leanne told him afterwards. 'She's twenty-one, and chastity has a short lifespan.'

Her wisdom did nothing to allay his foreboding. 'Leopold Mozart and I have something in common,' he told her.

'Did he have hair growing out of his ears too?'

'No, I'm referring to the burdensome worry of a dissolute son.'

'In eighteenth-century France, you could have had him thrown into the Bastille but, as things stand, you can only accept him as he is. You have to admit as well that he delivered the goods tonight.'

'At the concert, yes,' said Adam, looking at his watch. 'I just hope he's not delivering anything else.'

'You know, a daughter could be forgiven for feeling a tad upstaged just now.'

'I'm sorry, love. I don't know how I'd react if I thought some degenerate youth had designs on you.'

'A lot would depend on whether or not there was a letterbox handy.'

'Ah well,' he said, standing up, 'I'll see you in the morning.'

'Sleep well, Dad, and well done tonight.'

'Thanks, love. Goodnight.'

* * *

As Helen had to drive back to Huddersfield, Leanne expected Jimbo quite soon, and she was making coffee when he arrived.

''Evening, Jimbo. Well done tonight. You sang a blinder, as usual.'

'Thanks, Leanne.' He seemed less than his usual carefree self.

'Helen, too. Dad's thinking of writing a part into the cantata-thing for her,' she said, handing him a mug of coffee.

'Thanks.' He was clearly unimpressed.

'I take it she no longer rings your bell.'

He made no reply, but stared morosely into his coffee.

'Oh, Jimbo, don't tell me that after two dates and a successful concert, your last duet ended with a hey nonny *no!*'

He gave a forlorn nod. 'She's old-fashioned,' he mumbled.

'What's wrong with that? I mean, an enthusiastic train spotter or a dedicated do-it-yourselfer could bore you for hours on end, but an old-fashioned girl is harmless enough.' She struggled to mask her amusement. It was wrong of her, she knew, to tease him in his hour of frustration, but she couldn't let the opportunity pass her by.

'She believes in pre-marital chastity. Don't you see what that means, Leanne. She's a virgin.'

Leanne gaped. 'Wow! Did you get her autograph?'

'I didn't get a thing.'

'So Don Giovanni met his match. Poor old Jimbo.'

'Don't mock me, Leanne.'

She took his free arm and patted it. 'This is where I'm supposed to remind you that there are plenty more fish in the sea, but I wonder....'

'You wonder what?'

'If it's ever occurred to you that there might be more to a relationship than the horizontal rhumba. I know it stretches your imagination, but it's a possibility you might explore.'

'I can't live like a monk, Leanne.'

'You've told me that already, but you need to realise that there are other pleasures to be gained from a relationship.' She gave him a shrewd look and said, 'Besides, if you make a girl feel valued and respected, all kinds of benefits might follow.'

'Do you think so?'

'I'm sure of it.'

He hesitated. 'But you've had no experience.'

'I've been a girl for more than eighteen years,' she reminded him.

'I mean, you haven't.... Have you?'

'That's none of your business. What you need to concern yourself with now is building a relationship instead of just... counting conquests.'

It was something for him to think about.

* * *

139

With Jimbo still in bed, Leanne came down in her dressing gown to deliver the news to Adam at breakfast.

'Your darling girl is as innocent as the day she was born,' she told him.

'I'm delighted to hear it.' Puzzled though he was, he patted her hand to reinforce his approval.

'I don't mean me, Dad. I'm talking about Helen.'

'Oh, you found out about that, did you?'

'Mm, Jimbo came in looking woebegone. It's all over between him and Helen. It would be wrong of me to elaborate, so I shan't.'

'Quite right, and thank you for telling me, because I was concerned.' He poured her a cup of coffee.

'I knew you were.'

'Jimbo doesn't often look woebegone, does he?'

'No, and never for long, but I've always wanted to use the word, and Jimbo's appearance last night gave me the opportunity I needed.'

He poured coffee for himself and sat down. 'It's just a shame,' he said, 'that Jimbo can't be persuaded to look a little further than....'

'Serial bonking?'

'Yes.' He always felt uneasy when Leanne was explicit.

'I spoke to him about it last night.'

'Did you?'

She nodded. 'I gave him food for thought, although whether or not he'll act on it is anybody's guess.'

'We can only hope.'

Something occurred to Leanne as she buttered a slice of toast She asked, 'Isn't the funeral tomorrow?'

'Tomorrow afternoon, yes.'

'Poor Jenny. She was very close to her granny, wasn't she?'

'Yes, but she'll be all right.'

'Are you going, Dad?'

'Yes—' The bleeping of the timer in the kitchen interrupted him and he went to deal with the eggs. A few moments later, he deposited them into the two eggcups on Leanne's plate.

'Thanks, Dad.'

'I should go to the funeral,' he said. 'I knew Mrs Sanderson quite well from reading to her.'

'Did you do all the voices, the way you used to when we were little?'

'Of course.'

'That was one thing Mum didn't do at all well.' Curiously, she smiled as she said it.

'We can't be good at everything, and your mum did most things well.'

'Yes, she did. Did Mrs Sanderson appreciate it when you read to her?'

'Not so as you'd notice. She preferred to criticise me, but I didn't mind.'

'What did she say?'

'She told me I conducted everything far too slowly. The woman in the next room used to have Classic FM playing very loudly, and Mrs Sanderson thought I was doing the conducting.'

'Weird.'

'That's dementia for you.'

As Leanne attacked her egg, she asked, 'What else did she criticise you for?'

'Oh, just the usual failings that women see in men.'

'Yes, it's funny, isn't it?'

'What is?'

'Nature dictates that men and women have to get together, if only to procreate the species, but we're so different that we spend much of our time criticising and trying to change each other's ways.'

Adam gave the matter some thought. Eventually, he said, 'Many don't make the right choice, and those of us who do, still have to work at getting along.'

'You and Mum always got on well.'

'Yes, we did. Others are not so fortunate.' He went into the kitchen, leaving Leanne to finish her breakfast in peace. When he returned, she was ready to leave the table.

'Thanks, Dad,' she said, pushing her plate with the two eggcups and broken shells aside. 'That was great.'

'Are you going to have your shower now?'

'Mm.'

He held out his arms for a hug.

'What's this for?'

'For reminding me of your mum, for talking sense to Jimbo, and for being as innocent as the day you were born.'

'It's no trouble, Dad,' she said, crossing her fingers behind his back.

20

Adam made his own way to the crematorium. Jenny was bringing the children, so it made sense. Neither Gareth nor Nicola had ever been to a funeral, and Jenny had no idea how they would react.

Adam found himself in a slow-moving line of traffic, which made him anxious until he saw the hearse several cars ahead, and then he realised he was behind a cortege. He hoped it wasn't going to make him late for Mrs Sanderson's funeral.

When he saw the hearse and several cars caterpillar into the entrance to the crematorium grounds, he realised that it was her cortege he'd been following, and he was able to relax and enjoy the crocuses and daffodils that lined the driveway. He welcomed the crocuses particularly, as a colourful and vibrant prelude to spring.

He had to look around the carpark for Jenny. Again, he was so used to seeing her in jeans that he found her hard to identify from a distance. He saw the two children first, and then she turned and saw him.

'It's good of you to come, Adam,' she said.

'Not a bit of it. After visiting your gran and getting to know her, I feel almost like one of her intimate circle.' He turned to the children. 'Hello, you two. You're looking very smart, Gareth. Smarter than some of the grown-ups from the last funeral, I'd say, and that's a lovely dress, Nicola.'

'Thank you. Dottie couldn't come.'

'That's a shame.'

'She could,' explained Jenny, 'but we left her at home because of the hair problem.'

'Very wise.'

The funeral director began calling for the family.

'I'd be happy for you to sit with us,' said Jenny, 'but I think five of us will fill a pew.'

'I'll sit behind you.'

With Jenny, the children and Jenny's parents mustered, the funeral director led them to the front so that they could follow the coffin. Adam stationed himself behind them and watched the bearers shoulder the coffin. Bearing in mind Mrs Sanderson's tiny, bird-like physique, it occurred to him that it must be a bonus for them to carry someone as light as her.

He followed the family into the chapel and slid into the pew behind them. The organist was playing a chorale prelude by Siegfried Karg-Elert. Adam knew that because, on the way in, he'd sneaked a look at the cover through the clear Perspex desk on the organ. It sounded good, and he was pleased for the family. He tried not to think about Kate's funeral.

The minister welcomed everyone and then announced the first hymn, 'The Lord's My Shepherd', the words of which were printed on the order of service. It seemed that only four copies had been placed on each pew, and Jenny's parents were sharing one. Adam handed them his. He knew the words from childhood.

Jenny's mother read her tribute, gamely fighting back tears towards the end, but more interesting, at least from his point of view, was the eulogy, read by the minister. Adam learned that Mrs Sanderson had been a conscientious but shy pupil at school, and that she'd been particularly successful in her School Certificate and found a job as a secretary until the war intervened. She spent the next three years serving as a pay clerk in the Women's Auxiliary Air Force and, during that time, she met Geoffrey and married him, leaving the WAAF in 1942, when she became pregnant.

He half-listened to the rest, thinking about the person he'd known and how dementia had changed her.

After the funeral, Jenny introduced him to her parents, who invited him to join them at The King's Head.

'That's kind of you,' he told them, 'but I have it in mind to ask

144

Jenny if she'd like me to take the children somewhere. They're a bit unsettled, and I don't think a reception is much in their line.'

Jenny looked immediately relieved. 'Would you mind, Adam? It's ever so good of you.'

'Not at all. Gareth and Nicola, would you like to come back to the café where Leanne works?'

'Yes, please.' As usual, Nicola was the first to speak.

Gareth asked, 'Will Jimbo be there?'

'I don't know, but I can phone him.'

'You'll need Nicola's seat for the car, Adam,' said Jenny. 'Gareth's tall enough not to need one.'

'Okay, let's deal with that now, and I can take the children.'

He took his leave of Jenny's parents and walked over to his car.

'I don't really need the seat,' said Nicola, walking beside him.

'It's the law,' Adam told her. 'Leanne had one until she was twelve.'

'Did she?' It was an expression of total surprise, as if she'd never thought of Leanne as being anything other than grown up.

'Jimbo had one when he was little.'

'I don't believe you.'

Jenny brought the child seat over. She asked, 'Has your car got Isofix connectors?'

'I don't know. I only bought it last year, and both of mine were grown up.' On brief reflection, he added, 'Leanne was, anyway.'

Jenny searched the rear seats and found what she was looking for. 'You'd better let me do it,' she said.

'You're more up to date than I am,' he agreed, watching her plug the seat into the connectors.

'Come on, Nicola.' Jenny strapped her into the seat.

'Can I go in the front?'

'I don't see why not, Gareth.'

'Thanks again, Adam.' Jenny offered her cheek.

'It's a pleasure.'

As she went to re-join her parents, Adam turned up Jimbo's number on his mobile phone and wrote a text message.

I'm taking Gareth + Nicola 2 the T rooms. R U coming? Pop. Then, on reading it through, he added *Lol* after *rooms.* Sending it on its way, he congratulated himself on using a new foreign language for the first time.

As he drove out of the carpark, Gareth asked, 'Do you like my mum?'

'Yes, we're good friends.' It seemed an odd question. 'Why do you ask?'

'You keep kissing her.'

He wished he hadn't asked. 'That's just a friendly thing to do,' he said.

'In the olden days,' said Nicola, 'when a man kissed a lady, he had to marry her. They said so in *Chitty Chitty Bang Bang*.'

'We've got the DVD at home,' explained Gareth. 'It's a really old film, but it's still good.'

Adam joined the main road. As he did so, his mobile phone buzzed. Silently thanking his son for the interruption, he handed the phone to Gareth. 'It'll be Jimbo,' he said. 'Would you like to see what he has to say?'

Gareth read the message before expertly texting his reply. 'He says, "See you there."'

'What did you say to him?' It was a learning experience, after all.

'Just "See you there."'

'Whatever happened to poetry?' Adam knew the messages would have single letters in them, but he supposed it was progress of a kind.

The conversation that followed was of a non-challenging kind, and Adam could relax once more.

Gareth asked, 'Have you written any more things like *Donkey Ride to Bethlehem*?'

'Yes, I've written two since we moved here.'

'I'm going to the High School in September. They don't do them there.'

'I imagine they do rock musicals.'

'No, they don't do shows at all.'

'What a let-down.'

'What they need,' said Nicola, 'is a music teacher like you, Adam.'

'No, they don't need me, Nicola. They need someone who's young and keen.'

She appeared to give that some thought, because then she said, 'Someone younger than you could do all the running around, but you could write the shows sitting down.'

He turned into the tea rooms carpark. 'I could just about manage that without running short of breath,' he agreed. As he switched the engine off, he looked across to the Craven Heifer carpark and saw that there was a clear field of view from the tea rooms, just as Leanne had told him.

He herded the children inside, where Jimbo sat waiting for them at a corner table.

'Hello, you two,' he said to the children. 'I've been waiting for you.'

'We had to come from the crematorium,' Adam told him.

'Of course, you've been to a funeral, haven't you?' He looked at the children and said, 'You did the right thing coming here. Leanne will be along in a minute.'

In the event, Leanne came to their table in less than a minute. Taking Nicola's beaming face between her hands, she kissed her on the forehead. She did the same to Gareth, who blushed, to Adam, who greeted her warmly, and to Jimbo, who said, 'Now we've all had one, it doesn't seem so bad, does it, Gareth?'

Gareth merely continued to blush.

'I'll come back when you've all decided what you want,' said Leanne.

'Yes, have whatever you like,' said Jimbo. 'Pop's paying.'

'Don't I always?'

'You can always be relied upon, Pop.'

There was a lot to choose from, and that made it a difficult decision for the children, so Adam simplified the process. 'You could have sandwiches or boiled eggs, and then you could have cake or ice cream, or possibly both, as it's a treat.'

'I'm having boiled eggs and toast soldiers,' said Jimbo. 'Leanne has them on Sunday mornings, so it's my turn today.'

'The only reason you don't get them on Sundays is you're never out of bed before lunchtime,' Adam reminded him.

'A feeble excuse for ill-treating your son and heir.'

Leanne returned, notepad in hand.

'The children, all three of them, would like boiled eggs, please. I'd like the set tea without the scone.'

'What's wrong with our scones, Dad?'

'Nothing at all. The problem is my waist measurement.'

She took a step backwards to survey the problem and nodded sagely. 'Very wise, Dad.' She made a note on her pad. 'And what would the children like to drink?'

They made their choice, Jimbo opting for Coke with a bendy straw, and Adam for a pot of English Breakfast tea.

'Gareth and Nicola, would you like your toast cut into soldiers? I know Jimbo would.'

'Yes, please.'

'Yes, please.' Now recovered from his blushing ordeal, Gareth was eager to follow Jimbo's example in all things, and that included drinking Coke through a bendy straw.

As they waited, Adam became aware that a woman and a young boy were looking in their direction. A minute or so later, they got up and came over to the table.

'I'm sorry to trouble you,' said the woman, speaking directly to Jimbo, 'but aren't you the young man who sang in the concert on Saturday?'

'I'm afraid so. I've only just come out of hiding.'

Adam closed his eyes and lowered his head.

'I'm sure you don't need to hide. My son would be very grateful for your autograph. He was very impressed at the concert, and so was I.'

'Thank you, and no sooner said than done.' Jimbo picked up one of the advertising leaflets from the windowsill and found a conveniently blank space on it. 'Have you got a pen, Maestro?'

Adam took out a ballpoint and handed it to him.

'Oh,' said the woman, 'you're the conductor, aren't you? Do you think he could have yours as well?'

'By all means.' Adam waited until Jimbo had appended his flamboyant signature and then added his.

'Thank you so much.'

'Not at all.'

She turned to go, but the boy suddenly overcame his shyness. 'I took Grade Two on the piano last week,' he said.

'We're waiting for the result,' said his mother.

'Oh well, good luck.' It was all Adam could say.

'Thank you.' She took her son back to their table.

'That's the price of fame, Jimbo, signing autographs, but try not to make flippant remarks when people pay you compliments.'

'Sorry, Pop, it's just second nature.'

Nicola asked, 'What's Grade Two?'

'It's an exam some people take,' explained Adam. 'There are eight grades. After Grade Eight, you can go further and take a diploma.'

'Or,' said Jimbo, 'become a student and take a degree.'

'For which you have to work hard,' said Adam, looking pointedly at his son.

'My piano teacher moved away to Derbyshire,' Nicola told him.

'You can't have been as bad as that,' said Jimbo.

'No, I wasn't. She was a teacher at the High School and she got another job and had to move.'

'I wonder if she used to put shows on at school,' said Adam.

He would never know, but it didn't matter for long, because Leanne arrived with a tray loaded with more important things. As Jimbo pointed out, it would be better than anything the grown-ups were having at the King's Head.

21

Two days after Jimbo's return to London, Leanne received a text from him couched in the usual language plus a few additions of his own.

C ing Helen ag N. 2k your advice. Lol. Tell Pop I'm a re4med character. Luv, Jimbo.

Leanne decided to see how long Jimbo's resolve lasted before she raised her father's hopes. At the same time, she mentally crossed her fingers. After all, miracles still happened.

Meanwhile, she had her own life to live. Craig would be going back to university in September, for his final year. She would also be leaving then, and it was probably a convenient time for them to part company. Going out with him had been pleasant but unexciting.

Her greatest pleasure came from attending Jenny's watercolour classes and spending time with her on her photographic forays into the countryside. She'd learned a great deal from her about both of those media, and that was important to her. Equally important, at least from Leanne's point of view, was the natural friendship that had developed between them despite the difference in their ages. No relationship would ever equal the bond that had existed between Leanne and her mother, but Jenny had provided as much as anyone could. She was a comfort, a confidante and, most often, a like-minded companion.

* * *

Adam's preoccupation was with the cantata. There was a dearth of original poetry, and he was once more obliged to fall back on folksongs. It was far from easy; most of the songs of love and courtship seemed to be about maidens who succumbed to the wiles of passing sailors, drovers and itinerant workers, and who paid the usual penalty. He found two songs, however, that Helen could sing without embarrassment. They were 'Safe Home', which was sung by a wife waiting for her fisherman husband to return from the sea, and 'Scarborough Fair'. He thought he could include it, even though Scarborough wasn't in the Dales. It was actually just outside the North York Moors, but it was worth the inclusion. Jimbo's solos were 'The Lass of Richmond Hill' and 'Fourpence a Day', an echo of the Dales' lead-mining history. Together with the chorus, the two singers would tell the legend of Semerwater, and the whole cantata would be introduced, interspersed with, and concluded by Mrs Golding's poem 'From the Depths'. Adam got to work arranging the folksongs and setting the rest. He worked without a break, frequently forgetting to look at the time, so that dinner became a succession of take-aways. As Leanne pointed out, though, she'd always thought of take-aways as a treat, so she viewed his lapses in a positive, almost eager, light.

Eventually, *White Rose Cantata* emerged from Adam's printer and, after a final check, he was able to deliver it, spiral bound, to Jenny, who was surprised by the thickness of the score.

'It looks huge,' she said. 'How long is it?'

'Half an hour at the outside. Do you want to hear it?'

'Oh, yes.' She pulled out the piano stool for him.

'I'll have to ask you to turn the pages,' he said.

'It'll be an honour.'

He saw that she wasn't entirely serious. 'Okay, here goes.' He began the introduction, realising it was the first time he'd played it. It was all familiar, though. The music he'd heard only in his head was now filling the room. It would be infinitely better with Jimbo, Helen and the chorus singing it, but he did his best to fill in the missing voices as he played. Dottie was amusing herself in the garden, so he was able to sing 'Scarborough Fair', 'Fourpence a Day', 'The Lass of Richmond Hill', 'Safe Home' and snatches of solo from 'Semerwater' without competition. Eventually, he played out the end of 'From the Depths' and brought the piece to its grand close.

'Oh, Adam,' said Jenny, 'it's magnificent.'

'Thank you, it was hard work.'

'Are you satisfied with it?'

'I'm never satisfied, but there isn't the time available that I'd like to spend on it.'

'Well, I think it's wonderful.'

As she laid her cheek next to his, he became conscious of her perfume and wondered what it was. He was reluctant to ask, because it was an intimate matter, and he had no intention of creating the wrong impression. 'I think Dottie wants to come in,' he said in response to a succession of shrill barks. It was a timely distraction.

* * *

Netherdale Publishing Ltd called on a print-on-demand agency to turn out 400 copies of the test piece. Twelve choirs had expressed interest so far, but more could follow. They printed sixty copies of *White Rose Cantata*, and delivered them in a matter of days, so that William and the Choral Society were able to begin work. Adam and Jenny discussed the arrangements at her home.

'It's a lot for them to learn from scratch,' said Jenny. 'When we were learning something new, Nicholas used to bring in a friend, who took the sopranos and altos while he took the tenors and basses.' She added, 'He was never keen on women's voices. He always felt that the high parts should be sung by small boys.'

'What a strange man.'

'They both were. Nicholas was abrupt and impatient, but his friend favoured camp sarcasm. I really don't know which of the two was worse.'

'It makes you wonder why they did it,' said Adam. He'd been giving the subject some thought. 'I'm in favour of sectional rehearsals,' he said, 'but I need an assistant. Do you think you could rehearse two parts while I take the other two?'

'I've never done it before, but maybe I could if I watch you doing one.' She didn't sound terribly confident.

'Okay, we'll get the full chorus together and I'll teach them the first movement. Then, if you're still ready to have a go, you can take the tenors and basses while I take the sopranos and altos. It's just a matter of teaching by rote, four bars at a time, tenors and then basses, and then both together.'

She still looked uncertain, but nodded slowly.

'I wouldn't put you on the spot, Jenny, and your standing with the Choral Society is such that I'm sure they'd be completely supportive too.'

She came to her decision. 'All right,' she said, 'I'll do it.'

* * *

Adam took most of the first rehearsal unaccompanied, asking Jenny only for occasional notes, so that she could observe him and learn what for him, after years of experience, was a basic procedure, but one that demanded a new skill from her.

It was a successful rehearsal. At the end, Adam thanked the chorus members for their hard work. 'For the first hour, next Thursday,' he told them, 'you'll be split up into sections. Sopranos and altos, you'll be in the music room down the corridor with me. Tenors and basses, you'll be in here with Jenny. Now, it'll be her first time as a chorus coach, but I have total confidence in her, just as I know you'll give her your full support and co-operation.'

There was a loud murmur of agreement, during which one of the basses said, 'You'll be all right with us, Jenny love.'

The discussion continued afterwards at the Craven Heifer.

Steve Metcalfe, the bass who had been the first to voice his support for Jenny, said, 'It's grand, the way things are now we've got the right team in charge. It's a pleasure to come to rehearsals again.' Steve had been ill at the time of Adam's appointment and the *Messiah* performance, but had returned on the recommendation of others.

'It's big of you to say so, Steve,' said Adam, 'and I'm glad you said "team".'

'Aye, Jenny's got an important job to do an' all.'

'I'm beginning to feel as if the spotlight's on me,' said Jenny, 'and I'm not used to it.'

'But you see what I mean,' said Adam. 'Everyone's behind you.'

* * *

He was right, as Jenny discovered. Her first task was to teach the chorus of 'Fourpence a Day' to the tenors and basses.

'The verse ends with, "We're bound down to slavery for fourpence a day", and then, tenors, you sing. "To slavery, to slavery. Come, let's away. We're bound down to slavery for fourpence a day." Now, with me. One-two-three-four, "To slavery....".' She ran through it twice with the tenors and then, when the basses were sounding confident, she put the two together. 'You know,' she said, 'that sounds really good.'

'There's no need to sound so surprised,' said Steve Metcalfe.

'I'm sorry, Steve, I was just encouraging you.'

'Aye,' said Mark, 'an' you're doin' a grand job an' all, Jenny.'

Her best moment came when the whole chorus assembled for the second hour, and Adam took them through 'Fourpence a Day'.

'Well done, everyone,' he said, 'and well done, Jenny. You've done an excellent job with the tenors and basses.'

'Aye,' said Steve, 'you'd best look to your laurels, Adam. You've got competition there.'

'I know I have. Now, we'll go through the first movement and then the song. I can't sing it half as well as Jimbo will, but I'll sing the verses for now. Ready, Jenny?'

The end of the rehearsal came, and Jenny joined everyone at the Craven Heifer.

Adam asked her, 'How do you feel after it all?'

'Elated, really. It's such a marvellous feeling when you get them singing together in harmony.' She shrugged self-consciously. 'Does that sound silly?'

'Not at all. It's why I do it. The great thing about singing or playing together is that it's a shared thrill, and that's what makes it worthwhile.'

'I'm glad you feel the same about it. I wondered if it was just me, being a beginner.'

'The day I stop getting shivers down my spine when I hear something special, that's when I'll retire from music and collect stamps.'

She smiled at a memory. 'I felt that kind of shiver at your audition, when Jimbo began to sing in the cloakroom.'

'Yes, he tends to trade on that quality.'

'So you said.'

Adam picked up his glass and asked, 'Are you going to stay for another one?'

'No, I'd better get back for Leanne. Thanks all the same.'

'Okay. Goodnight and well done.'

'Goodnight. Thank you.' She threaded her way past various members, all of whom echoed Adam's words of praise, and the knowledge that she'd earned their approval, too, completed her evening's enjoyment.

She drove home, satisfied and contented. When she let herself into the house, she heard Leanne's voice, and wondered what might have happened. She opened the sitting room door to find Nicola snuggled up to Leanne but very much awake.

'What happened? A bad dream?'

'No,' said Leanne, 'Nicola couldn't sleep, so she came down for a chat. I think she's ready to go to sleep now, aren't you, Nicola?'

'Mm.'

'Good girl. Kiss Leanne goodnight and I'll take you up to bed.'

When Jenny returned, she asked, 'Was something troubling her? I asked her just now, and she said not.'

'She said she thought she hadn't done enough to make her dad happy, and that was why he left. Don't worry, I dealt with that.'

'What did you tell her?'

'I told her that when men want to misbehave, they don't need an excuse. They just get on with it.'

'Did she accept that?'

'Yes, no problem.'

'Thanks, Leanne. I'm grateful. Are you going to stay and have a drink?'

'Oh, I could be persuaded.'

Jenny brought a bottle of wine and two glasses. 'I shouldn't really,' she said. 'I had a glass of wine at the pub.'

'Throw caution to the four winds, Jenny. I would. Anyway, how did the rehearsal go? It was your debut on the rostrum, wasn't it?'

'It was amazing. I was so nervous at the beginning, but everyone co-operated, and... it just felt marvellous.'

'Great. I'm glad.'

'And, you know, the funny thing is that when I told your dad how I felt, he said it was always the same for him. He said the day he doesn't get goose bumps when he hears something special, he'll retire and do something different, like collecting stamps.' She smiled. 'He always says the right thing.'

'Ah, but you have to realise that whatever he says, unless he's larking around, he means it. That's something Jimbo and I learned when we were little.' She inclined her head towards the stairs and said, 'That's something else that Nicola and I discussed tonight. She was saying what a treat it was to come to the café after the funeral. She enjoyed everything about it, the food, Jimbo playing the fool, and some people who asked for his autograph because they'd been to the concert. Then, when it was time to go, she thanked my dad very properly, and he told her it was a pleasure to take her anywhere.'

'How sweet.'

'I'm sure he included Gareth in that compliment. It's just that he was talking to Nicola at the time. Anyway, she asked me if I thought he meant it, and I told her what I've told you, that he always means what he says.'

'It's lovely that you could tell her that.'

'Absolutely.' She wrinkled her nose briefly, and said, 'Of course, I told her that a fortnight in Bermuda was probably a wish too far, but he basically meant that the children were so well-behaved and good to have around that they'd made it a pleasure for him.'

'I was very grateful, all the same.' She gave a tiny shrug. 'I seem to spend my life being grateful to him. Take tonight, for example. He'd prepared me, shown me exactly what I had to do, and then made it even more worthwhile with his remarks after the rehearsal.'

Leanne nodded. 'He wouldn't chuck you in at the deep end, Jenny. It's not in his nature to do that, especially when he's so fond of you.'

22

It was always a mistake, fixing a bookshelf higher than he could reach, and it was bad luck that the complete set of Dickens' novels was on the top shelf. Adam had thought for some time that a musical based on *A Christmas Carol* was a feasible project, and he wanted to begin planning it.

He was tempted to stand on a chair, but it was much more sensible to fetch the aluminium stepladder from the service room. He opened it up and climbed up to reach the book. He had an idea that it was something like Volume 17, but when he looked, he realised his memory had deceived him. It was Volume 8, and he had to reach sideways for it. The books were packed tightly on the shelf and it was difficult to gain a purchase. Frustrated, he took his left foot off the rung and placed it on one arm of the rotating office chair beside the stepladder to gain a little more leverage.

The next sequence of events took place within little more than a second as the chair revolved, as it was designed to do, and he fell to the floor, landing heavily on his left shoulder.

His initial reaction was one of anger at himself for making such a ridiculous mistake, and then he became conscious of the pain. Even levering himself up with his uninjured right arm caused an agonising spasm to shoot through his left shoulder. Eventually, though, he was able to kneel and then stand.

He knew he wouldn't be able to drive; moving his left arm caused the pain to pierce his shoulder with renewed spite, making gear-changing impossible. Having no alternative, he picked up the phone and dialled Jenny's number. It rang several times, and he thought she must be out. Then, as he was about to put the phone down, she answered.

'Hello?'

'Jenny, I have a problem.'

'What's happened, Adam?'

'I've fallen on my shoulder and I think I've broken something.'

'Hold on tight. I'll shut up shop and be with you in a moment.'

'Thanks, Jenny....' He was about to say more, but the phone went down. Moving slowly and carefully, he locked the back door and went to the front just as Jenny drew up outside.

'I don't even know where to go, Jenny. It's something I've never had to consider.'

'Never mind that. I'll do you a temporary sling to support your arm until we get there.' She took out her car first-aid kit and removed a triangular bandage. 'I'll take you to Airedale Hospital,' she said. 'That's the nearest A and E department.' Gently, she folded the sling to accommodate his arm and fastened it round his neck.

'This is very good of you.' He eased himself into the front passenger seat, where he found that even the effort of pulling out the seatbelt caused a twinge of pain.

'After all you've done for me? It's nothing at all. Anyway, I'm just glad to be able to help.'

'Bless you, Jenny. Where did you learn first-aid?'

'In the Guides.' She said it as if it were obvious, which it probably was.

'Of course.'

She turned in the usual place and drove down the lane. 'What were you doing, anyway?'

'Reaching a book from a top shelf. It was a mindless thing to do. I put one foot on a revolving chair.'

'We all do these things. I broke my ankle last year, stepping backwards without looking where I was going.' She gave him a quick look and asked, 'Is it awful?'

'It's not my favourite experience so far, and I haven't even got a wine gum to take my mind off it.'

'No, the glove compartment's bare, I'm afraid.' She smiled. 'Did you always give the children wine gums when they hurt themselves?'

'No, wine gums are my weakness. They always got jelly babies.'

'So that's why you had them in your car.' She overtook the car in front and increased speed.

'I occasionally bribe Leanne with them.'

'I'm surprised you need to bribe her.'

'She can be very feisty.'

'If you say so.'

'But I'll miss her when she goes to university.'

'I think we both will.'

He had to clench his teeth each time the movement of the car caused him to shift in his seat, but the knowledge that they would soon be in Accident and Emergency gave him some relief, and he was able, to some extent, to appreciate the signs of burgeoning spring.

After a while, Jenny asked, 'I'm being nosey, but what were you looking for on the top shelf? It must have been important.'

'Dickens's *A Christmas Carol.*'

'Lovely, but in June?'

'I'm planning a musical based on it,' he told her, 'a scaled-down version of it, anyway.'

'What a good idea, and to simplify it for a school play is a good idea too.'

'Yes, deciding what to leave out will be interesting.' He gave an involuntary gasp as the car hit a pothole.

'I'm sorry, I should have seen that one.'

'It wasn't your fault.'

Jenny concentrated on the road, careful to avoid anything that might cause the car to jolt. After a while, she asked, 'Do you analyse books the way you analyse music?'

'Not in exactly the same way, but I do analyse them if I'm going to use them in my work.'

'I could look forward to a musical version of *A Christmas Carol.*'

'In that case, I'll give the school a freebie when it's published. It should serve as a gentle hint.'

'I'm sure they'll appreciate that.' She slowed down to negotiate two temporary repairs.

'Thank you.'

'It's no trouble.'

The sign for Airedale General Hospital appeared, and Adam began to relax.

'I'll drop you at A and E, and then I'll find a parking place.'

'Let me give you some change,' he insisted.

'I don't know how much it will be, and I shouldn't need it yet, anyway.'

He settled for being helpless until Jenny drew up outside the entrance, and then he climbed out of the car unassisted.

'Will you be all right while I'm parking the car?'

'Absolutely,' he assured her, confident that the end of his sorrows was in sight.

It seemed that he'd chosen a good time to injure himself, because the waiting room was half empty. He gave his details to the receptionist, who invited him to take a seat.

He was reading the profusion of posters and notices on the walls when Jenny joined him.

'What do I owe you for parking, Jenny?'

'It depends on how long we're here.'

He felt in his pocket. 'I've just realised,' he said, 'I've no money on me.'

'I'll put it on the slate,' she told him generously. Looking around her at the frieze of literature, she asked, 'What have you learned?'

'Nothing terribly useful. I'm not taking the contraceptive pill or any other medication, so they can do pretty well anything they like to me.'

'You're very brave.' She patted his hand encouragingly, just as a nurse opened the door marked *TRIAGE*, and said, 'Adam Watkinson?'

Adam rose to his feet, immediately regretting his eagerness, as the pain shot through his shoulder and chest.

'I fell off a stepladder,' he told her, taking the seat she offered. 'I fell on my left shoulder, and I think I may have broken something.'

'I see. You'll be relieved to know that I'm not going to manipulate it. Just tell me where the pain is.'

'Shoulder and chest,' he said, adding, 'and the shame of it.'

'Most accidents in the household are caused by carelessness.' She examined the sling and said, 'That's a very professional-looking sling.'

'My neighbour was a Girl Guide,' he explained. 'She's very resourceful. I imagine she has badges for every known skill.'

'Including first aid, I imagine, luckily for you.' The Triage Nurse left her seat and said, 'Sit in the waiting area until you're called. It shouldn't take long.'

He sat with Jenny until another nurse called his name, and he went through to be examined.

'It sounds like a broken collarbone,' said the doctor, a sympathetic Sikh with an immaculate turban. 'I'd like an X-ray.'

Adam followed the nurse obediently and was X-rayed. It was over very quickly.

When he returned, Jenny asked, 'How did it go?'

'I didn't know if I was supposed to smile, or if it was like having a passport photograph taken,' he said. 'In any case, I was nervous.'

'You poor scrap.'

The X-rays returned, and it was established that Adam's collarbone was fractured. Accordingly, the nurse applied a padded dressing and supplied tablets for the pain as well as a quantity of advice, for which he was suitably grateful.

'I need to call at the supermarket,' said Jenny when he was settled in the car. 'You can't cook with your arm in a sling, so the best thing will be for you and Leanne to come and eat with us.'

'I hadn't thought about that. You're very kind, and I will chip in.'

'We'll sort that out later.' She turned left at the end of the drive and continued to the supermarket. 'Take it easy,' she said, 'while I do some shopping.'

Adam sat helplessly in the car and waited for her. Eventually, she returned with two carriers filled with food. She put them in the back and took her place in the driving seat. She was carrying two cellophane bags, one of which she tore open and handed to him.

'Wine gums,' he said, surprised and delighted.

'They're for being brave,' she explained.

'Thank you. What's in the other bag?'

'Jelly babies,' she said, dropping them into the passenger glove compartment. 'They're for Leanne.'

'Leanne hasn't broken her collarbone,' he protested.

'No, but she deserves a treat now and again.' She gave him a stern look and said, 'I hope you're not going to be difficult and expect all the attention to be on you.'

'I don't think I dare,' he said, looking at her warily.

'Good.' She started the engine. 'Let's go home.'

'Would you like a wine gum?'

'Go on. Just one, and then they're all yours.'

When they were nearly home, she asked, 'Where did you leave *A Christmas Carol*?'

'On the floor beside the stepladder. Why?'

'If you give me your key, I'll get it for you, and then you have something to read while you're resting.'

After several years, it felt strange but pleasant to have someone care for him.

* * *

'Leanne doesn't know yet, does she? She'll go home and find the place deserted.'

'Relax,' Jenny told him. 'I phoned the café while you were asleep.'

'Thank you. I didn't mean to fall asleep.'

'No one ever does, Adam, but maybe the medication thought you needed the rest.'

'It's a conspiracy.' It didn't worry him, because, as conspiracies went, it was a cosy one.

'If you didn't need a rest then, you will soon,' said Jenny, picking up her bag. 'I have to collect the children.'

'Of course.'

'Do you need anything before I go?'

'Not a thing.'

'Good. I'll be back shortly. 'Bye.'

''Bye.'

He opened *A Christmas Carol* and looked again at his notes. Much of Dickens' narrative was scenic description, and scenery itself took care of that. There was a danger, however, that if he concentrated on what to leave out, he would be left with a ragged skeleton that neither recreated the atmosphere nor told the story adequately. It was an infinitely better strategy, he felt, to concentrate on what to preserve. He began to make a list of important characters in Stave One. These were: Scrooge, Bob Cratchit, Fred, and the two gentlemen collecting for the poor. Those characters helped to paint Scrooge as a misanthropic miser. The next important player was Marley's Ghost, and there were the ghosts of long-dead businessmen as well.

Stave Two was harder, because he needed to include the Ghost of Christmas Past, the young Scrooge, his sister, possibly some un-named acquaintances of his youth, Mr and Mrs Fezziwig, and some revellers. He decided to leave Scrooge's fiancee Belle out of it. It would be a large cast, and young children weren't usually interested in love interest.

He stopped work when he heard Jenny's car draw up outside. He would have time to work later.

First to come into the sitting room was Nicola, who stared at Adam.

'Hello, Nicola. What's the matter?'

'Why haven't you got a pot?'

'They can't put plaster casts on shoulders. I've got padding instead.'

Gareth pushed past her to look.

'They can't put plaster on shoulders,' Nicola told him with great authority. 'That's why he hasn't got a pot.'

The absence of a plaster cast was evidently a disappointment for them both, but then Nicola changed the subject and asked, 'Are you going to sleep over?'

'He can't,' said Jenny, closing the door behind her. 'You know we only have three rooms.' As an afterthought, she said, 'I could make you a bed on the sofa, but it wouldn't be very comfortable.'

'Don't worry,' said Adam, 'I'll be fine at home.'

Gareth saw the notepad and pencil, and asked, 'What are you doing?'

'I'm writing another musical play.'

'What about?'

'*A Christmas Carol.*'

Gareth looked puzzled. 'Which one?'

'Not an actual carol. It's based on the story by Charles Dickens that's called *A Christmas Carol*. Do you know it?'

'No.'

'Not to worry. I shouldn't be surprised if it crops up at your next school, although you could read it at home. You should start on the nineteenth of December, and read a stave – that's a chapter – each night. That way, you'll finish it on the twenty-third. You'll be too excited to read anything on Christmas Eve, but you'll never forget it.'

Conversation continued in its usual chaotic way, with the children changing the subject frequently and with no notice, until Jenny got up to go to the kitchen.

Adam asked, 'Is there anything I can do?'

Jenny shook her head. 'I can't think of a single one-handed job that needs to be done,' she said. 'In any case, you're supposed to be taking things easy.'

'All right.' He resumed his relaxed position and answered increasingly random questions put to him by the children, until Leanne arrived.

'Leanne,' said Nicola urgently, 'your dad's broken his neck.'

Adam heard her say, 'I'm not surprised. He's always breaking something. Last week it was the door on the woodshed, the week before last…. I can't remember what he broke. There are so many things. Let me in, Nicola.'

Leanne perched beside him carefully and kissed his forehead. 'Poor old thing,' she said.

'Not so much of the "old", and I'll mend the door on the woodshed as soon as I can.'

'Well, at least you won't have to go up a stepladder to do it. We don't have to worry about that.' Alerted by a noise from the kitchen, she said, 'I'd better see if Jenny needs a hand.'

'No, it's all ready,' said Jenny from the doorway. 'You can come through.'

Leanne crouched to take her father's good arm round her shoulders and helped him to his feet.

'I'm not completely helpless, Leanne, but thank you, anyway.'

'I'm just getting into training for when you're really old.'

165

'What kind of child have I produced?'

'Jenny,' said Leanne, seeing the quiche and salad on the table, 'this is brilliant of you. I'm sorry I wasn't here to help.'

'It was no trouble.'

'I'll help you clear away afterwards, and then I'll have to get showered and changed. Craig's picking me up at seven.'

'Oh.' The expression of disappointment came from Nicola.

'I'll see you later in the week, Nicola, and it'll be good practice for September.'

'What's happening in September?'

'I'm going away to university. I'll be back for Christmas.'

'Oh.'

'It'll be another treat at Christmas,' said Jenny. 'Help yourselves to salad, everybody.'

It was an excellent meal. Even Nicola agreed with that sentiment once she'd recovered from her initial disappointment.

Later, Gareth asked, 'Will you read us that story about the Christmas carol?'

'No, it's a ghost story, and it's not good to hear ghost stories at bedtime. Anyway, you can read it for yourself later.'

'Sometimes, it's nice to have a story read by someone else,' said Jenny.

'I've got one,' said Nicola. 'I'll get it.'

Gareth gave her a disapproving look as she ran upstairs. 'It'll be a silly book for girls,' he said.

'If it is, I'll read you a silly one for boys another time.'

Nicola returned with the book in question and handed it to Adam, who opened it and saw written inside:

Leanne Katherine Watkinson, age 8 years, 3 months
24 Slaithwaite Road,
Longwood,
Huddersfield
West Yorkshire
HD3 3ST
England,
Great Britain,

Europe,
The World,
The Universe.

'Leanne gave me it,' explained Nicola, stationing herself on Adam's uninjured side.

'That was generous of her. She loved this when she was your age.'

'What is it?' Gareth tried to peer over Adam's shoulder.

'*Five Get Into Trouble* by Enid Blyton. Are you both sitting comfortably?'

'Yes,' said Nicola.

Gareth declined to answer.

'Then I'll begin.' Adam began reading, using expression and changing the voices as he had years earlier for Jimbo and Leanne. Nicola snuggled up as far as she could, considering Adam needed his good arm to hold the book and turn pages. After a while, he put his arm round her, and that made it easier. Gareth eventually grew tired of feigning boredom and allowed himself to be drawn into the story. Jenny watched them and, from her lap, Dottie also seemed to be paying attention, at least for a minute or so, which was the limit of her concentration.

After half-an-hour, Adam tore a page from his notebook to use as a bookmark. 'That's enough for now,' he said.

'Oh.'

'It's better to be left wanting more than to fall asleep over it.'

Jenny voiced her agreement. 'It's time for bed, Nicola. You can come down and say goodnight when you've got your jim-jams on.'

'All right.' Persuaded that half a loaf, or at least the promise of a whole loaf in generous slices, was better than no bread, Nicola went upstairs to undress.

'You're an excellent reader,' said Jenny. 'It's a long time since I've seen them so absorbed.'

'Thank you. It must be the performer in me.'

'Or a lot of practice when Jimbo and Leanne were little, I imagine.'

'Jimbo had a favourite book,' he recalled.

'What was it?'

'*The BFG* by Roald Dahl. I don't think he ever moved on from it. Attempts have been made to ween him on to *A History of Western Music* by Donald J Grout, but with little success.'

'I like *The BFG*,' said Gareth.

'If Jimbo put ketchup on his cornflakes, you'd want it too,' said Jenny.

'Does he?'

'No, Gareth, I wasn't being serious.'

'Just don't make the suggestion when Jimbo's around,' Adam advised her.

Nicola stood between them in her pyjamas and asked, 'What haven't you to suggest?'

'Nothing. We were just being silly. Are you going to kiss Adam goodnight?'

'All right.' She joined him again on the sofa and reached up to kiss him. 'Thank you for the story. I hope your neck's better in the morning.'

'Thank you, Nicola.' Being kissed by her evoked memories of Leanne as a little girl. It was a special moment.

'It's time you were off to bed as well, Gareth,' said Jenny.

Gareth looked unsurely at Adam, who saved his embarrassment by holding up his right hand. 'High five?'

Relieved, Gareth responded. 'See you tomorrow,' he said.

Jenny kissed them both and bundled them off to bed before bringing a bottle of wine and two glasses from the kitchen. 'It's a screw top,' she said. 'No need for a corkscrew.'

Adam placed the bottle between his knees and unfastened the top.

'I didn't tell you that because I wanted you to open it,' she said.

'Just trying to make myself useful.' He poured two glasses. 'I got a text message from Jimbo,' he told her.

'What does he say?'

'I don't know. I usually get Leanne to translate them for me.'

'Maybe I can help.' She took the place beside him that Nicola had occupied earlier.

'It's beyond me,' he said, bringing up the text. It read, *LS told*

*me abt your precp x prepit x fall. Booze and old age, eh? Hope UR
recoveru x recuv x feeling better. Haven't yet got the hang of prec x
pridi x auto txting. B careful and GWS. Lol. Jimbo.*

' "LS" must be "Little Sister", I imagine "abt" is "about"; he's tried
twice to spell "precipitation", "recovering" and "predictive"; "GWS"
will be "Get well soon", and "Lol" means "laugh out loud".'

'He's just larking around. He can spell as well as anyone.'

'But he took the trouble to text you, Adam.'

'Yes, he did, but he couldn't resist teasing "the Old Man", as he
calls me when he thinks I'm out of earshot.'

Changing the subject, she picked up *A Christmas Carol* from the
table and asked, 'Will you read to me?'

'Yes, if you're very good and don't interrupt.'

'I just like to hear you read.'

'All right.' He opened the book and lifted his right arm so that
she could snuggle the way Nicola had.

'How will you turn the pages?'

'That's your job.'

'All right.'

He began. ' "Stave One. Marley's Ghost. Marley was dead: to
begin with. There is no doubt whatever about that. The register of
his burial was signed by the clergyman, the clerk, the undertaker,
and the chief mourner." '

He was conscious of her perfume and then, as he inhaled
discreetly, her shampoo. Her head rested on his chest and, as far
as he could make out, her eyes were closed. He wondered at first if,
worn out by the events of the day, she were about to fall asleep. For
the time being, however, he continued.

' "Scrooge signed it: and Scrooge's name was good upon 'Change,
for anything he chose to put his hand to. Old Marley was as dead as
a doornail." '

After a few seconds, she opened her eyes and looked up at him.
She asked, 'Why have you stopped?'

'I'm sorry. I was distracted.'

'What distracted you?'

'Your perfume. What is it?'

Surprised by the question, she said, 'Chanel. It's called "Allure".'

'Ah.' That made sense.

'Don't you like it?'

'Oh, I do. I find it very... alluring.' He was even more conscious of it now. He also realised that she was looking directly at him, as if she expected something to happen. It was a strange feeling, and not simply because he'd been a stranger to intimacy for so long. He hadn't woken up that morning resolved to move things on with Jenny; the possibility had occurred to him at odd times, but never with any sense of immediacy. Now, however, it felt like something he'd wanted all along.

Tentatively, he touched her lips with his and felt her respond. They hesitated and teased, finally giving in to a prolonged and indulgent kiss.

23

Jenny arrived at Adam's doorstep with lunch packed in a bag.
'As you're busy, I thought I'd bring it to you,' she said.
'How thoughtful.' He stood aside to let her in.

'Did you sleep all right?'

'Off and on. More off than on, really. It's only to be expected.'

'I'll take this through to the kitchen, shall I? It's only cheese and *pâté* and some salady bits, but we'll have a substantial meal tonight.' As she spoke, she seemed somehow hesitant, as if she were unsure of her reception.

'It sounds excellent.' He held out his right arm to her and drew her into a long kiss, after which he said, 'It'll be better when I have two arms again.'

'I'm not complaining.' She lowered her eyes to say, 'I did wonder, actually....'

'If last night was a flash in the pan?'

'Yes, considering... you know.'

'That I'm a fragile widower? Don't worry.'

'Just as long as you don't regret what happened.'

'As I recall, very little happened, but the little that did happen was rather special.'

They kissed again, and then, visibly relieved, Jenny said, 'I'd better unpack these things before the butter melts.'

'Is that a euphemism for something?'

'No, it's quite warm in here, and squelchy butter's not very appealing.'

'Let's take it into the kitchen.'

They unpacked French bread, *pâté*, Wensleydale cheese and butter.

'We could eat here, at the kitchen table,' he suggested.

'Yes.' She looked around her and said, 'I'd love a kitchen this size.'

'Feel free to use mine. I only need a small part of it.' He laid plates and cutlery, and they sat down to eat.

'You have a lovely, big service room as well,' said Jenny, inclining her head towards the kitchen outer door.

'The wet zone, yes.' He smiled fondly at the memory of Jimbo carrying Leanne into the kitchen. Then, changing the subject, he said, 'This *pâté* is very good. Which animal donated it?'

'It's chicken liver.'

'Lovely. Where did you get it?'

'I made it.'

He looked at her with fresh interest. 'Clever,' he commented.

'It's easy enough.' She peered at the side of his face that was nearer, but said nothing.

'What's the matter?'

'Oh, nothing.'

'Have I grown an extra ear?'

'No,' she laughed, 'but shaving must have been difficult this morning.'

'Ah.' He examined the area with his right hand. 'I use my left hand to help create the grimaces and contortions that are essential for a close shave,' he explained. 'This morning's was a half-hearted job. I'd use my electric shaver, but Jimbo took it with him to London.'

'I wish I hadn't pointed it out now,' she said. 'I didn't mean to criticise you.'

'But, being a woman, you can't help it. I blame it on the chromosomes.'

'You said something like that the day we met, when I was being inquisitive.'

He recalled the incident with some nostalgia. 'That was a good day,' he said. 'You know, Nicola and I had a very grown-up conversation that morning, all about sheep and dog hair.'

She nodded. 'You would. Nicola will never be tongue-tied in company. My big worry at the time was Gareth. That was until Jimbo worked his charm and restored him almost to his former self.'

'Yes, Jimbo has his moments. He'll be home before long.'

'Gareth can't wait. If he knew the date, he'd have it marked on the calendar.'

'So would I, if only for convenience's sake, but Jimbo usually manages a gig at the end of term as well as several during it, and that delays things somewhat.'

'Help yourself to *pâté*. Take as much as you like.' She moved the dish towards him. 'Jimbo gets a lot of work, doesn't he?'

'Yes, but he's good, and word gets around.'

'He's very popular with the Choral Society.'

'Jimbo's been universally popular since he was a toddler. His teachers couldn't bring themselves to tell him off, he was such a charmer. I had to do the job for them.'

'That was a shame, but you have a good relationship with him, don't you?'

Adam thought. 'I do, really. I have to apply a steadying hand occasionally, to maintain a degree of control, whereas Leanne believes she has no need for parental influence.'

'You've brought them up well.'

'Thanks.' He reached across the table to take her hand for a moment. 'You're doing a good job too.'

'Thank you.' As she released her hand, she looked at her watch. 'I have an appointment this afternoon,' she said, 'and I'll pick up the children after that, but I'll be back by about four-thirty, if you want to come down.'

* * *

At story time, Gareth declared himself happy with *Five Get Into Trouble*, although he insisted on sitting on the floor with Dottie, rather than on the sofa with Adam and Nicola. Accordingly, Leanne sat on the sofa, with Nicola sandwiched between Adam and herself, both of them listening with quiet concentration.

When Adam inserted his bookmark and closed the book, Leanne said, 'You can still do it, Dad.'

'Do what, love?'

'You can still bring all those characters to life, including Timmy, the dog.'

Hearing the last word, Dottie looked up for a moment, but resumed her supine position when she realised that nothing special was happening.

Jenny simply looked thoughtful.

'Thank you, darling,' said Adam. 'It's good to know I have your approval.'

'It was like going back in time.' Leanne seemed to dwell on that thought until she looked at her wristwatch and said, 'I should go. I have things to do. Thanks for a lovely meal, Jenny.'

'You're welcome. It's a pity you have to leave so soon.'

'I'll hang on 'til Nicola's ready for bed, and then I must go. For one thing, I have a pile of ironing waiting for me.'

'Okay. Nicola, get undressed and into your jim-jams and then you can kiss Leanne goodnight before she goes home.'

Nicola scampered upstairs whilst Gareth looked uncomfortable.

Leanne said, 'You don't like to be kissed by girls, do you, Gareth? You'll change your mind soon enough, but I'll respect that for now.'

Gareth blushed all the same.

When Nicola came down, she kissed Adam and her mum, leaving Leanne until last. Leanne played up to the arrangement by making it into a mini drama, which entertained Nicola but appeared to make Gareth wish even more fervently that he could become invisible.

Leanne left, and Nicola went to bed. Before long, Gareth decided that embarrassment was best suffered in private, and he, too, went to his room.

'It's only natural at his age,' said Adam, 'but he'll be as different again in a few months' time.'

Jenny nodded, but clearly with something else on her mind.

'A penny for them,' offered Adam.

She hesitated, perhaps reluctant to voice her concern, and then she said, 'Leanne said that listening to you read was like going back in time.'

'Yes, she and Jimbo used to enjoy it.'

'It's an important part of their past, then.'

'When it occurs to them. It's not something they think about every day.'

'But it happened when their mum was alive.'

'Yes, but reading to them was my department. Kate read to them occasionally, but her reading never gained their approval. She read like someone who dealt in numbers and formulae, which was what she did. They used to laugh about it.'

'I just wondered when I heard Leanne refer to it.... Maybe I was being too sensitive.' It was her turn to be embarrassed.

'Let me tell you something important, Jenny. Leanne is very intuitive. Somehow, she's twigged that something is happening between you and me, and she's accepted it.'

'How do you know?'

'Because there was no ironing for her to do tonight, and she knew that, because she did it all on Sunday. She was simply leaving us on our own. Also, she told me when I took her to the Golden Lion, that if something were to happen between you and me, it would have her approval.'

'I'd no idea.'

'Of course not. It wasn't the kind of thing I'd have told you at the time.' He patted the seat beside him. 'Come and join me.'

Relieved, she moved across to the sofa. 'It was never going to be straightforward,' she said.

'No, but it'll be easier now, or it should be when this collarbone's healed.'

'It does tend to cramp your style,' she agreed, moving forward so that he could slip his good arm round her.

'What style? Don't you recognise a caveman when he grabs you by the ponytail?'

'I don't believe you,' she said, submitting to a long, searching kiss.

After a while, she said a little breathlessly, 'I don't want to appear forward....'

'Be as forward as you like. Feel free to use all five gears.'

'The thing is, I'm afraid there's a limit to what we can do.'

'With children in the house, of course,' he agreed.

'Yes, but even when the children aren't here.'

'Oh?'

'At least, for the next seven days.'

'Ah.'

'Then we'll be all right.'

'Mm.' It was a murmur of anticipation.

'I went back on the pill today. That was the appointment I told you about.'

Adam adopted a thoughtful pose. 'I take back what I said about being forward,' he said. 'You're a shameless hussy.' He underlined the statement with a kiss. 'But don't change, whatever you do.'

24

As a member of the Festival Committee, Adam was obliged to attend meetings in which he had no more than an incidental interest. They covered such aspects of the festival as parking, catering and toilet facilities for those staying in caravans, campervans and mobile homes. Mention of tent camping aroused a negative reaction from Councillor Beasley.

'Do we really want rows of tents all over the place?'

'I think it's a good idea, Mr Chairman,' said Adam, rousing himself to full consciousness. 'A clean and tidy campsite would be an example to those who descend on Glastonbury and similar places of deprivation.'

One committee member asked, 'Why is it deprived?'

'Is that what I said? I'm sorry, I meant depravation, although they are deprived, in a sense, of culture.'

Councillor Beasley rapped on the table with his Overton Pharmaceuticals ballpoint. 'Will you kindly address your remarks and questions through the chair?'

The member who'd questioned Adam about deprivation said, 'Through the Chair, I feel that Mr Watkinson's remark about pop festivals and depravity, not to mention deprivation, was elitist and offensive.'

'Through the Chair,' said Adam, 'I was stating an opinion, that's all.'

'Through the Chair,' said his opponent, 'he was being a classical snob, so there.'

'Through the Chair,' said Adam, 'I take back what I said about depravity. We don't know yet what's going to happen in Netherdale.

For all I know, we might have to deal with tobacco pouches and man bags filled with cannabis, not to mention mountains of tonic wine bottles.'

'Stop,' ordered Councillor Beasley. 'We haven't come here to discuss elitism and depra... that sort of thing.'

'Through the Chair, Mr Chairman,' insisted the champion of pop festivals, 'it's your fault for being elitist about camping.'

Adam was glad he'd stayed awake.

* * *

He told Jenny about it the following day, but she was preoccupied with another matter.

'You've given me far too much for housekeeping,' she said.

'It's not just housekeeping. There was travelling to and from the hospital as well.'

'Even so, it's a lot.'

'You could give the children a treat,' he suggested, 'and that reminds me.'

'Of what?'

'How are you fixed this weekend?'

'In what sense?'

'Have you anything planned for Saturday?'

'Nothing at all.'

'Good, because I've booked a table for six at the Craven Heifer. Jimbo says he'll be here by then, and Leanne's taking the day off work. It'll be good for us all to be together again.'

'It will. Thank you, Adam. The children will love it.' She looked at the time and said, 'Speaking of the children, I must leave you for a short time while I pick them up.'

* * *

The children were excited when they arrived home, because Jenny had told them on the way home about Saturday. Most of the excitement was because Leanne and Jimbo would be there. In fact, their delight lasted until Leanne arrived, when Adam noticed, although it wasn't immediately obvious, that she was less than her usual chirpy self.

Adam asked, 'Are you all right, darling?'

'Yes,' she said, 'I'm fine. I'll see if Jenny needs any help.'

It was only after dinner, after bedtime reading and after Leanne had gone, that Adam learned the reason for her sober frame of mind.

'She'll be all right by tomorrow,' Jenny told him as they settled on the sofa. 'Craig called at the café today. He's going home to Somerset before he returns to Wye College, and he was expecting things to go on as before with Leanne, whenever they could get together, but Leanne had other ideas. She told him today that it was over, and because he was upset, she was upset too.'

'When did she tell you this?'

'When she came in from work.'

'Ah.'

'Don't feel excluded, Adam. It was a girl thing.'

'I don't. Thank you. I'm sure you dealt with it better than I could. I get tongue-tied and embarrassed when I talk to Leanne about... that kind of thing. It's easier with Jimbo.' He felt awkward just talking about it.

'I imagine Jimbo's love life is fairly basic.'

'No, Jenny, it's extremely basic.' He thought of a harmless example. 'We were outside a butcher's one day, and Jimbo saw something in the window he didn't understand. He asked, "What's a loin?" Leanne told him, "It's where you do all your thinking." He was eighteen at the time. She was only fifteen, but she had him weighed up.'

She lifted his arm in a way that had become familiar and snuggled up to him. 'Jimbo's such a lovely, sunny character,' she said. 'I'm sure he's not a lost cause.'

'Your faith in him does you credit, Jenny.' Suddenly, he remembered something. 'I got another text from him today.' He picked up his phone to bring it up. It read:

LO Pop. How RU coping? CU Friday. Did a 4A Requiem last week. Baritone, but better than 0. Btw, look out for me in Vincente advert on TV!

CU soon. Bike no more. Will hire car. Luv, Jimbo.

Jenny translated. ' "LO" is "Hello", "RU" speaks for itself, so does "CU"....' She hesitated for a moment. ' "Btw" is "by the way", but I must confess "4A" has me guessing.'

'Gabriel Fauré, the composer,' said Adam.'

'Of course. "Requiem" should have given it away.'

'There's a baritone solo in it, but Jimbo didn't find that too demeaning, so there's hope for him yet.'

Jenny looked at the text again and said, 'It looks as if he's started a side-line in TV advertising.'

'It doesn't surprise me. What's Vincente?'

'Haven't you heard of Lorenzo Vincente, the fashion designer?'

'No, the name doesn't mean a thing to me. Jimbo can't be modelling his clothes, surely.'

'Not unless he's taken to cross dressing,' she assured him. 'Vincente designs women's fashions. No, I think it's more likely that he's advertising one of the men's fragrances.'

'I suppose we'll find out soon enough.' He would also find out why Jimbo's bike was no more.

* * *

Jimbo arrived late on Friday afternoon and found the house deserted, so he texted Adam.

I'm at the family pile. Where R U?

Adam texted back: *We R at Jenny's. Join us.*

He arrived minutes later.

'Sorry I'm a bit late,' he said. 'I had to drop Helen in Huddersfield.'

'Your timing is spot-on,' Jenny assured him.

'I meant to tell you,' said Adam, 'that Jenny's been looking after us this week.'

'How kind of her. Thank you, Jenny.'

'Jimbo!' Leanne had leant forward to greet her brother, but now she moved away from him. 'What is that stuff you're wearing? You smell like a tart's handbag.'

'*Pas devant les enfants*, Leanne,' warned Adam.

'I'm sorry, but he does.'

'It should be possible to get used to it in time,' said Jenny. 'What is it?'

' "Fixation", the new fragrance from Vincente,' Jimbo told her proudly. Haven't you seen the advert?'

'Not yet,' said Adam. 'We're still bracing ourselves.'

'They say a prophet has no honour in his hometown.'

Leanne finally accepted a kiss from her brother. 'If you go around wearing that stuff, they'll run you out of town,' she said.

'Maybe a little goes a long way,' suggested Jenny.

'I think it's nice,' said Gareth.

Nicola asked, 'What's a tart's handbag?'

'Just an ordinary one,' said Leanne, 'but if you kept tarts in it until they went mouldy, it would smell horrible, wouldn't it?' Turning to Jimbo again, she asked, 'What does Helen think of it?'

'She's getting used to it,' he told her.

'Brave girl.'

'Here, Jimbo.' Jenny handed him a glass of lager. 'After all that, welcome home.'

'Thanks, Jenny. I knew I could count on you for a civilised welcome. My family disappoint me at times. They just can't adjust to my runaway success.'

'It's a considerable adjustment,' said Leanne, 'quite daunting, in fact.'

'Anyway,' said Adam, changing the subject, 'what happened to your bike?'

'I sold it.'

Adam waited, knowing that an explanation would follow. Leanne listened in uncharacteristic silence.

Jimbo duly obliged. 'The accident I had last winter wasn't the only one,' he told them. 'I've had several runs-in with London traffic and, basically, I'm bored with being knocked off my bike. Also, Helen's never been keen to ride pillion; she's given me quite a lot of earache about it, so I decided in the end to get rid of it.'

Adam absorbed the information. 'Two reasons,' he said, 'two very good reasons, even though one's a little surprising, coming from you.'

Leanne broke her silence by asking, 'Are things going well between you and Helen?'

'Very well.'

'Good,' said Adam. 'You'll be working together again in September.'

'No sweat, Pop. We sing together quite often.'

* * *

The lunch party at the Craven Heifer was everything Adam had intended. The children had a delightful time with Leanne and Jimbo, who was wearing a more discreet quantity of 'Fixation' than on the previous day, and was all the more welcome for it. Adam and Jenny were able to relax and watch the others enjoy the event, without having to contribute too much to the proceedings.

That evening, Gareth asked if they might be allowed to watch something on commercial TV. Everyone knew he wanted to see Jimbo's advertisement, so his request was granted. They watched the whole of a programme that none of them really understood, and were beginning to despair until the end, when the advertisements came on and they were treated to a close-up of Jimbo looking trendy and confident; in fact, he was much like his normal self. As he walked through a busy town square, one pretty girl after another turned to look at him admiringly, and a voice-over said, ' "Fixation", the new fragrance from Vincente gets you noticed.'

'Well,' said Leanne, 'no one can say the advert isn't honest and truthful.'

Gareth gazed at Jimbo in admiration while Nicola sat on the sofa with *The Famous Five* open and ready for Adam to read.

* * *

A ray of bright, afternoon sunlight infiltrated the room between the hastily-drawn curtains. As it did so, it backlit Jenny's hair, creating a halo effect as she knelt above Adam. At least, that was how it appeared to him, and it seemed appropriate, because he was experiencing a kind of peace he hadn't known for years.

She leaned forward, carefully avoiding his damaged shoulder, and kissed him. 'That's for proving my gran wrong,' she told him.

'She had me worried for a while,' he admitted. 'I was well and truly out of practice.'

'So was I.' She ran her fingers through his chest hair, still by-passing the injured side. 'Still,' she said, 'if you'll allow me a pun, it all came together.'

'It's just as well. If it hadn't, you might have taken your gran's advice and persuaded me to read to you instead.'

'I like it when you read to me.' She narrowed her eyes mischievously and said, 'I like what we just did, as well.'

'Good, because reading's been quite difficult lately.'

'Do you mean the long words?'

'And the short ones. I've been getting headaches as well. I think I need to have my eyes tested.'

She lowered her head to kiss him again. 'What a romantic conversation we're having. Is there any other part of your body that needs special attention?'

'Yes, but you've just seen to that.'

'So I have.' She glanced at the bedside clock and said, 'I'll have to pick up the children soon.'

'Yes, that's what makes it seem naughty.'

'The children?'

'Clandestine meetings, like this, when they're at school. I feel guilty, somehow.'

'Married couples sometimes do it when their children are elsewhere, as you know.'

'It's the furtive element that makes it different.'

'I know. It's like being teenagers again, dodging our parents.'

He gave her a searching look and asked, 'Is that how you spent your teens?'

'*Late* teens. I was a virgin when I went away to art school. Were you?'

'I've never been to art school.'

'You know what I mean. Were you a virgin when you went to music college?'

'Not quite.'

It was Jenny's turn to look stern. 'Either you were or you weren't. You can't be "not quite" a virgin.'

'It was a fiasco,' he admitted. 'Not so much *coitus interruptus* as whatever the Latin is for "over almost before it had begun".'

'Did you converse in Latin while you were doing it? I've heard of people introducing all kinds of games just to spice things up.'

'No, the main task was challenging enough.'

'All right,' she said generously. 'It's obviously a painful memory, so I'll allow you the "not quite".' She nodded as she spoke, and her small, neat breasts nodded, too, in comforting agreement. Then, she said with a hint of regret, 'I must put some clothes on and pick up the children.' She eased herself away from him and stood beside the bed. 'By the way,' she said, 'because they're not going on holiday this year, my mum and dad will be taking them on lots of day trips and treats in the school holiday.'

'Dare I ask why they're not getting a holiday?'

'I have too much to do here. I'll take them somewhere to make up for it when I'm not as busy. It's not easy, being a single mum, as you know from being a single dad.' As she picked up her clothes, she said, 'I mention the days out because it means there'll be times we can be together without feeling guilty.'

Adam still felt strangely awkward, although he would probably feel less so in a day's time, after a gruelling spell of car hunting with Jimbo.

25

It seemed a shame to begin on a negative note, but Jimbo's expectations were unrealistic, even by his impulsive standards. 'The Golf GTi is an excellent car,' agreed Adam, 'but not, I'm afraid, an option in your case.'

'Why not, Pop? It's not a huge car by any stretch of the imagination, yours or mine.'

'No, it's not. It's the price and the performance that rule it out.'

'But it doesn't have to be all that new, and I can handle the performance.'

'Jimbo, listen.' It was a lot to ask; Jimbo had many undoubted qualities, but listening to reason was a steep, uphill journey for him. 'For your peace of mind, you need to buy as new a car as you can, and before you tell me that VWs are renowned for their reliability, let me remind you of the other problem, which is your ability to find and afford insurance.'

Jimbo opened his eyes wide, as if a light had just been switched on. It happened frequently. 'There's the firm that insured my bike,' he said. 'I have a year's no claims discount with them.'

'Okay, Jimbo.' Adam was tired of arguing. 'Give them a ring and ask them to quote you for a Golf GTi.' He went into the kitchen to make coffee while Jimbo searched for the telephone number of the insurance company.

He returned with the coffee to find his son in a despondent frame of mind. He asked, 'What's the verdict, Jimbo?'

'They don't want to know.'

'Hard luck, old son, but I'm afraid it's one of those disadvantages you'll carry around until you're maybe twenty-five or thirty, and even then, your occupation could be a problem.'

'What do you mean, Pop?'

'It's not just students. The insurance companies aren't all that carried away with opera singers, either.'

Jimbo's expression brightened as another idea occurred to him. 'Suppose I told them I was an actor? It's basically true, now that I'm doing commercials.'

Adam shook his head sadly. 'Actors, opera singers and students are all out-crowd where insurance companies are concerned.' Looking at his downcast offspring, he felt sorry for him. Jimbo had a puppy-like way of inspiring sympathy, and Adam couldn't help being affected by it. 'Let's go and look at some cars, Jimbo,' he said. 'You never know, you might easily find the car that's been waiting for you. With any luck, the two of you could become inseparable.'

* * *

The first on Jimbo's list was a VW dealership in Skipton, where they looked at a couple of Polos, neither of which appealed to Jimbo. It seemed that, with a Golf GTi parked nearby, the poorer relation never stood a chance.

The salesman asked, 'What do you really fancy?'

Jimbo told him, and the salesman gave him an appraising look. 'Do you mind if I ask your age?'

'No, I'm twenty-two.'

The salesman pursed his lips and shook his head. 'What job do you do?'

'I'm a student.'

The salesman closed his eyes tightly. 'If I were you,' he said, 'I'd forget the GTi.'

'Come on, Jimbo,' said Adam, 'I'll buy you an ice cream.'

A '99' later, they returned to the hire car.

Jimbo asked, 'Where are we going now, Pop?'

'I thought we'd try the Peugeot dealer,' he said, tactfully directing his son towards that destination.

'I haven't considered a Peugeot,' said Jimbo.

'Well, it's always best to keep your options open.' He continued to give directions until they reached the Peugeot dealership.

Jimbo surveyed the lines of new cars without discernible reaction.

'The used cars are over here,' prompted Adam, pointing the way.

They looked at several cars, and a salesman, a young man with spiky, gelled hair, approached them. He asked, 'Have you decided what model you fancy?' He addressed the question to Adam.

'It's my young friend here, who's looking,' he said.

'Right. What sort of price do you have in mind?'

Jimbo told him, even though he seemed unimpressed by the cars he'd seen.

'We've got a lovely Two-Oh-Five. One careful lady owner from new and a full service history. We've maintained it, so we can vouch for it.' He led Jimbo to where the Peugeot 205 stood with its doors opened invitingly.

'It looks like a nice car,' said Jimbo, 'but it's not what you'd call a "puller", is it?'

'I don't know,' said the salesman. 'Stranger things have happened. One of my mates once pulled with an ex butcher's van. Its spacious interior came in handy later on, as well, so he told me.'

'It would,' said Jimbo.

It was time for Adam to intervene. 'Jimbo,' he said, 'you don't need a puller, and you know it. You could pull with a builder's wheelbarrow. You already have everything you need. You're tall, dark and handsome enough to make other men wish you'd bugger off somewhere else and give them a chance.'

'That's true, Pop. All the same—'

'Hear me out, Jimbo. What you really need to go with all those qualities, not to mention your beloved bass voice, is respectability, and a Peugeot Two-Oh-Five gives you that on wheels. A girl would look at that car and say to herself, "This man looks and sounds too good to be true, but wait a minute. You'd expect him to drive a performance car, such as a Golf GTi or a Lotus, like the other posers, but he doesn't. He drives a respectable car, and that kind of quiet, masterful self-confidence is what sets my pulse racing." '

'Do you really think so, Pop? I mean, when all's said and done, it's a bit out of your area.'

'I know what I'm talking about, Jimbo.'

'He does,' agreed the salesman. 'He's dead right, Jimbo.'

Jimbo sat in the driver's seat and put his hands on the wheel.

The salesman asked, 'Have you got your licence with you?'

'Yes.' Jimbo took out his card wallet and produced his driving licence.

The salesman gave it a cursory inspection. 'That's fine,' he said. 'Take it for a spin if you like.' He closed the car's doors and waved Jimbo away. Then, turning to Adam, he said, 'You should be doing my job.'

'No,' said Adam modestly, 'I just know my son.'

'Would you like a coffee or tea while you wait for him?'

'That's a good idea.' As he walked into the showroom, Adam thought about the forecourt price on the Peugeot. 'You may well have a sale there,' he said. 'I imagine there's some leeway with the price?'

The salesman picked up a plastic cup. 'Tea or coffee?'

'Tea, please. Milk, no sugar.'

'I could come down fifty,' he said.

'Is that all?'

'All right. A hundred.'

Adam looked doubtful.

'One twenty-five, then.'

Adam shook his head.

'Look, one seventy-five is as far as I can go.'

'Oh, well, if that's your absolute limit, I suppose we can work round it.'

'One seventy-five, a set of rubber mats and a full tank of petrol.'

'Okay.' Adam accepted the tea and waited for Jimbo. Experience led him to expect a whole new relationship to emerge between his son and the Peugeot.

When Jimbo returned, it was clear that Adam was right.

'What a lovely car it is, Pop.'

'I thought you'd like it.'

'I do.'

'Enough to buy it?'

Jimbo hesitated. 'That depends on the price, Pop.'

'I've whittled it down a bit.'

'How much?'

'One seventy-five.'

Jimbo frowned with concentration. Mental arithmetic was an effort for him. Eventually, he said, 'It's still five hundred more than I've got.'

Adam was thinking. 'Do you remember the dress suit I bought you last birthday?'

'Of course I do.'

'That was only part of your birthday present. I'll stump up the balance for the car.'

* * *

That evening, Adam had a serious conversation with Leanne.

'You know I'm helping Jimbo with this car, don't you?'

'Yes.'

'The thing is, I haven't forgotten you. You're going away in September, shortly before your birthday, and I want to make sure you have everything you need.'

'If you're thinking about a car, Dad, that's really generous of you, but can I bank it for later?'

'Of course.' It wasn't the response he'd expected, but it was a harmless request.

'You see, I don't see myself contributing to London's traffic congestion. That's okay for Jimbo, but it's not a part of me.'

'As ever, Leanne, yours is the voice of reason.'

He wondered, as he often did, how his children could have turned out so different. He was devoted to them both, but the contrast continued to entertain and exasperate him, roughly in equal measure.

'Dad,' said Leanne after visible thought, 'I've been thinking about your headaches, and I suspect they could be down to eyestrain.'

'That's very considerate of you, darling. I've made an appointment for an eye test next week. The only trouble is, I'll have to change it, because Jenny has something happening that morning.'

'Which morning?'

'Tuesday.'

Leanne thought again and said, 'Don't postpone it, Dad. I'll take you.'

'What about work?'

'I fancy a day off, and you can buy me lunch afterwards. If Jimbo comes as well, it'll be a family outing.'

Argument would be pointless. It would be an expensive eye test, but it would be interesting.

26

Jimbo had arranged to return the hire car and collect his new car on the day of Adam's eye test, so they agreed to meet him later. It was a sensible arrangement, as Adam explained to Leanne.

'Taking delivery of a new car is a special rite,' he told her. 'You have to observe it in your own time so that you can enjoy the experience to the full.'

Leanne started the Rover, unimpressed by the immature ways of the male sex. 'You'll find some wine gums in the glove compartment,' she told him, reaching across to take the packet from him so that she could tear it open.

'What are these?' He took out another packet.

'Jelly babies. I'll open them and then you can feed them to me later, while I'm driving.' She performed the operation before putting the car in gear and moving off.

They covered a few miles before Leanne spoke again. 'Dad,' she said, 'will you do me a favour?'

'What's that?'

'Will you pop a jelly baby into my mouth and then be ever so quiet and not bother me for about a minute?'

After almost nineteen years, nothing surprised him, but he had to ask, 'Why?'

'So that I can take my time over it and enjoy the experience to the full.'

'I sometimes think,' he said, carrying out her request, 'that I gave you too much freedom when you were growing up.'

'Shh,' she reminded him.

'Sorry.'

After about a minute, she said, 'If you'd allowed me as much freedom as you gave Jimbo, I might have ended up like him, and then you'd have had a nymphomaniac for a daughter. Think of that.'

'I'd rather not. Actually, I've been wondering about Jimbo. His waters are not usually all that still, but they seem to be running fairly deep, just now.'

'Last I heard, he was being very good. I think it's down to Helen Little's influence.'

'Very likely.'

After a while, she took the turning for Skipton. 'This eye test,' she said, 'represents an important stage in your life. It's one of several that Shakespeare left out when he wrote *As You Like It*.'

'It's certainly important,' he agreed, expecting a wind-up.

'They may put drops in your eyes,' she warned. 'If they do, you must be very grown-up and not make a fuss. Remember there are wine gums at stake.'

It was time for Adam to assert himself. 'Do I have to remind you,' he asked, 'about your anti-tetanus injection?'

'I was only five,' she protested.

'You were six.'

'Oh, now you're splitting hairs.'

'Six years old. Talk about a fuss....'

'If you must.' She was clearly thrown by the counterattack.

'It was the tiniest of needles, and when the nurse pushed it into your little bum—'

'Dad!'

'You went berserk.'

'Is nothing sacred?'

'It cost me a fortune in jelly babies.'

'Hardly a fortune.'

'Enough. I had to calm your mum down, too.'

Leanne gave him a strange look. 'Why?'

'Because she had the injection as well. All three of you did after that day in the garden.'

After a moment's consideration, Leanne asked, 'What about Jimbo? Did he make a fuss?'

'No, he was playing with the toys on the desk, and he wasn't aware of anything else happening.'

'That figures. Anyway, I think we'll leave that reminiscence in the dustbin of history. Truce?'

'Truce,' he agreed.

They reached the outskirts of Skipton before Leanne spoke again. 'Before we get to the optician's and before Jimbo turns up, hopefully at the right pub, can I ask you something personal? I've asked you this before, but things may have changed.'

'The mystery deepens. Go on, ask me, but I can't guarantee to answer your question.'

'Are you involved with Jenny?'

'Yes.' He'd been half-expecting her to ask.

'I thought so.'

'Has Jimbo noticed anything?'

'I doubt it. It's like the anti-tetanus injection. His mind's been on other things.'

'Do you mind?'

'No, I told you that a few weeks ago, if you remember.'

'I just wondered if you'd changed your mind.' He broke off to point ahead and say, 'That carpark on the left.'

'Right. I just want to say that I'm glad it's Jenny rather than anyone else.'

'Thanks.'

'Also, I'll break the news to Jimbo. He's bound to approve, and then he'll go back down his burrow and life will be pretty much as before.'

'You're old beyond your years, Leanne.'

She parked the car, and they walked to the optician's, where the receptionist invited them to wait in a seated area.

'I wonder if anyone wears a monocle nowadays,' said Leanne, looking at the multitude of spectacle frames that covered the walls.

'One of the Deputies at Aspley High did. If it comes to that, he probably still does. He got an infection in one eye and lost the use of it. After that, he couldn't see the point in buying a pair of glasses, when he only needed one lens.'

'I could see you with a monocle, Dad, like one of those posh people from the nineteen-twenties.'

'Let's just wait and see.' Grateful though he was to Leanne for her services, he knew that the journey would have been more peaceful if Jenny had brought him.

A door at the far end of the shop opened, and an elderly woman came out, followed by a younger woman carrying a document of some kind, which she handed to a man seated behind a desk. The elderly woman took her seat opposite him.

After a short time, the younger woman re-emerged and called Adam's name.

'Wait here, Leanne,' he said, getting up to follow the optometrist into her examination room.

It was a place of mirrors, lights and letters, a grown-up maze as far as he was concerned.

'There's nothing to fear,' the optometrist told him cheerfully as she closed the door. 'Take a seat, please.'

He lowered himself into the examinee's chair, feeling rather like a competitor on *Mastermind*.

'You don't wear glasses, do you, Mr Watkinson?'

'Not yet.'

'Don't worry, it comes to us all sooner or later. Tell me, what kind of work do you do?'

'I write music.'

The optometrist gave him a mischievous smile. 'Like Beethoven?'

It wasn't the first time he'd been asked that. 'Not exactly,' he said. 'For one thing, I've written more symphonies than he did. He only wrote nine, and he got so bored with the last one that he had to chuck a choir in to liven things up.'

'Really?' The optometrist looked surprised.

'No, I write educational resources. That's musicals, tutor books and that sort of thing.'

'Ah.' Realising that her leg had been pulled, she gave a nervous, snickering laugh. 'So you do a lot of close work, I imagine?'

'I spend most of my time looking at a computer screen. That's how music's written nowadays. I use a mouse to put the notes on the stave.'

'I see.'

The questions became more serious, and were followed by tests of various kinds, one of them involving drops, as Leanne had warned him, although the experience was painless. Eventually, the optometrist finished writing. 'Your eyes need a little help with close work, and that includes working on the computer. You've presumably enjoyed excellent vision until recently, but most people with six-six vision find, when they reach forty or so, that they begin to need help.'

'What's the difference between six-six and twenty-twenty?' He had an awful feeling that, with her sixth-form sense of humour, she might be tempted to say something like, 'fourteen-fourteen'. In the event, he wasn't far wrong.

'Almost four thousand miles.' Again, the snickering laugh. 'Americans talk about twenty-twenty vision because they deal in feet. Six-six refers to metres.' She snickered again. 'It's the same thing.' Becoming serious again, she said, 'You just need to wear your glasses for work or reading. Let's go to the dispensing optician to see about some glasses. That's unless you want to take your prescription somewhere else.'

'I wouldn't know where to go.'

She opened the door for him to leave, and he thanked her for her services.

'Good morning, Mr Watkinson,' said the dispensing optician, taking the prescription from the optometrist. 'Take a seat. Have you any particular kind of frame in mind?'

'None at all. Do you mind if I whistle up my daughter? She'll help me choose something that doesn't make her wet herself with laughter every time she looks at me.'

'If she's on the premises, by all means.'

Adam leaned backwards in his chair and called, 'Leanne.'

His daughter came dutifully to his side.

'Will you help me choose some frames, love? I haven't a clue.'

'That's what I'm here for.' She examined her father, as if for the first time, and said, 'You've got a long face, Dad.'

'That's because buying glasses for the first time is a serious business.'

'It's what we call an "oblong" face,' said the optician.

'Oblong?'

'It's a technical term. It just means that its length is greater than its width,' he explained. 'It has nothing to do with sharp corners.'

'That's a relief.'

'You should forget those trendy, shallow frames and go for deeper ones,' advised Leanne.

'Your daughter is right,' said the optician.

'She usually is.'

'Your hair colouring's mainly dark brown,' said Leanne, 'the bit that's not grey, so you'll be okay with warm or cold colours, although I'd be inclined to go for something quite dark.'

The optician, who was possibly feeling a trifle spare at that moment, said, 'Let's try a few frames.' He took some from the wall behind him and placed them on the desk. Leanne examined the price tags on them.

'These are designer frames,' she pointed out. 'Let's not forget the other end of the market. My dad's a struggling composer. Of course, he may decide to push the boat out, but you need to let him choose.'

'Certainly. I was coming to them.' The optician went to the other side of the room to find more frames.

Hiding his embarrassment as well as he could, Adam asked her, 'How did you learn all this?'

'I went shopping with Mum for her glasses. It's surprising what you can learn as a casual observer.'

First, it was buying and selling houses, and then glasses. He wondered what other areas of the consumer market his daughter had studied under her mum's tutelage.

The optician returned with several frames, which he put on the desk, and Adam tried them all. All glasses looked strange to a man who'd never worn any, but eventually, he selected a pair that he liked.

Leanne stepped backwards to look. 'I think you've got it about right, Dad,' she said.

Having chosen them, Adam allowed the optician to measure

him and made all final arrangements, which included taking the payment.

Leanne asked, 'Are you asking for the full amount up front?'

'That's the way we do it,' the optician told her.

'But he hasn't got his glasses yet.'

He hesitated uncomfortably. 'I suppose a deposit would be all right,' he said. 'Shall we say a hundred?'

Adam took out his debit card before Leanne could embarrass him further.

'It was the same when Mum ordered hers,' she told him as they left the shop. 'They only showed her designer frames to begin with, and when she chose budget ones, they tried to take the full price. I learned a lot from her,' she said, unlocking the car doors.

* * *

Jimbo was waiting for them at the pub.

Leanne asked him, 'Have you got your car?'

'Yes, I'll show you it later. Has Pop got his specs?'

'Not yet, but it's all arranged.'

'It's been a successful morning, then.'

The excitement of the morning had proved too great for Adam, who asked to be excused.

When he returned, he found Jimbo looking even more pleased than usual.

'Hey, Pop,' he said, 'Leanne's just told me you've got it on with Jenny. Good for you! I was wondering how much longer we had to wait.'

27

AUGUST

Sixteen choirs from various parts of the country had paid the entrance fee for the Festival and received their copies of the test piece. Hotels and guest houses reported an increase in reservations for the third to the fifth of September, and in most respects, the outlook was good.

'Considering it's the Festival's first year, sixteen choirs isn't bad at all,' observed Jenny.

'Mm, I'm not worried about numbers. It's the weather that's my concern.' As Adam spoke, a squall of rain hit the window behind him with renewed vigour.

'It won't keep competitors away,' Jenny assured him. 'It would take more than that.'

'I'm thinking of parking and caravans,' he said, 'or worse.'

'Well, we'd better keep our fingers crossed. In the meantime,' she said, 'I have another concern, and that is what to do about Gareth's birthday.'

'When is it?'

'The fourteenth, next Saturday.'

'Ah.' Adam assimilated that information and asked, 'What's the question about Gareth's birthday?'

'Basically, how to celebrate it. He's made a few friends since he became more outgoing, but he's still rather shy, and I can't help thinking that he's maybe a little old for a party, anyway.'

'Have you asked him about it?'

She shook her head. 'No, but I suppose he's old enough to know his own mind. Maybe I should.'

'Where are the children?'

Jenny gestured towards the stairs. 'Upstairs. Nicola's reading, and I don't know what Gareth's doing. My guess is he's combing his hair and trying to make it look like Jimbo's.'

'Designer bed-ruffled,' commented Adam. 'It's a difficult one to bring off without a hairdresser on the premises.'

'But he always looks smart when he sings in public.' As ever, Jenny was quick to defend Jimbo.

'That's only after a dose of Dr Jekyll's Patent Prescription, and it springs back into the post-rogering look as soon as he leaves the platform and unfastens his bow tie.'

'Didn't it work the other way round? As I recall, Jekyll became Hide when he took the mixture.'

'Jimbo gets everything the wrong way round. You'll get used to it after a while.'

Jenny shook her head in mock-despair. 'Anyway,' she said, 'what are they doing today? It's Leanne's day-off, isn't it?'

'I left them at home, watching *Bob the Builder.*'

'Both of them?'

'Yes, they're both fans. The only difference is that Leanne knows it's only a made-up story.'

With a look of resignation, Jenny went to the foot of the stairs and called, 'Gareth.'

There was a semi-audible response, so she called, 'Come down, darling. I want to ask you about something.'

Gareth arrived at the bottom of the stairs, still patting his ruffled hair into place. Nicola was behind him.

'There was no need for you to come, Nicola,' said Jenny. 'It's Gareth I want to talk to.'

Instead of returning to her bedroom, Nicola joined Adam on the sofa.

'Hello,' he said. 'What have you been reading?'

'*Five Go Off in a Caravan.*'

'That's a good choice.'

'Gareth,' said Jenny, 'I've been wondering what you'd like to do on your birthday.'

A look of alarm crossed his face. 'Not a party. Please.'

'No, there's no reason to have a party if you don't want one. I just wondered what you *would* like.'

Gareth bit his lip and examined his trainers. 'I don't know,' he mumbled.

'That's a shame, darling, because if you don't know, how can I?'

Gareth continued to stare downwards, and Adam sensed that tears weren't far away.

Jenny stroked his arm and said, 'Let me know if you have any ideas.'

As Adam considered the question, memories of the gathering after the funeral came to mind. He asked, 'Do you mind if I make a suggestion?'

'Please do.' Jenny was clearly grateful for any contribution.

'Suppose you had a very small party, Gareth, like the one we had at Leanne's café. How does that sound?'

Jenny asked him, 'Would you like that, Gareth? You could invite Jimbo, and Leanne would already be there.'

Nicola tugged at Adam's shirtsleeve and asked, 'Will you come as well, Adam?'

'That's up to Gareth, Nicola. It would be his party.'

Gareth nodded mutely, and Jenny, who was close enough to him to recognise his state of mind, drew him into her arms. 'It's all right, darling,' she said. 'We only want you to have what you want on your birthday.'

The boy's muffled sobs set Adam thinking.

Nicola lifted Adam's arm the way everyone else had, and wriggled closer to him. Her brother's discomfiture seemed to leave her unmoved, because she asked, 'Does that mean I won't have a party as well?' Her birthday was on the 18th of September. Adam knew that because she'd mentioned it several times.

'No,' said Jenny, 'you can have a party as usual if that's what you want.'

Nicola appeared to consider her mother's answer, because she said, 'I'll let you know if I have any ideas.'

Jenny made no reply. In any case, the dilemma had been Gareth's. She kissed him and asked, 'Are you all right now?'

A silent nod told her he was.

'All right, then. Will you two go upstairs and carry on with what you were doing? We want to have a grown-up conversation.' She waited for the children to disappear and then joined Adam on the sofa. 'I could commit murder,' she said, 'when I think of what that boy's father did to him.'

'I can understand why you feel like that, but I think there was rather more going on just then.'

'Do you?' She snuggled up to him. 'Don't keep me in suspense, Adam.'

'Okay. You've told me that Gareth became shy and withdrawn when his dad left, and he's made remarkable progress since Jimbo took him under his wing, but he's not completely out of the wood yet, is he?'

'No, he's not.' She waited for him to continue.

'So, being rather shy, he hates the idea of a big social occasion, but you rather put him on the spot when you asked him to suggest an alternative. I think most eleven-year-olds would have been tongue-tied.'

'I can see that now, but I'm his mum. Why does he suddenly feel threatened by me?'

'He doesn't.' Adam drew her closer, as he always did when the conversation ran deep. 'You're his source of love and comfort, and that's anything but a threat. No, he's at an awkward age, when minor problems assume mountainous proportions, and the threat is having to put newly-discovered and embarrassing feelings into words. It's a lot to ask of any lad going into adolescence.'

'Poor boy.' She stroked Adam's hand thoughtfully. 'I don't suppose Jimbo ever had that problem.'

'Oh, but he did.' Talking about Gareth's difficulty had already reminded Adam of an incident involving his son.

'I don't believe it.'

'When he was thirteen or so,' he told her, 'we received a letter from his year tutor at school, telling us that he'd been very rude to a member of staff, and when he was referred to his year tutor, he became hostile, angry and abusive.'

'Jimbo?'

'We couldn't believe it either. We asked Jimbo to tell us what it was about, and he did what Gareth just did. He stared dumbly at his feet, unable to tell us anything. We went to his school and met his year tutor, who was also baffled, although it transpired that Jimbo had been his usual, genial self with every other member of staff, so we did wonder a little about personalities. Anyway, we agreed to let the school know if we discovered anything more, and we left it at that.'

'How odd.'

'It was,' he agreed, 'and then one of the English staff showed the year tutor a short story Jimbo had written, that explained everything, albeit with fictional names. It was about an impatient maths teacher who told a girl that she would probably be able to read and understand a question more easily if she cleaned those bottle bottoms she called her glasses. As you can imagine, the girl was very sensitive about her eyesight problem and her appearance, so she was upset.'

Jenny raised her head to register her dismay. 'I'd be furious if a teacher said something like that to one of my children.'

'I don't know how the girl's parents felt about it, but I do know that the boy in the story told the teacher everything that lay on his mind. For all his amorous antics, Jimbo's always had a strong sense of justice and decency, and the incident was more than he could witness without reacting.'

'Good for him.' Jenny eyed him sternly. 'He's a remarkable young man, whatever you say about him.'

'I agree. We told him we understood why he'd done it and that, whilst it wasn't the most diplomatic manoeuvre to call his teacher an effing disgrace, we weren't going to hold it against him. I have to say I admired him for it.'

'Good.' Satisfied that Jimbo had escaped punishment and earned Adam's approval, Jenny was eager to hear the rest of the story. 'Did he have to go on being taught by that awful maths teacher?'

'No, Jimbo's modest exam results led to his being transferred to a lower set for maths, and he went on to become very much a favourite of his new teacher. I recall that Jimbo was rather fond of her too, even though she taught maths, but it wasn't surprising. He's always had a generous nature.'

* * *

Gareth's party was a complete success in that he enjoyed every second. The Tea Rooms provided the cake, which they delivered to the table with great ceremony, and he was allowed his favourite Tea Rooms delicacy, which was a soft-boiled egg with toast soldiers. That it happened also to be Jimbo's favourite was no coincidence, and Gareth's other menu choices mirrored those of his hero exactly. A special bonus was that his hair remained in its state of designer untidiness, albeit with the assistance of a discreet application of wax, right to the end, which was when he consented to be kissed by Leanne.

The party's success prompted Nicola to make her request, having learned that the Tea Rooms offered a children's party package.

'All right,' said Jenny. 'Give me your guest list and I'll book the Tea Rooms again.'

Adam was happy that his suggestion had been a success. Like everyone else, he'd come to enjoy the sixfold gatherings of the Watkinson and Thorpe families, regarding them very much as a part of his and his children's new direction.

His only concern, now, was the weather, which was turning the planned parking for the Festival into a quagmire.

28

Thundery rain continued so that before long, the question of parking was tabled at a meeting of the Festival Committee.

'I've had a look at that field,' said one committee member known for exaggeration, 'and it's reminiscent of Passchendaele.'

'I've told you before,' said Councillor Beasley, 'you can talk about your foreign holidays to your heart's content after the meeting, but let's concentrate on the Festival for now.'

'What's needed is hard standing,' said another. 'There's four motor caravans coming, thankfully no tents, but there's all their cars to accommodate as well.'

'Kindly address your questions and remarks through the chair,' Councillor Beasley reminded him. 'Councillor Hartley, I believe you have some suggestions you'd like to make.'

'Yes, Mr Chairman,' said Councillor Hartley, 'I have a contingent list of possible car parks.'

'Well, then,' prompted Councillor Beasley. 'We're waiting.'

'Through the chair,' began Councillor Hartley, 'there's the High School playground and staff carpark.'

'They don't call it the playground,' objected Councillor Moreton, 'not at the High School.'

'Well, whatever they call it,' said Councillor Hartley impatiently.

'Kindly address your remarks through the chair,' demanded Councillor Beasley.

'Through the chair, they call it the "Yard",' corrected Councillor Moreton. 'Only little children have playgrounds.' His eleven-year-old grandson was due to join the school in September and the distinction was important to him.

'All right,' said Councillor Beasley, 'I'd like to hear that list of carparks. That's if you can stop arguing about what to call them. Councillor Hartley, carry on, if you please.'

'Thank you, Mr Chairman. There's the carpark at the old Council Offices, and the landlord of the Craven Heifer has offered the parking to the rear of the pub. He needs the other parking at the side for his patrons.'

'That brings up the question of the Golden Lion,' said Councillor Beasley. His remark gave rise to a chorus of laughter from the meeting. Someone said, 'Oh no, not "The Happy Clamper."'

'Mr Chairman,' said Adam, 'I've dealt with Mr Harrison in the past. Perhaps I could persuade him to allow some parking on his premises.'

There was renewed laughter, and Councillor Hartley said, 'Aye, at least, if he clamps anybody, we'll have you to call on.' The story of Adam's ultimatum had become Netherdale folklore.

'Address your remarks through the chair,' demanded Councillor Beasley. 'I'm grateful for your offer, Mr Watkinson. Can I take it that's the feeling of the meeting?'

The chorus confirmed that it was the case.

'I think we're set for more rain,' said Councillor Mrs Priestley, making her first contribution to the meeting. 'My barometer's gone down as far as it'll go. Mind you, it's not a proper barometer with mercury and stuff. It's one of them aneroids, I believe they call them.'

Councillor Hartley asked, 'Doesn't your firm make ointment for them, Mr Chairman?'

'Nay,' said Councillor Moreton, 'you're talking about asteroids.'

'Through the chair,' Councillor Beasley reminded them.

'Mr Chairman,' said Councillor Hartley, 'are they aneroids or asteroids or what?'

'I believe they're called haemorrhoids,' said Councillor Mrs Priestley. 'That's the posh name, isn't it, Councillor Beasley? I've never called them that, though, and I've had enough dealings with 'em over the years. I've always called them—'

'I don't bloody care what you call them,' snapped Councillor Beasley. 'Can we go on to Any Other Business?'

* * *

The Choral Society's final rehearsal, which included Jimbo and Helen, ran much more smoothly, and Adam was feeling quite confident by the time he and Jenny walked into the Golden Lion.

'A glass of dry white wine and a pint of Thwaites, please,' he asked the barmaid, 'and I'd like to see Mr Harrison when he has a minute.'

'Tom?' The barmaid looked worried, possibly expecting a complaint.

'It's all right. I just want a word with him about the Choir Festival.'

Jenny looked around her at the unfamiliar layout of the bar and passed judgement. 'It wouldn't be my ideal pub,' she said, 'but it never has been.'

'If you're going to be like that, I shan't bring you again.'

'I only agreed to come out of curiosity.'

From the little Adam could overhear, Tom Harrison was treating a group of visitors to a reminiscence of some event that had taken place during his army career. He appeared to bring the recollection to a close and noticed Adam and Jenny across the bar. The barmaid spoke to him, and he nodded.

'Here he comes,' said Adam, as Tom Harrison approached them.

'Good evening, Mr Watkinson and Mrs....'

'Thorpe,' Jenny prompted him.

'It's good to see you both. I believe you wanted to speak to me.'

'It's about car parking for the Choir Festival,' said Adam. 'The weather's made a nonsense of the soft ground we had in mind.'

Mr Harrison nodded confidently. 'I've known huge areas of country swamped by monsoon rain,' he said in his important way. 'I've just been telling some people about it. That was when I was in the Royal Engineers. We used to drive piles of teak into boggy ground, and build bridges and platforms over them. Of course, that's not an option in this case.'

Adam wondered if Harrison's army service dominated the conversation every night. 'I can think of one councillor,' he said, 'who's had a lot of experience with piles, but you're right. It's not an option.'

'What do you propose?'

'We need hard standing for cars and possibly motor caravans. We've found some, and the landlord of the Craven Heifer has offered the parking to the rear of his pub. We wondered if you would be kind enough to offer some of yours.'

At the mention of his competitor, Mr Harrison's expression changed and he became thoughtful. 'I could probably accommodate a dozen vehicles,' he said.

'That would be excellent. Thank you.'

'We all have to do what we can, Mr Watkinson.'

'Adam.'

'Tom.'

The two men shook hands.

Adam couldn't resist saying, 'It'll do your reputation in the community no harm at all.'

'Ah, yes,' he said sheepishly, 'there is that.'

As they left the pub, Jenny said, 'He knows perfectly well he'll pick up trade from anyone who parks there.'

'Yes, I think we know where his loyalty lies, but he's helping us solve a problem, and that's what really matters.'

The walked on, and Jenny said, 'I'll probably wish I hadn't asked, but what was that about a councillor and piles?'

'Councillor Mrs Priestley,' he told her, 'has been a martyr to them these many years.'

'How do you know?'

'She brought them up at the last meeting of the Festival Committee, just before Any Other Business.'

'Of course.'

* * *

Adam's fellow judges confirmed that they would both arrive on the afternoon of the 5th, the caterers announced that everything was in place at the High School, the local press signalled their intention to mark the event, and local TV news reporters made initial contact. All that was needed now to make the occasion particularly memorable was a break in the weather.

29

SEPTEMBER

I t was as if the thunderstorms and heavy rain of August had been a cruel tease, because, to everyone's relief, the new month dawned sunny and dry.

The day came, and Adam and the other two judges, both experienced choral conductors, took their places in a screened-off area at the rear of the hall, where they would hear the competitors most clearly. Taking the names of the choirs in reverse alphabetical order, they would hear eight in the morning session and the rest in the afternoon.

After a welcoming speech from the Chairman of the District Council, the first choir came to the platform. It was a disappointing start; the ensemble was uneven and diction was poor. Even the item of their choice was a lacklustre offering, and Adam could only hope for an improvement as the competition continued.

It came with the third choir to take the platform, a mixed choir from Lincolnshire. Their performance of the test piece was excellent and they went on to sing their chosen item, 'Like to the Damask Rose' by Sir Edward Elgar, superbly well. Such was the impression they left, that Adam and his colleagues had to dismiss it from their minds when the next choir came to perform. Like it or not, though, it was the highlight of the morning and was memorable as such.

The afternoon session included four outstanding choirs as well as some that were good but not exceptional. Of the sixteen taking part, there were five in the reckoning. Even so, the judges had no difficulty in choosing a winner. The hardest task was that of determining which were to be second and third.

Eventually, the decision was made, and Adam communicated the fact to the Chairman. An announcement was made on the public address system that the presentation was about to take place, and competitors returned to the hall to hear the result.

Adam stepped up to the platform, uncomfortably conscious that he was under the scrutiny of the local TV studios and the press. He announced the third and second prize-winners, and when he came to make his final announcement, the atmosphere in the hall was almost tangible. This was the prize he and the others had created; not the Rose Bowl itself – that was a mere token – but the accolade of being judged the best, even in a competition that had only recently come to the public's notice.

'As I said earlier,' he began, 'we have heard some exceptional choirs today, and it has been a most enjoyable experience for my fellow judges and for me, but it gives me the greatest pleasure to invite to the platform, to accept First Prize and the Netherdale Rose Bowl, the conductor of the Wellerby Choir from Lincolnshire.'

There was a spontaneous barrage of cheering and applause, mainly, he imagined, from the Wellerby members and supporters, and then a diminutive, grey-haired woman joined him on the platform. He stared at her for several seconds.

'I'm the conductor,' she prompted.

'And an excellent conductor you are, too.' He shook her hand, still stunned and ashamed that he'd been taken by surprise. The competitors had been hidden from the judges' sight, and this tiny matron was not at all what he'd expected. He collected himself, however, and spoke to her again. 'Congratulations,' he said, 'on a superb all-round effort, and on a particularly enchanting performance of the Elgar.' He stepped backward to allow the Chairman's wife to present the Netherdale Rose Bowl.

* * *

'I couldn't believe it,' he told Jenny at the Craven Heifer that evening. 'I was astounded that such a tiny, modest woman could be so full of music. That performance alone made the effort of organising this thing worthwhile.'

'Remember what the Chairman of the District Council said as well,' Jenny prompted him. 'It's a tremendous thing you've done for the Dale, and you'll be remembered for it. That must have made it worthwhile, too.'

'That was a small repayment I made. No more than that, but let's not dwell on it.'

'All right.' Sensitive as ever to his feelings, Jenny changed the subject. 'I wonder how many of the competitors will stay for tomorrow's performance.'

'And your exhibition.'

'And Leanne's, don't forget.'

It was difficult, leaving the day behind, even after the bonus of an excellent TV news item. The Festival had been the culmination of so much effort and planning that it seemed wrong for it to occupy only two days, with one of them gone already, but now they had to concentrate on the Exhibition and the Choral Society's performance of Adam's *White Rose Cantata*.

* * *

The art exhibition was also held in the school hall, and Adam was gratified to see Leanne in a dress, possibly for the first time since the Easter concert. The same applied to Jenny, although in her case, he was careful to frame his observation as a compliment. Jimbo and Helen looked very much a pair as they viewed each painting and photograph in turn.

'Someone's actually bought one of my paintings,' Leanne said excitedly. 'Isn't that cool?'

'Well done, darling,' said Jenny, 'but try not to sound so surprised. It's better to let people think you've been selling pictures all your life.'

'But it's my first.'

'I'm delighted for you,' said Adam, 'and so is Jenny. She's just giving you good advice.'

* * *

Leanne managed to catch Jimbo alone while Helen was examining some studies of Upper Wharfedale.

'You and Helen are looking very much the part,' she said.

'Yes, it's going well.'

Looking around her to make sure there was no one within earshot, she said, 'I can't believe you've managed to abstain for so long.'

Jimbo's attention was drawn suddenly to a painting of Kilnsey Crag.

'Oh, Jimbo.' Her expression told him that words failed her. 'You haven't, have you?'

'Let's just say that Helen came round to my way of thinking.'

'You haven't got a way of thinking, Jimbo. You let your willie do it all for you.'

Jimbo looked hurt but said nothing.

Helen came over to join them. 'Hello, you two,' she said. 'You're not having a disagreement, are you?'

'Disagreement? No,' said Leanne, 'just a difference in perspective.'

'Speaking of perspective,' said Helen, switching to safer ground, 'I think you're ever so talented.'

'Thank you, but so are you. Are you looking forward to this afternoon?'

'Yes, very much. I've never taken part in a first performance until now.'

'My dad spent ages finding suitable songs for you. It seems that the Yorkshire lasses in most ballads suffered the usual fate through frolicking in the hay with passing ne'er-do-wells.'

'Let's hope for the girls' sakes,' said Helen with a hint of mischief in her eyes , 'that the ne'er-do-wells occasionally did it rather well.'

Leanne was so surprised that she could think of no response.

* * *

Several choirs, including the prize-winners, stayed for the final part of the Festival, so it was a capacity audience that attended the cantata's first performance. Most welcome of all, though, was Mrs Elizabeth Golding, author of the poem 'From the Depths'. She and Adam had met on her arrival, and he was acutely conscious of her presence when he took his place in front of the chorus and principals.

The music began, mysterious and enticing, with the opening lines of the poem sung by the female chorus, joined then by the tenors and basses as the ocean receded to expose the first glimpse of land. Helen's mezzo voice described the advance of the glaciers, and Jimbo's sombre bass painted the peaks and crags they left behind. The mood of the music changed then, as the temperature increased and the hills felt their first warmth.

Jimbo's song 'Fourpence a Day' was about a young boy who had to spend each week away from his home, washing the lead ore that was extracted from the Dales mines. It was a story of heartbreak and misery told with the solid stoicism that was the mark of the Dales folk who mined the lead. Adam had calculated that, taken away from its usual folk-style rendering, the pathos of the song would be conveyed most effectively by the rugged timbre of the bass voice, and Jimbo's interpretation was impeccable. Again, Adam found himself wondering about the contrasting sides to his offspring's personality.

In a more light-hearted interlude, the chorus prepared the way for Helen to sing 'Scarborough Fair'. Everyone in the audience would know it well, although not Adam's arrangement of it, and a quick glance to one side told him that the song and Helen's singing were working their usual charm.

The Ballad of Semerwater changed the mood of the cantata again, and Adam was conscious that the audience was completely involved in the brooding legend.

Helen's solo 'Safe Home' and Jimbo's 'The Lass of Richmond Hill' were interspersed by contrasting choral interludes, and the music went on to reach its glorious, triumphant finale.

As the last chord ended, there was a moment's hiatus before the audience broke into unrestrained applause. Adam gave a hand to the chorus and then the two principals. He kissed Helen on the cheek and offered his hand to Jimbo, who forgot himself again and hugged his father. Finally, he waved Jenny and Mrs Golding to their feet, and the chorus, principals and audience showed their joint appreciation. Adam kissed Jenny on the cheek and whispered a private message in her ear.

'Me too,' she said, beaming, but they were in the public gaze, so their conversation would have to be concluded later.

* * *

Jenny's parents brought the children back from their two-day visit, fed, tired, and ready for bed.

When Nicola came down in her night things to say goodnight to everyone, she appeared to have something on her mind.

'Mum,' she said, 'Daisy Duncan is going to be a bridesmaid at her cousin's wedding.'

'Oh, and who is Daisy Duncan?'

'She sits in front of me. Well, she did last term.'

'That's lovely. Every girl should have that experience.'

Nicola said impatiently, 'I want to be a bridesmaid.'

Jenny gave her a hug and said, 'I can see how that appeals to you, darling, but there's just one tiny problem. You see, for you to be a bridesmaid, someone has to get married.'

Leanne said, 'I'll tell you what, Nicola. I'll give you first refusal, but don't hold your breath, because it's not going to happen for some time.'

'Don't worry, darling,' said Jenny. 'One day, perhaps, it will happen.'

The children went to bed, and Leanne made a discreet exit. Jimbo and Helen were elsewhere, so Adam and Jenny found themselves alone.

Jenny asked, 'Did you mean what you said to me this afternoon?'

Adam made a pretence of thinking.

'When you kissed me,' she prompted.

'Oh, that.' He thought again. 'Of course I did. I wouldn't have said it otherwise.'

'Say it again, Adam.'

'All right. I love you, Mrs Thorpe.'

'I love you too, Mr Watkinson.'

'That's a relief. It would be awful if you were to spurn my advances after all the groundwork I've put in.'

'Don't be silly.'

'All right.' Instead of being silly, he kissed her with the easy confidence of one whose final objective is in sight.

After a while, he said, 'I think Nicola would be a lovely bridesmaid, and she's obviously keen. I can't just see Gareth as a page boy, and I don't think he'd be all that enthusiastic, but I can see him as Assistant to the Best Man, as long as the Best Man is Jimbo.'

Jenny shook her head in mock-puzzlement. She asked, 'Have I missed something?'

'Didn't I say? I meant to ask you something earlier, but in the excitement of the day, I forgot.'

'If it'll help you remember what it was, the answer's "yes".'

'Oh, good.'

'Having settled that,' she said, heading for the drinks cupboard, 'shall we drink to it?'

'Yes,' he said. 'It's just a shame we can't celebrate properly, things being as they are.'

'Adult content must wait until the children are back at school and settled there, particularly Gareth in his new school.'

'I agree absolutely. First things first. We must be grown-up and responsible, and let the occasion take us by surprise.'

'It wouldn't be a new direction,' she pointed out, handing him a bottle and the corkscrew, 'if we didn't encounter an occasional surprise along the way.'

'You know,' he said thoughtfully, 'I can't help thinking we've flogged that one to death.'

'Which one, Adam? You've lost me again.'

'The new direction.'

She studied him gravely. 'After everything you've achieved during the past year, what's wrong with the new direction?'

'Only that it doesn't sound positive enough. It needs a name that's both positive and final.'

'Have you thought of one?'

'Yes. I have. As of this evening, I think we can safely rename it "The Right Direction." Let's drink to that.'

'Yes,' she said, 'let's.'

THE END

Lightning Source UK Ltd.
Milton Keynes UK
UKHW041833050920
369410UK00001B/2